DANGEROUS LOVE

Lauren walked slowly down the hallway, stopping only when she noticed the red light on her answering machine blinking. She walked in and depressed the button, listening to the muted whir of the tape rewinding.

"Did you honestly think I wouldn't know the two of you went off together, Laurie dear?" The whispered voice struck a dark chord. *"You don't like being called Laurie, do you? No one with the snooty-bitch name of Lauren would. Then I think that's exactly what I'll call you until I can give you a more appropriate name."* Her voice turned harsh. *"Did you tell Josh all the dirty details behind your divorce, Laurie? Or did the two of you find a motel room together for some down-and-dirty sex? No, I don't think you did, because if you had, he wouldn't have wanted you, would he?"*

Shaking so violently she couldn't stand, Lauren dropped into the chair next to her desk as she listened to the insidious voice bring up memories she had buried months ago.

"Josh isn't a man to take things lightly, Laurie," the taunting voice continued. *"But I can make it very easy for you. Just leave him alone and give him back to me, and I'll forget all about it—I promise. And Laurie, I always keep my promises."*

Her demonic laughter whipped across Lauren's frayed nerves just before the click indicated the answering machine had cut her off.

"A must read for anyone who loves to have white knuckles while reading."

THE PAPERBACK TRADER

"Linda Randall Wisdom ha[s] incredible talent who adds [to the sus]pense field."

LINDA RANDALL WISDOM
DOUBLE JEOPARDY

ZEBRA BOOKS
KENSINGTON PUBLISHING CORP.

ZEBRA BOOKS are published by

Kensington Publishing Corp.
850 Third Avenue
New York, NY 10022

Zebra and the Z logo Reg. U.S. Pat & TM Off.

First Printing: August, 1994

Printed in the United States of America

Prologue

Obsession hung in the air. The fragrance, that is.

That evening Carol had taken Josh out to dinner to celebrate his birthday, then taken him back to her apartment to give him his present in private. After a few hours of heavenly comfort in her bed he regretted having to return home because of a early morning court appearance the next day.

It wasn't until he entered his house via the back door that the musky perfume lingering in the air penetrated his sated brain. Josh quickly flipped on an overhead light and viewed the scene before him.

"Shit!"

He wouldn't dream of placing a snowy white linen cloth on the butcher-block table set off to one side in the breakfast nook. He also didn't own the two china place settings facing each other, nor the delicate crystal bowl filled with honeysuckle blossoms set precisely in the middle of the table.

Dominating a serving tray next to it was a birthday cake decorated with the appropriate number of candles . . . except it didn't look very festive with a champagne bottle upended in its center. Equally unappetizing was the extremely overdone roast he found dumped in the sink. Ironically, he noticed that the coffee cup and plate which had held his toast that morning had been washed and set in the drainboard. And the dishwasher had been run and the contents emptied.

He didn't touch anything as he quickly checked out the rest of the house. As he walked down the hallway, looking into the other rooms, he could still smell the exotic designer fragrance that seemed to increase in strength as he reached his bedroom. It was the only room that showed signs of the unknown visitor's touch. He used his elbow to push the bedroom door open.

The scene before him was worse than anything he could've imagined. It was easy to guess the room had originally been set up with seduction in mind.

Now, it looked more like a scene out of a nightmare.

Candles had been mashed into the top of the bureau and nightstands. The burgundy-and-silver paisley comforter hung askew off the bed, while the burgundy sheets had been pulled back and slashed by an angry hand. What really got his attention was the sight of the open closet doors with piles of ripped clothing thrown across the floor.

That was when he noticed the faint light shining from the partially closed bathroom door. He crossed the room slowly as he wondered what he would find in there. He stopped short at the doorway as the door slowly swung open the rest of the way. The drawers were pulled open and their contents dumped onto the floor.

But the unsettling part was the words written in bold red lipstick on the mirror.

That slut will regret taking you from me!

Josh was back outside in a matter of seconds to use

his car phone to contact the police. He had another break-in to report.

She parked her car far enough up the street not to be noticed by Josh or anyone in the neighborhood, but close enough that she had an excellent view of him sitting inside his car, talking on the phone.

She kept her gaze fastened on him as her right hand stroked the front of her black dress in a long, slow lover's caress. Her eyelids drooped to half-mast as she imagined it was his hand loving her. It was his hand reaching inside the deep V-neckline to stroke her, his voice whispering in her ear that she was the only woman for him and how much he loved her. Her other hand dropped to stroke herself between her legs. Her breathing grew harsh in the cramped space as her passion escalated. Then reality took hold as she remembered why she'd sat in the house for hours waiting for him and he hadn't come. An animalistic sound of pain mingled with fury escaped her throat.

The gentle touches turned rougher, until her red polished nails scratched and tore the fabric. The sequined material shredded until the top of her bra showed before even that delicate material tore under her savage motions. She was so caught up in her mental pain she didn't feel her skin burning from the deep scratches she'd self-inflicted, nor care about the warm trickle of blood trailing down her chest.

Chapter One

"Would you mind if I asked you a simple question, Mr. Brandon?"

"Not at all, Your Honor."

The judge stared at the prosecuting attorney over the top of his reading glasses. His gaze was most definitely not kind. "Does the county not pay the assistant district attorney enough so that he can afford a tie? Or is there a personal, perhaps religious, reason why you don't wear one in my court?"

Josh Brandon grinned, not the least intimidated by the older man's sarcasm. "More like a personal reason, Your Honor. I feel they restrict my breathing."

The judge frowned at an age-old argument. "I suppose that also goes for your refusal to wear a suit."

"I figure I'm getting paid to prosecute the guilty, not for my fashion sense."

Judge William Collins sighed. "All right, let's get on with it." He nodded toward the defense attorney. "Mr. Martin, I believe you had a motion to make before the court. And try not to be too long-winded for once. I'd like to wrap this up before lunch." He settled into his high-backed chair.

* * *

So this was Assistant District Attorney Josh Brandon. Not bad—not bad at all. She leaned forward and rested her arms across the back of the bench as she studied the man questioning the witness. Her expert eye estimated him to be a couple inches over six feet, two hundred pounds, two ten at most, and it looked to be all muscle, which was good for a man who was in his early forties. She continued to take her mental photographs.

His thick, dark brown hair and moustache were slightly peppered with gray, which made him like a man who more likely fought with a gun than with a law book.

She remained in her seat for a little over an hour, watching Josh argue his case with a drawling ease that she sensed was deceptive. Now that she knew what she'd be dealing with, she was ready to get back to her own work.

As she walked down the courthouse hallway, more than one man took a second glance.

"Get a load of that lady, Frank. Now, those are the kind of legs I'd like to have wrapped around me," one of the bailiffs muttered to a friend.

"The lady might look like a walking sex ad, but I wouldn't want to lie down around her. And you don't, either." He leaned over and whispered in the other man's ear.

"She's doing *that?*" The first man looked green around the gills. "Someone who looks like her works down there?"

Frank nodded.

The other man shook his head. "There ain't that many good-looking women around, and now one of

the sweetest-looking ones around turns out to be
. . . well, I don't even like to think about it. No good-
looking woman should be doing something that disgusting."

Josh considered cocktail parties on a par with a visit to
the dentist. If he could have gotten out of this one he
would have. Except this get-together was thrown to
honor Sam Daniels, who was retiring from his position as district attorney due to ill health after partial
recovery from a near-fatal heart attack. The restaurant's banquet room was decorated with black and
white streamers overhead and posters listing his con-
victions and a few listing less-than-victorious cases.

"Talk about a miracle—do my eyes deceive me, or
am I seeing you wearing a tie tonight?" Judge Collins
walked up to Josh and nodded at his shirt front. He
peered at it a bit more closely. "For a minute, I
thought you might have had it painted on," he joked.

"Oh, Judge, you know very well Josh never does the
expected," Beth Langley, one of the other prosecutors,
cut in as she passed them. She cocked her hand, holding the glass of Scotch out of harm's way as she paused
long enough to get her dig in. She pursed her lips in an
exaggerated kiss to Josh before moving on to another
group who were seated at one of the round tables set
along the sides of the large room.

Josh shook his head in exasperation at her outrageous behavior. "I figure Sam's only going to retire
once, so I thought I'd give him a treat and wear a tie
in his honor."

"Are we sure the man can survive the shock of the
county's own cowboy looking respectable?" A
woman's laughing voice intruded.

"Hi, Gail." Josh wrapped an arm around her waist and kissed her on the cheek. They'd dated a few times after Gail's divorce, but he'd soon realized she might be putting more emotion into the few dinners they shared than he did, and he'd gently broken it off. "How do you like working in Vice?"

She wrinkled her nose. "I can think of better ways to spend my evenings than in the company of hookers. Trouble is, Bill doesn't have the legs for a miniskirt, and Larry's chest is too hairy to carry off a tube top. I wish I could get into Homicide. At least there, all you deal with are dead people. They don't talk back or try to strike a deal when you arrest them."

Josh chuckled. He looked over her shoulder. "No date?"

The pretty brunette shrugged. If the gaze in her eyes was a trifle hopeful, he chose not to see it. "Not tonight."

"Hey, Josh, who'd you steal the tie from?" one of the defense attorneys laughed as he walked past.

"I only hope he'll accord me the same honor when I retire," Judge Collins joked.

Josh started to reply when he looked past the judge's shoulder and froze. His arm, still draped loosely around Gail's waist, dropped to his side.

Judge Collins turned his head to see what had caught Josh's attention. "I see you've noticed the county's newest member."

"Who is she?"

The older man chuckled. "I can't believe you haven't met Dr. Hunter before and tried to impress her with that good-ole-boy charm of yours."

"There's no reason why I can't do that now." He wondered if he was grinning like a fool. A hint of a woman's smoky voice reached his ears. "That and more."

The judge chuckled. "Maybe I should warn you that rumor has it the lady has turned rejecting a man's advances into a fine art. Although, I admit if I wasn't a happily married man for the last thirty-two years, I'd be willing to try my hand at it."

"Then it's a good thing I'm stubborn guy. If you'll excuse me." Josh headed for the group.

As he approached them he looked again at the woman who was the center of attention of a group of men near the door. Long showgirl legs encased in sheer black stockings, a black silk wrap skirt that moved with her to reveal even more, and a black sequined low-cut top with skinny straps. Her ash-blond hair was pulled back in a coil that should have made her look demure instead of sexy as hell.

"Hey there, Brandon," one of the other prosecutors greeted him, when Josh stood just behind him.

"Ted." Josh looked around for a place to set down his glass. "I thought you and Missy had something going."

"Hey, I'm not dead yet." He lowered his voice. "Plus, Missy didn't want to come to this, since I told her it was a retirement party. And what she doesn't know won't hurt her. I'm only doing the political thing by showing up and now by getting to know Dr. Hunter." He lit up a cigarette.

"Political, hell. No man would mind having a doctor who looked like her," Josh said.

Ted laughed so hard he started coughing. "You might change your mind after you find out just what kind of doctor she is."

"Why, is she a vet for the K-9 units?"

He grinned as if he knew something very funny. He

patted Josh's shoulder. "Let's just say I hope the good doctor won't have to examine me for a long time."

Lauren Hunter turned her head just then and fastened her dusky blue eyes on Josh.

"Josh Brandon, isn't it?" She smiled and held out her hand. "I'm Lauren Hunter. I observed you in court a few days ago. You really enjoy throwing people off guard, don't you?"

Josh was never one to believe in love at first sight or that touching a person could send electric signals up his arm. But meeting Lauren Hunter changed his mind on a lot of points. The lady had a firm, no-nonsense handshake, an equally no-nonsense way of looking directly at a person that she liked, a throaty voice that had him thinking of hot sex, and best of all, she didn't wear Obsession perfume.

"I watched 'Perry Mason' when I was a kid, and to this day, I like to get a highly emotional confession from the guilty party while he's on the stand."

"And did anyone ever fulfill your dream?"

He grinned. "Not unless you count the guy who broke down and admitted he did tear out the parking meter in front of his store in the dead of night and plant a tree in its place."

Lauren nodded with the gravity necessary for the topic. "It must have made you feel powerful that you brought down such a dangerous criminal."

Josh leaned over and whispered in her ear, "The man's crime was that he overwatered the tree and killed it."

Lauren lifted her wineglass to her lips. "I'm grateful that was one homicide victim I didn't have to deal with."

Josh frowned. He hadn't missed the faint snickers going on around them or the cryptic statements made by the others. He decided it was time to find out why. "Okay, okay, you've all had your fun. Luckily, I'm adult enough to ask a stupid question. Why would you want to meet a homicide victim? You don't look crazy enough to be a cop."

"Once again, Brandon, you played wastebasket basketball with those all-important memos that get passed around. Which meant you didn't bother with the memo about Dr. Hunter that made the rounds last week, did you, Josh? That's how you end up with these surprises," Pat Kerns, one of the prosecutors, confided, winking at the others. "So who wants the pleasure of giving this guy the news?"

Josh handed his drink to Pat. "I read everything that's addressed to me."

Lauren's smile widened as she realized the reason for his confusion. "So you don't know exactly who I am."

Josh deliberately tuned out their avid audience. "You're Dr. Lauren Hunter, who happens to be a very classy-looking lady."

"I hate pretentious wines, and five-star restaurants, I can bait my own hook, I prefer to watch movies that aren't subtitled, and I once stayed up all night watching the Creature Feature marathon on cable. I love the older horror films that didn't need tons of blood and guts to scare a person." She ticked off each item on her fingertips. Josh's eyes lit up as he realized he was hearing the words of a kindred spirit.

"Oh no, another one!" Mike Kerry, one of the DA's office investigators, groaned, slapping his forehead with his palm. "Now they're going to compare notes on which B movie was the best."

"William Castle's *Homicidal*," Josh intoned.

Lauren began laughing. "It's one of my favorites!

Right next to *The Tingler* and *House on Haunted Hill.* What can I say? Vincent Price is one of my heroes."

"How can a coroner not like blood and guts?" Mike asked.

"When you deal with it at the office, you don't care to see it at home, too," she said.

Josh digested this surprising piece of news. Just at that moment, he glanced at the table filled with an array of hors d'oeuvres. He discovered he wasn't hungry anymore as he realized what she was saying. "So, you're the new coroner?"

She nodded. "I am the new coroner."

"How did Igor get so lucky?" Josh muttered with comic displeasure, mentioning the assistant coroner. "I get a Telly Savalas look-alike, he gets Kathleen Turner. Where did I go wrong?"

"You went to law school," Lauren quipped with a saucy grin, liking the fact that Josh was willing to laugh at himself. That and more. Although, as she stood there talking and laughing with Josh and others, she felt a chill travel along the back of her neck that escalated into faint nausea.

If she hadn't known better, she'd have thought someone nearby was directing waves of hate at her so strong she sensed they could knock her to her knees. She resisted the urge to look over her shoulder to see if she could find the source of this ugly sensation. Instead, she concentrated on Josh. Pretty soon, the feeling diminished and she was able to draw a faint breath of relief.

"I gather the Igor you're talking about is Pete Ignatius?" She mentioned the assistant coroner.

"Igor, Ignatius. He can't help looking like something out of a B horror film." He glanced around, a slight frown on his face. He moved his shoulders as if shrugging off something unpleasant.

"Lauren, I'm glad to have met you, and unfortunately, I'm sure we'll meet again under different circumstances," Mike intruded, deliberately stepping in front of Josh. "If I wasn't a happily married man and leery of people who prefer to spend their workdays with the dead, I'd carry you off to Hawaii and a beachfront condo."

"This from the man who hates to fly."

It took a few moments for the good-natured arguing to recede until Lauren and Josh were alone.

"How do you put up with it?" she asked.

He shrugged. "I ignore them. Or threaten to snitch to their wives when they misbehave."

She gave him a direct look. She never did believe in beating around the bush. "So I gather that means there's no wife they can snitch to."

"Probably because no one wants to put up with me."

Lauren noted the way Josh's smile lifted one corner of his moustache and warmed his eyes. That and his lazy drawl were pleasing. She had to remind herself that she was still experiencing the aftereffects of a nasty divorce and the last thing she needed was even considering interest in a man. She looked at her watch.

"Well, I have a busy day ahead of me; my house is still filled with unpacked boxes." She managed a bright smile and again offered her hand. "It was very nice to meet you, Josh. And I suppose we'll be seeing each other again."

"We will." He deliberately held on to her hand longer than necessary.

Lauren extracted her hand, very aware of Josh's gaze on her as she turned and walked out of the banquet room. And even more aware of someone else watching her with another emotion in mind. She never felt more grateful than when she left the restaurant and the unsettling feeling went away. It brought back unpleasant memories she'd succeeded in suppressing, and she didn't like the idea of having them resurface when she felt as if she'd finally put her life back together again.

By the time she reached her car, she felt the unease come back. She crossed the well-lit parking lot, eyes shifting from right to left, noting a couple walking into the restaurant, a man climbing into his own car after giving her a look of interest that caused her to turn away before he got the wrong idea. She was glad to reach her car and hit her car alarm remote. The extra beep told her the car had been touched. But then, how many times had she lost her balance and fallen against a car with an alarm? Besides, it was still here, wasn't it? As she started to unlock the door, she noticed the deep scratch scrolled along the side of her blue BMW convertible.

"Wonderful," she muttered, jerking the door open. "I park under a light, hoping my car won't get stolen, so instead some sicko has to scratch it up. And they claim the crime rate here is much lower than in LA." She shook her head. "Although I guess there, the idiot would have taken my stereo and anything else he could have gotten his dirty little hands on."

Lauren slid behind the steering wheel and started her car, unaware that a malicious spirit was watching her every move.

She found a dark corner to stand in just around the side of the building. From there she could claim an excellent view of the bitch's reaction to that nasty ole scratch that had somehow appeared on her pretty little BMW. She smiled her satisfaction as she watched Lauren's lips moving in a muttered curse and the look of disgust on her face. Obviously, she didn't like the idea of someone marring the mirror-finish surface.

She hadn't been the only one to notice the look of interest that had passed between Lauren and Josh when they'd first been introduced. Several comments were made about how the lanky ADA always seemed to fascinate the women. And she knew exactly the meaning of the look that flew between Josh and Lauren, a look she was only too familiar with. It was bad enough that Lauren looked like Celia. Did she have to act like her, too, and take away her man? And she knew Josh was all hers. From the moment she'd met him, she'd known he was the man destined to be hers, the one man who could make her happy. He wouldn't betray her, as the others had with Celia. She just couldn't allow him to hurt her anymore.

Did Lauren Hunter honestly think her fancy clothes and whorish looks could get Josh's attention? Didn't he understand he didn't need anyone but her? Was she going to have to deal with this one, too? She held onto her purse with clenched fingers while her nails dug furrows into the soft leather. She wasn't sure why she sensed Dr. Lauren Hunter might not scare off as easily as the others. But that was all right. She wouldn't mind preparing something very special for the woman if she didn't stay away from Josh.

Taking one last look at the retreating red taillights of the small car, she quickly smoked a cigarette before making her way back to the restaurant's rear door. Going out for a smoke wasn't anything unusual around here, since the restaurant had a no-smoking policy. While inside, maybe she should look around for Josh and see if she could persuade him to go somewhere more private for a drink. After all, she only needed time to prove to him she was all the woman he'd ever want.

As Josh talked to several judges, he suddenly realized the dark haze in his mind was gone as quickly as it had appeared. He glanced around, but couldn't find anyone looking at him with strong intensity. All he saw in the large room were business colleagues, friends, and a few people he couldn't put in any one category. He soon relaxed and moved on to another group.

Relaxed until he recognized a familiar fragrance seeming to surround him like a tightly woven net threatening to choke him.

He hoped it was nothing more than a coincidence that someone happened to be wearing the musky scent; after all, it was very popular. Still, he couldn't stop the feeling that it was worn as a signal pointed directly at him—something for him to think about. What if this person wanted him to know she could be anyplace he could be?

It wasn't surprising that all the fun had suddenly gone out of the party.

Chapter Two

"I have met my share of bastards in my time, but Josh Brandon, you take the grand prize when it comes to finding ways to humiliate a woman in front of her peers!" The woman's voice shrilled in his ear. "After what you did, I know no jury in the land would convict me if I shot you dead!"

Josh winced as her strident voice assaulted his eardrums. He quickly changed ears so the first one could recover. "Carol, honey, I don't—" he began, only to be cut off by her snarl.

"I don't want to hear any idiotic excuses! I thought you were the best thing to come along in a long time." She spoke rapidly, disgust in every word. "Since I consider my career important, I understood why your work had to take precedence at times. Besides, you were always sensitive to my feelings, and I value that in a man. Not to mention you were always great in bed. I just never dreamed you'd do something so cruel to me after everything we've meant to each other! You knew how important this promotion was to me! How could you do it?"

"Carol, what the hell are you talking about?" He cut in the moment she took a breath.

"You know very well what I'm talking about, you son of a bitch. You couldn't bother coming to my celebration party, yet you had the gall to send me two dozen black roses, delivered by the ugliest-looking man I've ever seen, and dressed like an undertaker. My God, he even showed up in a hearse!" Her voice grew shriller with each word. "As if that wasn't bad enough, he went around the room offering his condolences to my co-workers on their having to put up with me as the new VP. I have *never* been so embarrassed!" She finally ran out of steam . . . until she came up with a few more colorful terms for what she thought of him.

Josh closed his eyes. He was listening to a side of her he didn't know existed. And didn't like.

"Carol, you've talked about your hopes for getting a promotion, but I had no idea you'd finally gotten it," he tried to reason with her. "And I didn't know about any party held in your honor, and for once, I'm very relieved to say I didn't send you any flowers, black roses or otherwise."

"Listen to me, you son of a bitch." Her vicious hiss was further pain to his ears. "The card was not only addressed to me, but on the inside, you wrote down my nickname. And I don't think anyone could forge that unreadable scrawl of yours. So do us both a big favor and erase my name from your little black book, because I won't be accepting any of your calls from now on."

Josh held the phone a safe distance from his ear as the receiver was slammed down.

"Shit." He leaned over and flicked the intercom button, waiting for his secretary's voice to question what he wanted before he begged, "Ginnie, do we have any aspirin left? Say, fifty or so?"

The older woman walked into his office pulling a

white bottle out of her jacket pocket and handing it to him. "The minute I heard her screaming your name and demanding your genitals—see what a lady I am in not using the word she did?—I figured you'd need these. Good thing we buy them by the gross." She smiled without offering one ounce of sympathy. But that would have been out of character for her. "She thinks you're pond scum."

"That's putting it mildly." He grimaced as he followed the aspirin with a swallow of cold coffee. "This is all so crazy." He leaned back in his chair as he mentally replayed the conversation. "If I was the paranoid type, I'd think someone was deliberately sabotaging my love life."

"What did you supposedly do this time?"

Josh sighed as he tried to figure out something that really didn't make any sense to him. "She accused me of sending black roses to her promotion party, delivered by some ugly guy dressed up as an undertaker. A party it seems I'd been invited to and didn't even bother letting her know I couldn't attend. Hell, I didn't even know she had gotten a promotion. Much less know anything about the party."

Ginnie shook her head, still not offering any sympathy at her boss's snarled frustration. The older woman had worked for Josh from the beginning, even though she'd bluntly informed him she didn't believe fetching coffee and donuts was part of her job description, and if Josh ever dared ask her to work late, he'd better be prepared to listen to her mumbling the entire time. Not to mention that she refused to work for a fool, so Josh better make sure he didn't screw up anything she might have to put right. At the same time, she was as loyal as they came to those she felt deserved it, she was vengeful to those who deserved that, she had an excellent information network if Josh needed something he couldn't get by conventional means, and she made sure the job wouldn't give him an ulcer. She also ruled his office with an iron hand; that made his life easier. More than one prosecutor had trembled under the gruff secretary's wrath and slunk away to lick his wounds in private.

"Look at it this way, she finally showed you her true colors. And I'm not surprised she turned out to be such a cold-hearted bitch. She only smiled with her teeth, not her eyes. Maybe you had a good time between the sheets with her, but she was still one cold lady. Now, let's see. The score is, them six, you zip. That's unless you count the mystery lady who sends you flowers every Thursday. We've kept a list out there, and this week is Susan's turn."

He looked up. "All of you women are sick. Keeping a list as to who gets the next batch of flowers." He hadn't confided in Ginnie his uneasy feelings about the woman sending him the flowers perhaps being the same one who'd broken into his house the night of his birthday. But knowing the secretary, she'd already figured it out and was just waiting for him to voice it to her.

"It makes the days go faster."

Ginnie stepped forward to snag the ringing telephone. "Mr. Brandon's office." Her expression didn't give any indication as to the identity of the caller. "One moment, please." She punched the red hold button. "Are you available for the Wicked Bitch of the Eastern Seaboard?"

Josh raised his eyes heavenward. "Did my horoscope read this was the day to make Josh's life hell?"

"Buck up, Moondoggie, and take your lumps,"

Ginnie ordered him, without the least bit of sympathy. She held out the receiver.

Muttering curses, Josh snatched it out of her hand and scowled at his departing secretary.

"What do you want, Stephanie?"

"As sparse with words as ever, aren't you, Joshua? It wouldn't hurt for you to say hello and ask me how I am." Cultured tones that could be warm as honey or cold as ice assaulted his ears. Right now, he figured the arctic circle would look like the tropics compared to her.

"Since you only call to bitch at me, I don't see any reason to act polite."

Stephanie Carver's silence was as eloquent as her dialogue. "Your check is late again."

Josh silently counted to ten. "I suggest you take it up with the postal service, since it was mailed out on time. I have to get to court. Anything else?"

"Nothing you would understand, much less be interested in." The click was loud in his ear.

"Didn't she get her distemper shot for the month?" Ginnie walked back into the office carrying a file folder.

"She has a trust fund that could pay off the national debt, not to mention a father who's rolling in money," he grumbled. "But if her damned alimony check is one day late, she threatens to send out an enforcer." His scowl would have intimidated a lesser person, but Ginnie was familiar with her boss's moods.

"You should have gotten married in a state with community property laws. You might have been able to get alimony out of *her!*" She laid the folder on his desk. "Here's something that will improve your mood. I only read the first couple of pages, but I'd say it's a pretty interesting autopsy report. Just the kind you love."

He chuckled at her false cooing. "Ginnie, there are days when you can be a real bitch." He picked up the file and opened it.

She snorted as she walked back out to her desk. "Flattery will get you nowhere. Don't you have enough woman problems without adding me to the group?"

Josh scanned the pages until he came to the last one and found a signature. He chuckled. "And she says *my* handwriting is illegible." He returned to the first page and began reading.

By the time he'd muddled through several pages of medical terminology, he felt his suspicions growing. When he'd reached the last page and read the preparer's conclusions, he was ready to chew nails. He leaned forward to pick up the phone, then changed his mind. "If anyone needs me, I'll be in the morgue," he snarled on his way out.

Ginnie looked up from her typing. "A perfect place to find a woman, if I say so myself. The ones there can't scream at you or threaten to cut off your balls when your checks are late." She mocked embarrassment. "Oh me, and here I promised to be a lady. Well, hell, that's what she said. Something about using them the next time she played tennis."

Josh's answer was to whip his hand over his head with the middle digit standing proudly.

"Same to you, boss," Ginnie's voice followed after him.

Lauren sifted through her in-box. "Pete, I can't find your report on the Thompson post. Did you bring it by yet?"

Her second-in-command remained standing in the office doorway as if the last thing he wanted to do was cross the threshold into enemy territory.

Pete Ignatius wasn't known as Igor for nothing. Barely five feet seven inches, with a slightly hunched-over, narrow body and even more narrow features, colorless eyes that refused to look at a person, and pale skin from too much time spent under fluorescent lighting, he was a pitiful picture. The green cotton surgical scrubs he wore only made his skin look more sallow. It seemed he enjoyed capitalizing on his less than normal exterior.

"I haven't finished it yet." Even his voice came out in a slight nasal whine that grated on the ears.

Lauren silently counted to ten, something she'd been doing every time she dealt with her assistant. "You performed the post two days ago. You even said it came out pretty standard. You couldn't find a sign of foul play, unless something shows up in the toxicology tests. There's no reason why your report shouldn't have been turned in by now."

His face was tight with belligerence. "Dr. Faber never minded if it was a little late. He understood that I do have other duties to perform around here."

For not the first time, Lauren wondered if the man was this sullen to everyone, or if she was the only lucky one to receive this treatment. "We're all overworked here, Pete, and yet the others don't seem to have any problem getting their paperwork in on time. I expect your report on my desk before you leave today." She deliberately kept her voice soft but firm.

"Lady, you are in big trouble!" Josh pushed past Pete as he barreled into Lauren's office. "And I'm just the one to give it to you."

She didn't bat an eye at the unexpected intrusion.

"I'll get to you in a moment, Counselor." She turned back to her assistant, who was inching his way to freedom. "I mean it about the report, Pete. I want it in here by the end of the day." She ignored his muttered imprecations and turned to Josh, who'd dropped into the chair in front of her desk and was glaring at her as if he wanted to cut out her heart. She smiled at him, looking as unperturbed as if he'd dropped by for a friendly chat. "Now, what can I help *you* with?"

Josh leaned forward and slapped the report on her desk. "This details the post you performed on Cal Streeter," he reminded her.

She nodded as she picked up the report and scanned it to refresh her memory. "Oh, yes, your alleged rapist. Actually, I'd have to say he was the real victim in this case."

He barked a laugh of disbelief. "Wait a minute. He raped his victim and then tried to kill her before she somehow got hold of his gun and shot him in self-defense. Now you're playing cop and stating there's no way it could have happened the way she said; that there was no rape; but you didn't explain where you got this new information. Or did you happen to be hiding in the closet while all this was going on?"

She ignored his sarcasm. "I stated my findings in the report."

"Then do me a favor and cut through the medical bullshit you scribbled in here and tell me why he couldn't have raped her."

"I'll put it in simple terms that even you can understand. At some time in his life, Cal Streeter was castrated, and not by choice," she explained, settling back in her chair and propping her crossed legs on top of her desk. "Judging from the old scars, he must have been in a freak accident that left him your run-of-the-mill eunuch. The toxicology tests also revealed he had enough barbiturates in his blood that even if he had all his equipment he couldn't have gotten it up for the sexiest woman in the world. Why he was in her bedroom, I don't know, but I can't imagine he would have had rape in mind."

She held up her hand to stop his expected protest. "Yes, I'm well aware there was evidence that she'd been sexually assaulted not long before Streeter was killed. But let me play the devil's advocate." She waved her hands around to emphasize a point here and there as she talked. "The evidence that some call assault could also mean she was into rough sex. Did anyone check to see if she had a past history of playing around with B & D?"

Josh frowned. The police and medical reports he'd read hadn't brought that up. But now he could see how it could be a logical conclusion. "Let me make this clear to you. I don't like people telling me how to do my job."

He focused on her long legs. Funny, he'd never thought of those ugly green cotton surgical scrubs and white leather Reebok running shoes as sexy. Even if the white shoes did have tiny rust-colored spots on them that he uneasily figured had to be blood. Even her hair was pulled back in a no-nonsense braid that shouldn't have looked tempting, but did. He was barely tossed out of a relationship and he was already looking at other women!

"Neither do I, but I believe in looking at both sides of an issue." She smirked. "I'd say your so-called open-and-shut case has a few holes in it, Counselor."

Josh hated with a vengeance to have someone tell him there was a good chance he might be wrong. He hated losing, and he hated it even more when he couldn't argue with such good logic. "I didn't realize forensic pathologists had such a grasp of the letter of the law. Wait, don't tell me," he held up a hand, "you also have a law degree, but for the time being you're playing with the medical part, right?"

"It's a good thing you're a classic monster-film buff. Otherwise, I'd deck you for that. When you work in forensics, you become used to sometimes discovering surprise information that can blow open a case previously considered open-and-shut."

She lifted her legs off the desk and leaned forward. "Yes, I can see you didn't want to hear that. Too bad, Counselor, because if this case goes to court, I will be stating my qualified medical opinion that there is no way on earth Cal Streeter could have raped Sally Warner. I don't say it just for the hell of it, either."

He also leaned forward. "Tell me something, Doc. Since you didn't get to meet the man until he was dead, how do you know what he could and couldn't do when he was alive? Who says all men who've been castrated can't get it up? Maybe he ate a few dozen oysters beforehand."

Lauren got to her feet and braced her hands on her desk as she leaned across the cluttered surface until her face was close to his. The faint scent of formaldehyde, disinfectant, varied chemicals, and other odors he didn't want to think about perfumed her skin. He fought the urge to sneeze.

"Let's conduct an experiment, Counselor. Purely for the sake of research, of course," she said, in a sultry voice that hit him below the belt. "We'll start out the evening out with a special cocktail I've whipped up just for you. I'll pump you so full of downers you'll be a virtual zombie. Then, I'll seat you in a very comfortable chair where you can watch me stand in front of you while I slowly strip off my clothing in accompaniment to some bluesy jazz. Then I'll slip into a black sheer nightgown and walk over and curl up in your lap. There will be a backdrop of several rows of scented candles to add to the mood."

She slowly ran her tongue across her lower lip. Her physician's half easily noticed Josh's heightened respiration and color. Good; she was definitely getting to him. "Now," her lips formed a sexy O, "let's see if you can get an erection and do what your brain is screaming for you to do before you go insane."

For one moment, Josh was convinced his heart had stopped. The mental image of Lauren wearing a sheer nightgown was more than enough to perform a tap dance on his libido. He coughed to clear his throat. "Don't worry, Doc, all I have to do is look at you and a hard-on is the least of my worries."

She dipped her head in indication of his fast reply. "Very good, Counselor. You're hoping I'm going to be curious enough to check out the condition of your crotch. Isn't it a good thing I have such wonderful willpower? You know, I hate to sound smug, but this is a time when I know I'm right."

"You were the one to bring up the subject of erections, not me." Josh flicked a corner of the report with his fingers. "So the bottom line is, you're convinced Cal Streeter couldn't have raped Sally Warner."

"Not only am I now convinced, but if you'd fully read the report, you'd have noted that the blood type taken from the semen found in Sally Warner was O positive and Cal Streeter is A negative. According to the doctor who examined her at the hospital, only one blood type's semen was found in her. And it obviously wasn't Streeter's." She held up her hands. "But then,

I'm only the coroner, not a member of the bar. The rest is up to you and your investigators."

Josh mentally called himself every name in the book. "So it's up to my investigator to find out why Cal was shot."

"You're the prosecutor."

"Glad you're finally admitting it." He shook his head. "Doc, it's been interesting." He held out his hand.

"Glad to know you're man enough to admit when you're wrong." She allowed him to clasp her hand.

For a moment they stared at each other as if unsure where to go next.

"You use a unique kind of air freshener down here," Josh commented, for lack of anything else to say.

Lauren shrugged. "You stick around these smells long enough, you don't notice them. I've been used to it since medical school. No matter where we were on campus, people only had to take one good whiff and they knew they were near medical students."

"I'm glad that wasn't something I had to worry about." He picked up the report and moved toward the door. He stopped just before he reached it. "You've got quite a voice, Doc. The kind that some would say should be registered as a lethal weapon. You know, I bet you could make a fortune in the phone sex racket. Hell, I'd even call up and pay to let you talk dirty to me." With that he sketched a salute and left.

Lauren blinked, stunned by the abrupt change in conversation. She dropped back in her chair and laughed.

"Just remember, I wouldn't come cheap," she called after him.

* * *

It was late before Josh was able to get away from his office. He shifted his briefcase from one hand to the other as he made his way out to the parking lot.

"You look tired." A tall, red-haired woman started walking next to him.

"Probably because I am," he admitted. "How's it going for you, Mitzi? Is Steve still obeying the restraining order we filed?"

She nodded. "So far. Brian said he thought he saw him lingering outside the schoolyard a few days ago. He went to find a teacher and by the time one came out, whoever it was was gone. I talked to his teachers and they're keeping a close eye out, just in case."

Josh patted her shoulder. A product of an abusive home life where his father believed he had to use his fists to keep his family in line, Josh grew up determined to do what he could to make sure no woman would have to endure the kind of hell his mother had. When Mitzi, one of the clerks in the public defender's office, had been beaten up by her soon-to-be ex-husband and had tearfully begged to find a way to be free of him, he'd guided her through the process of pressing charges against the man and filed a restraining order to keep him away from her and their children. Since then, he'd received two dozen peanut butter cookies, his favorite, every Friday from the grateful woman. He never dreaded seeing the cookies the way he dreaded seeing the flowers.

"Don't ever hesitate to call me if there's a problem," he advised, standing by her small VW bug while she bent down to unlock her door.

Her smile was filled with warm affection. "I will, Josh. Thanks."

He stood there waiting until she drove away before heading to his own car.

By the time he walked into his house, he decided he wanted a cold beer. Jamming the small pile of mail in his mouth to free his hands, he pulled a bottle of Beck's from the refrigerator. Dispensing with a glass, he drank deeply from the bottle as he headed for his office. The blinking red light on his answering machine indicated he had only one call.

"Hello, lover." The woman's husky whisper sent chills through him instead of warmth. "I saw you at Judge Collins's retirement party a couple nights ago. That burgundy-and-gray tie you wore was quite a surprise, since it's well known you hate ties. But the real surprise was seeing you talking to that forensics specialist, Dr. Hunter. Funny, I didn't think you'd go for a woman who fondles dead men all day long. Especially since you've been screwing Carol for the last few months. Although I have heard she's far from a cold fish in bed. But I doubt she's better than me."

Josh's fingers hovered over the machine's off button as the voice taunted him. He thought about just turning it off, but he knew that wouldn't shut her out of his mind. He set the bottle down as he forced himself to keep listening to the deadly whisper.

"Oh, that's right. The lively Carol dumped you, didn't she? I wonder if it had anything to do with the flowers you sent her. She always liked unique things, so you'd think she'd appreciate the black roses. Unless she was a tad upset because you didn't go to her celebration party. I wouldn't worry; she only wanted to show you off to everyone. She wanted everyone to see how lucky she was to have the assistant district attorney in her bed. Don't worry, lover. She was a viper. You wouldn't have been happy with her for much longer, anyway."

Her whisper turned coarse. "Do us both a favor, lover. Don't get any ideas about replacing that bitch Carol with the new doctor of the dead. Pretty Lauren might not end up as lucky as the others. I can't allow you to hurt me anymore with all your affairs, lover. You're all *mine,* no one else's. *Don't you understand?* I did everything for you!"

As the rage in her voice escalated, so did Josh's tension.

He hit the off button and carefully dislodged the tape from the machine by using the tip of a pencil. He dropped it in an envelope and wrote across the front while punching out a phone number.

"This is Josh Brandon. Is Sergeant Peterson still around?" He sipped his beer while waiting.

"Peterson."

"Kevin, I've got another tape for our private collection."

"Your secret admirer strikes again, huh?"

Josh wasn't amused by his friend's black humor.

"Considering the number of murders committed because of fatal attractions, you'll understand why I'm not all that flattered. Do you want to swing by the house tonight and pick it up, or I can drop it off tomorrow."

"Is it like the others?"

"Pretty much. This time she talks about what happened with Carol." He quickly filled the man in on Carol's phone call that day. "She's also saying next time could be worse." He finished his beer, so furious he stopped short of throwing the bottle against the wall. "I can't believe there still aren't any clues about her identity! She knows everything there is to know about me and we know shit about her!"

"What can I say, she's one smart lady," Kevin admitted. "The one time we were able to trace one of her calls, it turned out to come from a pay phone at the mall. She never leaves any fingerprints in your house, and no matter how many times you've changed the locks and beefed up security, she's always been able to waltz right in. Every order of flowers she's sent out has been paid in cash, and no one can agree on what she looks like, so that tells us she's using disguises. So far, the description reads a tall or short redhead or blond with gray or blue eyes who wears glasses or not. One said she had a thick southern accent; another said she sounded European, but he couldn't even guess from what country.

"How can we catch someone who's doing such a good job at hiding her identity? Stalkers usually don't care if you know who they are because they believe their love for you is pure. She's not fitting any of the usual patterns, as if she knows what we'll look for, and changes at the last second. This is one smart bitch, Josh. She's not going to make it easy for us, because she's having too much fun playing games."

Josh looked over his mail, grateful nothing seemed out of the ordinary.

"I wonder why she doesn't talk to me directly. It's always done through the phone, where she disguises her voice, or through the mail. And nothing that can be traced."

The detective easily read his frustration. "Yeah, I'm not too happy about all this, either. Tell you what, I'll pick the tape up tonight on my way home. That way, I can get it over to the lab first thing in the morning and see what we can get. Let's hope we'll get lucky this time."

"You really believe that?"

"No, but hell, I'm one of those optimistic types."

"Probably a good thing someone is," Josh muttered, after he hung the phone up.

Chapter Three

"Good morning, Doc. I thought I'd make your day by letting you know that I'm a man who's only too happy to admit when he's wrong. And I'm ready to pay up."

Lauren shifted the phone receiver to her other shoulder as she worked to contain her smile at the sound of Josh's voice. It wasn't easy when she had to gaze at the surly expression of the young woman barely out of her teens Lauren had the misfortune to call her secretary. She stood in front of Lauren with a handful of papers scrunched against her hip as she rudely tapped her foot against the tile floor. Lauren wasn't sure which was worse—her toe-tapping echoing on the linoleum, the frizz of blond hair that haloed her anorectic features and heavily made-up eyes, or her jaw snapping that damn gum Lauren would love to claw out of her fuschia-glossed mouth.

"Don't tell me that Ms. Warner decided she may have made a mistake about poor old Cal after all," she said smoothly, holding out her hand to her secretary. The crumpled papers were rudely slapped in her outstretched palm.

"Something tells me you're not alone."

"That's correct." She winced as she read the reports

and found a number of misspelled words and not one of them more than a few letters long. She picked up her pen and circled the words. "How about I go over that report to refresh my memory and get back to you later?"

"I'll be here for another ten minutes." He hung up without saying goodbye.

Lauren looked up. "Sophie, the computer program you use has a spell-check program. If you don't care to use that, I'm sure there's a dictionary in your desk."

The young woman shrugged as she reflectively scratched her neck. "I guess so."

She handed the papers back. "Then I suggest you either call up the computer's spell-check program or get out the dictionary and check out the words I circled."

Sophie's jaw dropped as she stared at the inked circles. "Hey, I worked a long time typing that report up and there was nothing wrong with it."

Lauren ignored the younger woman's accusations. "To begin with, elbow doesn't have an a in it, femur doesn't have an h, and penis only has one e." *Which I thought even you would know,* she thought to herself. "From now on, if you're unsure of the spelling, look it up first. In fact, even if you think you know how it's spelled, look it up. I will not have any reports leaving this department with misspelled words or bad grammar. And I'm talking about words you should have learned to spell in the second grade."

Sophie snatched the report from her hand and stalked out of the office.

Lauren rubbed her forehead with her fingertips. She looked through her Rolodex until she found Josh's number.

"This is Dr. Hunter, returning Mr. Brandon's call,"

she told the woman who sounded like his watchdog. She didn't have to wait long.

"Hey, Doc," his gravelly voice rumbled in her ear. She tried to ignore the tingling sensation that went along with it by silently reminding herself the opposite sex was set almost near the bottom of her list. "Did I catch you in the middle of one of your infamous openings?"

"While there are people I wouldn't mind slitting open from stem to stern, and I truly don't care if they're not dead at the time, I instead had the great pleasure of giving my secretary a spelling lesson."

"Ah, yes, Sophie. You might as well pack it in where she's concerned. She can spell, she just likes to make people think she can type a hundred words a minute instead of twenty. Some of us have turned reading reports she's typed into a game to figure out what the words really are. I have to admit, she keeps us on our toes. Being a city employee, along with having the prestige of being the mayor's favorite niece, who dropped out of college a year ago because she didn't think she could handle the heavy load of three classes, makes her just perfect. Thanks to those qualifications, she's impossible to fire."

"And to think I was the lucky one. Now, as to your paying off your debt—I gather you're not going to pout if I gloat?" She buffed her nails against her shirt front in an 'I am so great' attitude. Even if Josh couldn't see her doing it, it made her feel better.

"Doc, you can gloat all you want. Turns out Sally has a nasty habit of bringing guys home and then rolling them. The guys never filed charges because they were too embarrassed. Except Cal forgot to tell her that he had trouble getting it up, or maybe he hoped she would wave some magic wand and help him get a hard-on. Anyway, she got pissed when he couldn't come through with the hot and heavy sex she expected and called him a few choice names. When he got up to leave, she shot him. Her lawyer says PMS made Sally go off the wall. I can imagine all that coming out in court."

"I guess no one told her a good vitamin regime could easily take care of that monthly problem. Since I won the bet, I get to choose the restaurant."

"Don't you trust me?"

Lauren laughed. She was already looking forward to spending the evening with him. "That hurt-little-boy routine went out of style a long time ago, Counselor. Besides, McDonalds doesn't carry the type of cuisine I enjoy when someone else is picking up the check. I intend to break the bank, big boy. I understand Rothschild's has excellent food. Tomorrow night at seven?"

"Sounds good to me."

"Good. And Counselor," her breathy voice didn't match the wicked grin on her face, "I have a *very* large appetite." She replaced the phone receiver on Josh's sputters before she burst into laughter.

Sophie appeared in the doorway. "I can't find asphyxiation," she announced, holding up the dictionary.

Lauren resisted that violent urge to again snatch the gum out of her mouth. She reminded herself to be grateful the woman didn't blow bubbles. "I'm sure it's in there under a-s-p-h."

Sophie blinked. "P-h? I thought it was an s-f."

"Perhaps if you viewed a few posts, you could figure out how to spell the words."

The girl blanched and quickly recovered. "You

can't force me to do that. Besides, that kind of thing is disgusting."

"I can't? You'd be surprised what I can do when I put my mind to it, Sophie." Her soft voice held a core of steel. "I will not have this department held up for ridicule just because you don't want to learn your job. You might also want to remember that the people doing that so-called 'disgusting' thing helps pay your salary."

With a quivering lower lip and dramatic sniff, Sophie left abruptly.

Lauren looked at the clock. It was barely 10 A.M. and she already felt as if she'd put in a full day.

"My next trick will be to pull the wings off several flies," she announced to the air.

The prospect of dining with Lauren the next evening flew out the window when Ginnie told Josh that Kevin was on line three.

"*Nada,* buddy," the detective told him, when he asked if there were any clues.

"Shit!" Josh slammed his hand against the desk top. "How can there be not one hint of a screw-up on her part? She hasn't left anything close to a clue. It doesn't make sense."

"It does if you look at it one way," Kevin suggested. "This lady knows everything there is to know about you. She gets in your house as easily as if she has a key to the front door, and we already know you didn't give any keys out when you moved in and you've even changed the locks. She goes through your things, leaves you home-cooked meals on nights you work late, cleans house, even does your laundry, sends you flowers when you win a case, and includes cute little gifts. Hell, she even baked you a fucking birthday cake! This is not your run-of-the-mill fatal-attraction–type broad. This is a lady who has more than a few screws loose, and I hate to think what would happen if those screws decided to fall out."

"Trying to figure her out is your problem! So why don't you find out what's going on and spell it out for me instead of playing these same damn games she likes to play" he ordered.

"Fine. Ten-to-one the lady is someone you see pretty much on a daily basis. This is a person who knows you almost as well as you know yourself. She's someone who seems to have constant access to your schedule. She's obviously jealous of any sign of you having a relationship, and she doesn't mind using some pretty nasty little methods to terrorize the women you've dated. Her methods are also turning more vicious, and I'll be honest, that scares the shit out of me."

Josh didn't like what he was hearing; it seemed too logical to him. "Are you thinking she could turn violent toward me?"

"That's already happening. Look what she did to your clothes. She ripped them up so bad you had to buy a whole new wardrobe. I don't know about you, but I see that as the action of a woman who doesn't have all her marbles. Although, there was the time my wife deliberately backed the car over my favorite fishing pole," he reflected on a sad note.

"If she wants me that badly, you'd think she'd want to meet with me face to face and get it over with."

"We still don't know a lot about stalkers, Josh," Kevin pointed out. "Some prefer fantasy to reality. That way they don't have to worry about rejection from their fantasy lover. They've set their victim on a pedestal. Made them seem larger than life. They want to worship them from afar because it's safer that way. That's why they creep into their houses when they're not home to be around their things or hang out in their offices where they can memorize their schedules and study them like some school assignment.

"They also don't want that person to have anyone else grow close to them, because if they do, those people will have to be gotten rid of. But that object of infatuation better not do anything that makes them less than perfect because they can be brought down, too. We both know what that means. And we have those where if they can't have their idol, they're going to make damn sure no one does."

Josh thought of stalking cases in the past, stories in the newspaper. Few ended happily. For a brief moment, his ex-wife came to mind. Would she do something like this? He couldn't envision the cold-hearted and very proper Stephanie doing his dishes, but anything was possible nowadays. She would probably bring her maid along to handle the dirty work. "Yeah."

"We've already increased the drive-bys in your neighborhood, but no one's ever noticed anything out of the ordinary. A lot of the houses around here are set far back from the street to offer privacy and a lot of women work outside the home now, so not that many people are home during the day. Do us both a favor and stay away from the opposite sex until we find out what's going on. And especially, keep your pants zipped. The next lady in your life might end up with something a lot nastier than black roses."

Josh felt the rage and frustration boiling inside. "I can't put my life on hold because one person has decided to fixate on me for some unknown reason."

"You can if you want to keep that life."

* * *

It was always so easy to just walk in wherever she wanted to. As usual, the deadbolt hadn't been secured, and the door lock was a joke. Obviously, she didn't expect anyone to stop by when she wasn't home.

"Hi, honey, I'm home," she called out, stepping into the kitchen.

She looked around. No dirty dishes in the sink, only a rinsed coffee cup left in the dish drainer next to a neatly folded red print towel. A Bekins box marked "China" stood against the wall. How easy it would be to drop the box a few times until she could only hear the sounds of broken dishes.

She found more packing boxes stacked in the center of the living room and family room. A cream-colored couch decorated with throw pillows in swirling pastel colors was pushed up against a wall to make room for the boxes and a chair in the same fabric was pushed up against a television set and stereo system. She walked inside and examined the glass-topped coffee table that held only a couple medical journals.

"The woman has no sense of how to decorate," she sneered, dismissing the room. She always believed in strong colors. They gave a person a feeling of power.

She also checked out the in-home office, studying the personal computer. She thought about turning it on and seeing what secrets it held, then decided it could wait until another time. She had a feeling she'd be back.

She continued down the hallway, pausing only to glance into a bathroom and what she guessed to be a guest bedroom with a double bed and chest of drawers inside before she found the master bedroom.

"Bland," she pronounced, studying the soft cream–

colored walls as she walked into the room. She examined a small floral painting on the wall by the door. "Just like her."

She ran her fingers across the top of the dresser, then looked at them for signs of dust. She wore thin latex gloves to ensure she didn't leave any prints behind, so she felt comfortable touching anything that caught her fancy. She enjoyed handling the things in front of her. She felt it gave her additional insight into the person that lived there.

And with that insight came power.

She slid open the mirrored closet door and surveyed the contents. She pulled out one dress and held it in front of her. She snarled when she noticed the size tag. She starved herself and exercised constantly to remain a size ten, while this bitch was a six. Some things just weren't fair. She carefully replaced the dress in the closet before she gave in to her inclination to rip it to shreds. This wasn't the time to declare her presence.

She moved on to pull open dresser drawers, to study the delicate lingerie folded neatly between layers of tissue paper. Not a jumble of brightly colored clothing, like her drawers.

"No one keeps things this neat," she sneered, closing the drawer that held bras in a variety of vibrant colors. "She's either very anal retentive, or has a housekeeper who puts it all away for her." She pulled open another drawer and found silk chemises. She resisted the urge to take one as she finished exploring each drawer. She recognized a cream-and-black silk nightgown as one she'd admired in Victoria's Secret at the mall a few weeks ago but hadn't bought because she'd known it wasn't her style.

The jewelry she discovered was good quality costume except for a pair of diamond stud earrings and a diamond pendant tucked away in a small midnight-blue velvet pouch in the bottom dresser drawer.

She angrily envied the brass head- and footboard, the quilted comforter splashed with shades of soft yellow, blue, peach, rose, and soft green. She clenched her hands to prevent them from picking up the comforter and ripping it.

She found the doctor's reading material in the bedside table; a few mysteries; and a horror novel featuring a female vampire. She smiled when she found a copy of the latest *Playgirl* in the drawer, picked it up, and leafed through it until she reached the centerfold.

"Josh is much nicer looking." Her fingers found something hard and unyielding under the pile of magazines. "Well, what do we have here?" She pulled out a deadly looking handgun. And found it loaded. "My, my, Lauren, aren't you full of surprises? I never would have imagined you for the violent type. I do hope you have a permit for this nasty little item. Josh doesn't like women who break the law."

She next wandered into the blue-and-peach–decorated bathroom, opening bottles of bath oil set on a shelf above the bathtub so she could sniff the contents of each. The dusting powder matched the fragrance of one of the bath oils.

After that, she dug through the drawer Lauren kept her makeup in, studying colors of eye shadow and blush, even feeling bold enough to try one of the blushes on her cheek, then wiping it off after she decided the color wasn't for her. The bathroom cabinet yielded little other than a bottle of Tylenol, some Alka-Seltzer, and a packet of birth control pills. The latter bothered her the most. Had they been seeing each other on the sly and she hadn't found out about it? She'd have to do a little more checking.

She only wished she could find some illegal drugs. Something to pin on her.

"Why bother with anything else? She's a doctor and can prescribe herself any old thing she needs."

Everything she picked up was replaced in the exact same spot with meticulous care. She didn't want to give Lauren any reason to suspect someone had been there. This was the best part of the game to her. She'd found out long ago she enjoyed walking through a person's house, touching their things, finding out their secrets while making sure she left no trace of her visit.

She should have gone to Josh's house. She enjoyed her visits there the most. No matter that he'd changed the locks a couple times and even recently added a security system. She was still able to go in whenever she wanted to.

She laughed to herself as a memory surfaced. She wondered if Josh ever noticed that one of his t-shirts was missing. She'd slept so much better since she'd exchanged her nightgowns for the shirt. In fact, at night, if she closed her eyes and thought real hard, she'd almost believe it was him wrapped around her instead of the soft cotton.

Her eyes flew open; the rage she'd kept so carefully tamped down was beginning to surface. For a moment her hand trembled violently, as if it would suddenly develop a mind of its own and sweep the counter surface clean. She turned away before her darker side emerged. It was time to leave.

Still, she wanted to leave Lauren with something to think about. She wanted her to wonder if someone had been in her house. She wanted her to worry a little. Nothing overt. No, it had to be something very subtle.

She looked around until she found the perfect method. She moved toward the dresser and picked up a bottle of perfume, touching the frosted glass tip to her pulse points. She waited a moment and sniffed her inner wrist. Not a fragrance she would normally wear, but the idea of wearing *her* perfume taken from *her* bottle was too much to resist.

She applied the scent to each wrist, behind each ear, between her breasts, and behind her knees. She then very carefully placed the bottle's top on the dresser's surface. A drop of perfume fell onto the highly polished wood, leaving a smudged spot. She stepped back to study the picture it made.

Perfect.

Chapter Four

Lauren sensed a difference in the atmosphere the moment she stepped inside her house. A dark memory started to intrude, making it hard for her to breathe. She abruptly shoved it out and found it easier to take in air as she decided to see if the uneasy feeling was only imaginary.

She first looked around her kitchen searching for something, anything, out of order that would cause the subtle shift in the air she felt. She even took a quick inventory of the contents of the cabinets and pantry.

"Stop with the imagination," she ordered herself, as she braced her hand on the counter while she used her toes to push her shoes off while reaching into a cabinet for a wineglass. "You're just overtired and looking for the bogeyman."

She pulled a bottle of wine out of the refrigerator and filled a glass. She decided a hot bubble bath was in order before she could even think about dinner.

But her unsettling feeling refused to go away as she looked around the kitchen. As she walked down the hallway, she couldn't stop herself from pausing at the doorway to each room and taking a quick look inside. That troubled feeling deep in her bones refused to leave her, although she couldn't find anything out of place. As she looked at her computer, she felt the urge to turn the power on and see if any of the files had been looked at. She suddenly shook her head to rid herself of the feeling and left the room before she gave in to her paranoia.

From the moment she walked into her bedroom she knew her imagination wasn't going overboard. Lauren's first thought was that someone had taken her gun, but a quick search in her night stand drawer proved it was still there. As she looked around, she finally realized what bothered her: the scent of her perfume lingered in the air.

"Good going," she chided herself, seeing the perfume bottle top lying on the dresser. She was disgusted with herself as she picked up the cut-glass stopper and stared down at the polished wood, now marred by the liquid dripping from the glass. She couldn't believe she'd been in that much of a hurry that morning that she hadn't put the top back on the bottle. She couldn't even use the excuse that perhaps her cleaning lady had done it, since this wasn't her day to come in. She replaced the stopper and promptly headed for the bathroom.

She began running her bath water and pouring in bath salts before quickly stripping off her clothing. It wasn't until Lauren had settled back in the hot water with a sigh of relief that an unsettling thought struck her so hard she almost bolted out of the tub to recheck all the door and window locks to make sure they had been secured.

She hadn't worn that particular perfume today.

* * *

"I want to thank you for talking to the group on such short notice, since our scheduled speaker had to cancel at the last minute." Gail walked with Josh out of the high school building into the parking lot. "There's always someone who can tell them how to build their self-esteem, but the important thing they need to hear is that there is hope, if they're willing to take the chance. And the only person they should hear it from is a member of the bar."

"I didn't mind doing it. Although I wasn't sure at first that they would want to listen to me; if they shouldn't have a woman prosecutor talking to them." Josh shifted his briefcase from one hand to the other as he pulled his car keys out of his pants pocket.

"Maybe so, but you're so active in helping the battered woman that I felt they would listen to you. You look about as nonthreatening as a teddy bear when you're in your small-town–lawyer mode," Gail insisted with an impish grin, as she patted his cheek.

He affected a mock snarl. "I have to admit, I was impressed by the size of the group. A lot of brave ladies were in there."

Her face darkened. "They have to be brave in order to endure the hell they live."

Josh stopped by Gail's small compact car, waiting as she unlocked the door. "Changes can't happen overnight, Gail. At least now, if the wife is physically abused by her husband, she doesn't have to press charges if she's afraid to. The abuser is automatically taken in. It's a step in the right direction, but women still need to take that next big step by getting up the courage to get out of the abusive relationship before it's too late."

"It's not always that easy."

Josh noticed her bleak expression. "You?"

For a moment he thought she was going to evade his question. She lifted her head and looked squarely at him. "Can you honestly think I would put up with an abusive relationship?"

He remembered the stories of the petite police-woman bringing in burly suspects more than twice her size without any problems and chuckled. "After what I've heard, I'd tend to think you were the one handing out the black eyes in a relationship."

She laughed at that. "Yeah, I'm a real tough guy." She glanced at her watch. "Say, would you like to go somewhere for a drink or a cup of coffee?" She immediately backpedaled when Josh hesitated. "Hey, it's all right. I understand if you have other things to do."

"Jury selection for the Watson case is tomorrow, and I like to take the night before to psyche myself up," he explained. "How about another time?"

"Sure." She opened the door and slid into her car. She switched on the engine. "Good night, Josh, and thanks again."

"Gail?"

She looked up.

"I think it's great you work so hard for this support group for battered women. That if, for one reason or another, they don't seek help from a shelter, they can find out they have another option until they feel strong enough to make a decision by coming to this group and learning they're not alone."

"You've always been very supportive in battered women's issues, so I knew you would understand why I wanted to find an alternative for them." She ran her palm along the steering wheel. "Unfortunately, too many women refuse to admit they're being abused or that it's wrong to be abused, but thanks to their relatives or friends urging them to find help, there are a few who are coming around to face the truth. For each one that happens I'll throw a party. For each one I lose," her face was a study in darkness, "well, I'll pray for the day the abuser gets his. Good night, Josh."

Josh tried to ignore the unsettling feeling he experienced as he watched her drive away. For all the time they'd worked together and the few times they'd dated, he still wondered how much of her he didn't know.

When he reached his car, he unlocked the door and stepped back in revulsion as he stared at a small square-shaped clay pot filled with an unfamiliar flowering plant that had been set with great care in the middle of the driver's seat. He leaned closer for a better look and recoiled as the heavy aroma of Obsession perfumed the car's interior.

"Interesting choice of plant life, Josh," Kevin said to Josh, who waited impatiently by a patrol car while his own car was dusted for fingerprints and the interior examined for a hopeful clue.

He was not amused. "Maybe she couldn't find any roses at this hour."

The detective inclined his head toward the car. "Hawkins, whose hobby is plants, told me what kind of plant was left. You're the proud owner of kudzu."

"Kudzu? What the hell is that?"

"Hey, I only know roses because if I don't buy them for the wife on her birthday and our anniversary, I'm in big trouble. One of the other guys says it's used as ground cover. Why you got it, we have no idea. Maybe she's finally leaving clues to her identity. Which I wouldn't mind one bit. The least she could do is give us a hint. It'd make my job easier." He scratched the back of his head.

"What the hell is she trying to do? Is she going to start following me wherever I go now?" Josh was ready to explode with the frustration boiling up inside him. "Am I going to have to look over my shoulder from now on? What's next? Is she going to freak out one day and kill me or some innocent person?"

"Hey, calm down, buddy." Kevin held up his hands to stem Josh's words. "Josh, we're going to make sure it doesn't go that far. Look, we may not have all the resources that LA has, but we do have a bunch of men who aren't going to let anything happen to you. You're the only prosecutor with a decent conviction rate."

He nodded. "I know. It's just making me nuts. I can't help but wonder. I've already lost a wardrobe. What's next?"

Kevin grinned. "If I were you, I'd make sure to keep my insurance premiums paid up."

"You are one sick bastard."

"Yeah, but a cop has to be. It's the only way we can do our jobs and remain somewhat sane."

"Then find this woman before I do. Because so help me, I don't care if she is a woman, if I find her first, I'll beat the living shit out of her for doing this to me and people I care about."

Lauren had no idea where they were going for dinner. She'd been kidding when she'd suggested to Josh that they go to Rothschild's and had given him a call back, asking him to surprise her. Although the choices in the small desert town weren't many, most of the restaurants were geared for the tourist trade that stopped to eat on their way to the Arizona border, and all served good quality food. She figured she was safe with her burnt-orange silk jumpsuit.

"I really should consider getting a dog," she told her reflection as she looked into the mirror and applied mascara. "Then I'd have a good reason to talk out loud and someone to keep unwanted visitors out." She lifted her head when she heard the doorbell.

Josh stood on the doorstep wearing slacks, instead of his usual dress jeans.

"Come on in," she invited, as she pulled open the door. "Would you like a drink?"

He shook his head. "No thanks. I made reservations for seven-thirty. I would have brought you flowers, but I've sort of developed an aversion to them," he explained, helping her with her coat.

"Just bring chocolate and I'll be your slave forever." She made sure the heavy-duty deadbolt was engaged when they walked back outside.

"I'll keep that in mind." He led her down the walkway to his car and opened the passenger door for her. "You're out of LA, right?"

"Right in the heart of it."

"Not many people would leave what had to have been ultramodern facilities to come out here, where the city complains every time we need pencils."

"I went through a bad divorce and needed a change of scenery. One of my instructors from medical school knew about this position. I think his letter of recommendation counted more than my qualifications. Plus, they wanted a forensics specialist out here so they could keep up with the times."

"Yeah, we have a bunch of good ole boys out here," he agreed. "How long were you married?"

"Six years." Her distaste was evident. "And not one of my favorite subjects."

Josh took the hint. "Well, let's see. I'm not sure I could discuss your work on an empty stomach, I haven't prosecuted any interesting cases for quite some time and I've never been one to talk about the weather or politics. Have any suggestions?"

"Did you watch the Christopher Lee festival on cable last night?"

"Of course." He rapidly warmed to his subject. "Although I admit I'm more a traditionalist and prefer the classics."

"Same here. I see enough blood and gore in my work that I don't need to see it during my time off."

During the short drive to the restaurant, they kept up a running debate as to which film epitomized a true horror classic.

"Karloff could scare anyone with nis eyes alone," Lauren insisted.

"You want to be scared?" he dared. "Look at Lon Chaney, Senior. The man was an artist at frightening a person," he told her, as he climbed out of the car and walked around to help her out.

The moment Josh gave the headwaiter his name, they were shown to their table and handed menus.

"What got you interested in pathology, anyway?" Josh asked after they were asked if they cared for a drink. Since he was driving, he decided to stick to club soda. Lauren ordered a glass of wine.

She smiled. It wasn't difficult to understand his curiosity. "I know. People, especially men, can't understand why, when it's not known as a specialty women doctors are interested in. Even more so with my subspecialty being forensics pathology."

"I admit it's not easy for me to visualize you down in the morgue with Igor, cutting up corpses."

Lauren thought of the problems she had with her assistant and began to think the nickname fit the man. "There's days I wonder why I got into it, but I've never regretted my decision. I became fascinated in the field during my intern's rotation in pathology," she said, looking up with a smile as her wineglass was set in front of her. "The head pathologist was one of these diggers. By that, I mean he enjoyed digging for the truth. He kept on top of everything new in his field, attending seminars dealing with new techniques and all. He always said why use a hammer and chisel to write when you can use a computer. So why not search for better ways to detect the cause of death? I did my residency under him and learned it wasn't wrong to question what might look like the truth and to keep an open mind in my work. I soon developed an interest in forensic medicine and took on studies of the subject and began some research. The first thing I learned was that the best qualification for that kind of work is a strong stomach, since there's no such thing as a clean murder."

Josh thought about some of the murder scenes he'd visited in the past. "You're right on that count. Although, you won't have the challenges here. Our homicide rate, knock on wood, is pretty low."

"That's why I liked the idea of having time to indulge in some research," she replied. "What will really take up my time for a while is organizing the records."

"Harvey never did like recordkeeping, which was a prime bone of contention with everyone."

Lauren thought of the state-of-the-art computer system and staff she'd left behind. She was grateful that she was familiar with the computer her new office used. "That was the first thing I noticed. I'm just glad I like a challenge." She eyed him as she set down her menu after deciding on chicken in wine sauce. "Such as, how does an assistant district attorney with a slight Texas drawl end up in a California desert town filled with more than its share of yuppies who think they've found nirvana and a bunch of old-time locals who wouldn't mind the town going back to the rural way it was? Not to mention the ongoing controversy over why you won't wear a tie in court."

He grimaced. "Someone's been talking."

"It seems your refusal to wear a tie has become a legend around the courthouse, since none of the other attorneys are allowed to get away with it," she pointed out. "And the drawl is not easy to miss for someone who spent two years in specialized training in Houston. Rumor has it you're too good a prosecutor to be out here and should be where you could properly utilize your skills. Sound familiar?"

"It just goes to show the town knows what it's doing in attracting quality help."

Her gaze didn't waver from his. "Such as prosecutors who have secret admirers?"

The tic in his jaw told her that wasn't one of his favorite subjects either. "Who told you about that?"

She ignored his abrupt tone. "Do you honestly think it could have been kept a secret? In fact, some people are thinking of starting a pool to guess the lady's identity. Although they didn't exactly give it the grim overtones you seem to be exhibiting. More like talk of flowers and small gifts and such."

His jaw worked furiously. "We're trying to keep it quiet."

Lauren understood immediately. "This isn't about

some shy little thing who has a crush on you, is it? You're really spooked about it."

He waited until their waiter left their plates before speaking. Even then, he lowered his voice to ensure he would not be overheard by neighboring diners. "A few months ago it was nothing more than something that flattered my ego. Flowers sent with thank-you notes, things like that. Before I knew it, it turned into an out-of-control situation with my home being broken into and women's things left there. I have no idea who's doing it or why."

"The only gossip I hear is about flowers and notes."

"Because the police are trying to keep it as quiet as possible," he explained. "This woman has broken into my house I don't know how many times. No matter how often I change the locks she finds a way to get in; she's played nasty tricks on women I've dated, she leaves messages on my answering machine and sends gifts, some so personal they're almost embarrassing. Not once has she given me any hint as to her identity. She acts as if I should know who she is."

Lauren nodded. "Typical fatal attraction. I'm sure you've investigated the women you might have parted with on less than friendly terms. I hate to say it about my own sex, but a scorned woman can be a very vengeful creature and eager to inflict horrible pain. I performed a post on a man who told a woman he'd dated a total of three times that he didn't think they were compatible and should start seeing other people. She couldn't handle the idea he was rejecting her and went after him with a carving knife. By the time she finished . . ." She left the rest unsaid.

Josh shuddered at the thought. "I've seen my share of these cases, which leaves me even more unnerved, now that I'm one of those statistics."

"I gather you don't suspect me if you're willing to talk so openly about it."

"You weren't in town when it all began and, to be honest, I can't see you terrorizing anyone. I have an idea you'd prefer to face your victim."

She laughed at that. "Funny you should say that." The brief look of pain crossed her face so quickly he wasn't sure if he'd imagined it.

Lauren waited until they began eating before bringing up the subject again. "Has anyone worked up a psychological profile on your stalker?"

Josh winced at the term, even if it did fit. "We're a small town, Lauren. We don't have the resources, probably because so far, we haven't had the crimes to warrant them. Plus, so far, no one has thought it was serious enough to go on the outside for help."

"From what you've said, it sounds as if the problem is increasing, which means it isn't anything you can take lightly." She sipped her wine before continuing. "I have a friend who used to work as a suspect profiler for the FBI. She now has a private practice and does some police consulting on the side. Dana's been looking at the growing number of stalkers and their victims. She's already done some very extensive research on the subject and worked up some interesting views about them. I'm sure she could work up a profile, or at least offer some ideas. So far, she's been right on the mark with her profiles, so she might come up with something that will give you a clue to the woman's identity."

He sighed as he contemplated his steak. "Right now, I'd settle for a name, address, and telephone number. Even a vague location of where she lives would be helpful."

Lauren smiled her sympathy at his frustration. "If it

was that easy, we wouldn't need to worry, would we? But I'm sure she can come up with some ideas that might help you get a clearer view of your unwanted admirer. She will need to look over the police reports so she can have an overall picture of what's gone on."

Josh never believed in thinking things over, but he gave his answer immediately. "If you're willing to call her and see if she's interested, I'm more than willing to put together a file of whatever information she needs to figure this out. I'll accept help from anyone who offers it. I want this woman out of my life."

Lauren held up her wineglass in a silent toast. "Don't worry, Josh, we'll learn the identity of your secret admirer and pay her a visit. And while we're there, we'll suggest she wait for an invitation before she decides to drop in again."

He tapped his glass against hers and said on a grimmer note, "That's an invitation she won't see in this lifetime, because when this is all over, I plan to see her sitting in a cell for a very long time."

Chapter Five

"Hey, Doc." Detective Kevin Peterson stuck his head around the door to the autopsy room. He deliberately kept his gaze averted from the naked form lying on the stainless steel table in front of Lauren. "Any chance you're almost finished cuttin' up that stiff? I'd like to have a talk with you."

Lauren looked up. Her features were hidden by her surgical mask, and the goggles she wore to prevent bone splinters and dust from flying into her eyes made her look like something out of a futuristic film. "Come on in, Detective. I have no problem in talking to people while I work. And, by the way, the word we use around here is 'deceased,' not 'stiffs.' We do try to keep a little class." Her eerie appearance belied her words.

He inadvertently looked in her direction and turned a nasty shade of green as he watched her hand her assistant a kidney to be weighed. "I make it a practice of not being present at any openings I don't absolutely have to attend." He swallowed the nausea crawling up his throat.

Her face mask shifted as she smiled. "I'm almost

finished here. Why don't you wait for me in my office?
There should be some coffee left in the pot."

"I'll see you there." He didn't hesitate in taking her
up on her offer.

Ten minutes later, Lauren walked in her office to
find Kevin lounging in the chair opposite her desk. He
whistled an off-key ditty as he idly leafed through the
contents of a manila folder. By reading the label on the
folder, she knew it was one he'd taken from her desk.

"I swear, you cops are worse than a five-year-old
child. Can't you respect anyone's privacy? Or is it just
a habit with you that you feel you have to read other
people's reports?" She plucked the folder out of his
hands and dropped it back on her desk as she walked
around to her chair.

He shrugged, not the least embarrassed to be caught
snooping. "There's pretty gory stuff in there. Judging
from the pictures, I'd say his body was out in that
house for quite a while. That's the Thompson case,
isn't it?"

Lauren nodded as she opened a desk drawer and
pulled out a tube of hand cream. "Chemicals are hell
on the hands, even when you're wearing gloves," she
explained, squeezing a dab in the palm of her hand and
rubbing the lotion into her skin. The faint scent of
vanilla mixed with the more tangy chemical smells.
"There's no evidence of foul play—nothing more than
a straightforward heart attack. I'd say he'd probably
been dead a good four or five days before anyone
thought to check on him, and with the warm days, his
body started decomposing pretty fast. Seventy-four
years old, no family." She seemed to shake herself out
of her doldrums. "So what can I do for you?"

Kevin smiled. "No 'Make an appointment with my

secretary' or putting me off like a big city hot-shit coroner would?"

"Since we're not in the big city anymore, I don't see why I should act like a big-shit coroner. And, knowing my secretary, she'd probably not write you down anyway. I also doubt you'd come down here unless you had a good reason, although I'm not complaining. It's so seldom we get drop-in visitors who can still breathe and function on their own."

She settled back in her chair and propped her feet on top of her desk with the ankles demurely crossed as she watched him with a steady gaze. If he didn't want to get to the point right away, she wasn't going to push the issue. She noted the sandy blond hair, bright blue eyes, and lightly tanned features of a man who would always look like a boy. She imagined he had no trouble soothing older women with his boyish charm or intimidating men with that darker hidden side of his. His teal polo shirt tucked neatly into khaki trousers lent to his boyish appeal.

He grinned. "I can't believe it. A doc with a sense of humor. Can you cook? And if you can, will you marry me? I have this weekend free. We don't need to have a big wedding, do we? I hate crowds, and white makes me look so washed out. Of course, we have to make sure not to let my wife know about this. She hates the idea of sharing."

She stretched her arms over her head as she rotated her neck to relieve the tension. "This weekend looks good for me. I wouldn't worry about wearing white. I'm sure if we searched around we could find something in a nice, soft shade of cream for you."

Kevin's smile warmed even more. He knew this was one lady he could work with easily. The word was already out that she was whipping the department into shape, and reports were reaching detectives on time instead of their having to call down, demanding and making threats when they didn't get them. "You're not only prettier than ole Harvey, you're quicker. Or maybe I should say that Josh is the quick one. He didn't waste any time in snapping you up before anyone else had a chance to say more than hi," he elaborated.

"From what I've heard of what happens to women snapped up by Josh Brandon, I don't think I would consider it the chance of a lifetime."

His only reaction was a slight narrowing of the eyes. "Do you listen to rumors, or did Josh tell you?"

"Josh."

He leaned back in the chair, resting his clasped hands across his belly. "How much did he tell you?"

Lauren shrugged. "Enough to know there's a woman out there making his life hell. She's graduated from simple adoration to a bit of terrorizing his past lady friends, and she's even starting to retaliate against him. I'm not an expert, but I'd say if she isn't found and stopped soon, someone could end up badly hurt."

He nodded. "Then you know we're talking about your typical fatal attraction here. The lady leaves no concrete clues, but she does make sure that Josh knows she was on his turf."

Lauren thought of the day she'd sensed someone had been in her house.

Finding the open perfume bottle top on her dresser still bothered her, and she hadn't been able to wear the fragrance since. She now took the extra time to make sure all the doors were locked securely before she left home and she made arrangements to have a security system installed. She offered the company a bonus if it was installed fast.

"Even without finding any clues, I would think you could come up with some idea of who she could be. Or has he been that popular with the women over the years that the list is practically endless?" She only hoped she didn't sound as if she was fishing—even if she was.

"Josh works with a lot of women's issues—spousal abuse, rape, you name it." Kevin pulled out a pack of cigarettes and looked hopefully around for an ashtray. "Mind if I smoke?" He held up the cigarette and a lighter.

"Don't light that unless you want to end up on my table before the end of the day. I quit a year ago and still don't have the willpower, not to mention tolerance, to sit around a smoker," she told him, as she reached into a drawer and pulled out a squirt gun. "Just a little insurance, in case anyone doesn't believe I mean it."

"You reformed nonsmokers are a pain in the ass, you know that?" With one last, wistful look at the pack, he put it back in his pocket. "Okay, back to Josh. Because of all the women's causes he's worked with, Josh has a lot of ladies who're grateful to him. We're figuring one of them is behind this. As we've learned from past cases, it's the overly grateful women who turn out to be the most dangerous ones."

"They decide he's done it for them personally, not because of the issue involved. They see it as a declaration of love."

Kevin nodded. "Josh pulled a copy of the files. Said you have a friend who has experience in this area."

"Dana has a pretty strong background in the subject. She was one of the first to follow some of the stories on stalkers and see patterns in their behavior just as there are patterns in serial killers," she explained. "She's written some informative articles on stalkers and has since become an expert in the field. I thought it might not hurt for her to look the case over and see if she has any suggestions. I realize I'm venturing into your territory, and I apologize for that, but I didn't think you'd mind any help you could get."

"It may be my territory, but I'm adult enough to welcome it." He shook his head. "This bitch has me up against a wall. She's so clever it's downright scary. Sometimes I pray she'll just disappear down some hole or move to another town. I figure she'll make some other guy's life hell. And become another cop's nightmare. But next time around, someone might get lucky."

Lauren tented her fingers, peering over the tips. "Is there a reason why you're talking so openly about this case to a civilian?"

"The best kind of reason."

"Meaning?"

Kevin didn't believe in pulling his punches, and he figured the woman seated across from him was strong enough to take the worst he could throw at her. And if his hunch about her and Josh turned out right, she was going to need to know what could happen.

"We don't know very much about this woman, but the few clues we have tell us she's decided she's put her brand on Josh and she's going to make sure anyone who tries to poach on her territory will get hassled in the process. She's getting a lot nastier about it, too."

She grew still. "Give me some examples."

"What we once figured was nothing more than random vandalism and harassment to a few people we're now giving more serious thought to. And that's because each of them had dated Josh at one time. And they were usually the ones to call it off." He didn't need to pull out his notebook to refresh his memory. "It started out as little things at first. Prize roses cut. Paint thrown against front doors. Obscenities painted on outside walls. Phone calls in the middle of the night, then the caller hangs up. Two women Josh saw a few times had their tires slashed. When he broke up with them, the tricks stopped as suddenly as they'd started. The latest was a pretty nasty joke involving the lady's job promotion. She now considers Josh lower than dirt."

Lauren leaned forward in her chair and laced her fingers together, resting them on top of her desk. "This may not be anything at all, but you may as well know that one evening when I got home from work, I sensed someone had broken into my house. Except I couldn't find anything taken."

Kevin's gaze sharpened. "Is this feeling more than a woman's intuition? Was there proof someone had been in there even if nothing was taken?"

"Have you ever been somewhere and had the hair stir on your arms or on the back of your neck because something just doesn't feel right? It was that kind of feeling. I couldn't find anything concrete, nothing even looked out of order in my drawers, but the stopper to one of my perfume bottles was lying on top of the dresser next to the bottle and I hadn't worn that fragrance that day. I had all the locks changed the next day and a security system will be installed tomorrow."

He nodded his approval. "Did you tell Josh about this?"

She shook her head. "No reason to. Mr. Brandon and I are not an item, no matter what anyone thinks."

Kevin muttered a curse. "That doesn't mean his 'friend' doesn't think so, since she has a habit of jumping to quick conclusions about women Josh so much as talks to. I suggest you start acting a hell of a lot more cautious when you're anywhere on your own."

"I'm not foolish enough to think I'm invincible, but I'm not going to look over my shoulder every thirty seconds, either," she retorted, thinking back to a time when she'd done just that and, as a result, ended up a nervous wreck. It took a lot of inner strength for her to take back her life. "I can't imagine why this woman considers me a threat."

Kevin pushed himself out of his chair. "Maybe it's *her* woman's intuition at work. I want you to call me if you ever again think an unwanted visitor dropped by. Next time, we'll dust for prints and see if we can find anything." He dropped a white business card on her desk. "Changing your door locks is a good idea, but I'll warn you now that she's gotten around new locks and security systems before."

She nodded.

"Dr. Hunter, Pete needs you." A bored-looking Sophie appeared in the doorway. "Now."

Kevin shot Lauren a sympathetic glance as he walked past the secretary. "Good luck, Doc."

"I should have listened to my mother. She wanted me to be a dermatologist," she muttered, dreading to think what problem her assistant had gotten himself into.

Let's see how the new doctor for the dead likes this turn of events! she laughed to herself, as she exited the elevator and easily merged with the building employees going to lunch. It wasn't difficult to blend in. Not when she was one of them.

She wondered how long it would take them to discover the paperwork mix-up. Considering how inept

Pete Ignatius was at times, it was incredibly easy. Which was why she'd made sure the all-important file error would be blamed on him. How far along would he get before he realized the error? And his only recourse would be to tell *her* what had happened. It would throw their precious schedule off but good, which would then throw the blame on her. Yes, she even made sure of that happening.

Her chuckle stopped cold at the reminder of why she'd chosen to make this woman's life miserable. They had no idea she'd seen them at the restaurant Saturday night. She tried to tell herself it was a business dinner. Until she saw the way Josh looked at Lauren. A look of wonder, as if he couldn't imagine a woman like her could ever come into his life. As if he was the luckiest man in the world to have her with him. That was when the pain struck. A pain that sent white-hot darts through her body as she watched Lauren look back at him with that same faint wonder. How dared she think she could seduce him away from her?

She knew that type of woman. They liked to tease a man, lead him on, and promise him all sorts of things. Look how all the others did just that to Josh. They were nothing more than trash. She made sure to show him exactly what they were like. She wanted him to see how evil they could be. And, in the process, she'd let him know how devoted she was to him by rescuing him from these women.

"Hi, haven't seen you in a while. JoAnne and I are going over to that new salad bar. Want to come along with us?" Lauren laughed. "I even promise not to talk about how my morning went or how I spent it!"

Her lips stretched in a natural smile as she looked at the object of her hate. Her expression was so bright and cheerful as she gazed at Lauren that the coroner could never guess how much she really despised the woman. "Thanks, Lauren, lunch with you and JoAnne sounds like something I really need. You would not believe the crazy morning I've had."

"The bastard came by the school this afternoon and told the office that he was supposed to pick up Brian for a dental appointment!" Mitzi sobbed, twisting her shoulderbag straps between her fingers.

Josh handed her a Kleenex. "The school is aware of the restraining order you obtained. Did they call the police?"

She nodded, taking several deep, calming breaths. "The secretary was alert enough to write a note to one of the clerks to call the police while she stalled Steve by claiming she didn't know what class Brian was in and would have to look up his file. He got suspicious and started screaming that they were keeping him from his son. When the police showed up, he was running down the halls, yelling Brian's name and frightening the children, especially the smaller ones." She covered her nose with the Kleenex and blew noisily. "By the time I got there, Brian was in hysterics. He . . ." she stopped to catch her breath, "he thought Steve had killed me and had come to kill him."

"Shit," Josh said under his breath, easily visualizing what had to be a chaotic scene as he glanced over the notes of the incident. He knew the official report wouldn't be written up yet, and therefore, he'd asked Ginnie to get any information on it she could. Naturally, she came through with flying colors. He decided Mitzi wasn't ready to learn that the officer who arrested Steve found a loaded handgun in her ex-husband's jacket pocket.

"Mitzi, the man was uncontrollable when the police officer tried to arrest him. He was taken to the hospital because his behavior was so erratic and they thought at first he might be on drugs. He's since been placed under psychiatric observation, so you have nothing to worry about."

"Until he gets out." She swiped at her tears with her fingertips. "I can't live this way, Josh. I'm always afraid that he'll show up again. Afraid that he'll break into the house one night and hold a knife to my throat, the way he did that one night. I'm so scared he'll lose what little control he has."

Her words ended in a sob. "What if he turns all that anger on Brian? He's just a little boy, and he sometimes acts as if he's lived through a major war. He jumps at the slightest sound. He has nightmares. He's suffering emotional problems at school. His teachers understand, but it can't keep on this way," she appealed to him, grabbing hold of his hand. "Josh, you're the only one I feel safe saying these things to. It's times like this I'm embarrassed to work in the public defender's office. They work to keep people like Steve out of jail when I'm begging the system to keep him in there!"

"Honey, it's their job to worry about a person's rights," he soothed, uneasily aware she was right.

Ginnie slipped inside the office and placed her hands on Mitzi's shoulders. "Come on, honey, let's wash your face. You'll feel much better." Her gentle voice was at odds with her usual acerbic nature. She pulled the younger woman to her feet and led her out while shooting a telling look at Josh over her shoulder. *Okay, hotshot, do something!*

He picked up the phone, at first having no idea who he was going to call or what he was going to say. He only hoped he could come up with something in the next few minutes that would ease Mitzi's mind. "Why not just come right out and ask for a damn miracle while you're at it? That might be the easiest thing."

As Josh quickly made several calls, a question nagged at the back of his mind. Could Mitzi be the one behind these nasty jokes? Could she have misunderstood his assistance for something on a more personal level? The idea of his not daring to trust any woman he came in contact with, no matter how casual, wasn't a pleasant prospect. He didn't consider himself a perfect individual, and the hellish limbo he felt himself in at times wasn't anything he was used to.

"Dr. Hunter's on line two for you," one of the other secretaries called through the open door. "Shall I tell her you'll call her back later?"

"No, I'll take it now. She can't have any worse news for me than what I've already been hearing," he muttered, picking up the phone. "Lauren?"

"One and the same."

He grinned. "By calling me, you've made my day. What can I do for you?"

"It's more what I can do for you. Kevin sent over copies of the reports last week and I immediately faxed them to Dana, my psychiatrist friend. She called me last night and said if you're available, she'd like to get together with you next Friday afternoon around three to discuss what she's come up with. Shall I tell her that's all right, or would you like to call her directly?"

He turned the calendar pages until he came to the appropriate day and scanned his schedule. "There shouldn't be a problem, as long as you're free, too, and I don't need to talk to her ahead of time."

"Then I'll let her know we'll be there." A man's voice sounded faintly in the background. Lauren uttered a sigh of disgust. "Excuse me, but I have to go kick some butt and carve up a few bodies to earn my living. Try to keep yourself out of trouble, Counselor."

"I'll see what I can do." He was still smiling when he hung up.

"Josh?" Mitzi hovered just inside the office, still tearstained, and uncertain whether to walk into the room the rest of the way.

"Come on in." He quickly returned to the present and gestured for her to enter as he looked over the notes he'd taken during his phone calls while she was gone. "I was right. Steve has been hospitalized for a thirty-day psychiatric evaluation. During his first five minutes in there, he's already punched out an orderly and slammed a nurse against a wall. At the rate his popularity is growing, I have an idea he's going to be there a hell of a lot longer than thirty days."

The woman looked as if she wasn't sure whether to smile her relief or cry. "You've been a great help, Josh," she said, in a husky voice bordering on tears. "I don't think I'll ever be able to repay you for your help."

He shook his head. "Don't worry about it."

"It's just that few men care about women victims the way you do, and I want you to know how much I appreciate all you've done for us," she insisted, clasping his hand between hers as she reached up and kissed him on the cheek. "Thank you."

After she left in the midst of another wave of tears, these of relief, he leaned back in his chair, feeling as if he'd just gone through an intense session. For a moment he felt as if there had been more than your normal everyday gratitude in Mitzi's voice when she'd thanked him. He hated to consider that she might be the one making his life hell. But then, he couldn't discount anyone, and Mitzi did have access to his schedule.

Right about now, he hated anything and everything that had to do with women.

Chapter Six

"What, no flowers?" one of the other attorneys kidded Josh, as the two men walked past the desks of clerks and secretaries. "Did I lose track of time, or did your secret admirer move on to someone else?"

"Up yours, Hampton," Josh told him.

"That's right, Brandon, keep that stiff upper lip! You can always find another woman."

"It *is* pretty odd, no flower delivery," Ginnie told him, as she followed him into his office. "They're always here first thing in the morning. Sheila's devastated. It was her turn this week."

"Then call a damn florist and have something delivered to her," he growled, starting to drop his briefcase on his desk, but he changed his mind after seeing the pile of message slips. He sifted through them and grimaced at one in particular. "Did she say why she was calling?"

"Just that she's been thinking about you a lot lately and she's so sorry for all those horrible things she said to her honey bunny the last time you were together." Ginnie uttered the last few words in a syrupy drawl. "I'd say she wants you back. She exuded enough hormones over the phone that even I could have gotten horny."

Josh crumpled the message slip in his hand and dropped it in the wastebasket.

"You know she'll call back."

"And if I'm here, I'll talk to her and remind her she was the one who broke up with me and I have no desire to get back with her again. But I won't bother calling her back."

If that was to be his only dark spot for the day, he didn't care. He was only relieved that his unknown admirer hadn't somehow found out about his appointment with Lauren's friend. There were days he'd felt so paranoid, he even wondered if his phone was bugged, and he'd had it electronically swept on a regular basis to make sure it was clean.

He'd also taken special steps by not putting his meeting with Lauren's friend down on his desk calendar or mentioning it to anyone. Not even to Ginnie. While he trusted his assistant implicitly and knew she couldn't be the one, he still couldn't trust that a certain someone might find out without Ginnie realizing what was going on. Ginnie could keep her mouth shut, but what if it was someone around here who knew how to push all the right buttons? He didn't even want to consider it.

Not when he could feel a faint cold spot on the back of his neck. Heather wanted back in his life, and she had been strange to begin with. Funny, he hadn't even considered her when all this began. He was grateful he was going to see that psychologist friend of Lauren's. Too many strange things were happening in his life. He needed something to balance it. Other than thoughts of Lauren.

First thing Friday, he merely told Ginnie he was

taking off early that day and that she could do the same. Feeling the need to be cautious, he took a circuitous route to Lauren's house, to be on the safe side.

"Our crime rate isn't that bad, you know," he commented, inclining his head toward the security alarm keypad bolted into the wall by the front door.

"I'm from LA and believe in being safe and not sorry. I don't appreciate unwanted visitors." She pulled on a dark green blazer and rolled up the sleeves to reveal patterned fabric cuffs.

He was positive there was a lot more to her not so casual statement. He told himself there was no reason to have those unsettling feelings; he wasn't officially dating Lauren. But lately, he'd gotten suspicious of everyone, including the paperboy. "Have you had any lately?"

"No more than most people. I just like to be prepared." She paused and looked back as she picked up her shoulderbag.

"Such as?" he persisted.

Lauren shook her head. "Somebody with kinky thoughts decided it was fun to rummage through my clothing and makeup. No big deal."

He wasn't convinced. "It could be."

She looked up. "I prefer to keep it low key, all right?"

Josh was frustrated by her refusal to take it seriously, but he figured if he said too much she'd think he was merely being paranoid. He'd let it drop—for now.

"How many people know about your appointment with Dana today?" she asked, as they walked to his car.

"You, naturally, and me, and I guess Dana. I figured it was better if no one else knew. I only told Ginnie I was taking the rest of the day off for personal reasons. I recently finished a heavy-duty case, so it's not surprising I'd want to get off by myself for a day."

Lauren didn't speak again until they were in the car and on the road. "Has anything happened recently?"

Josh shook his head. "So far, the lady has been quiet. There weren't even any flowers delivered yesterday. That was the most noticeable. And the house has even been left undisturbed. I guess I'm just one of those who always waits for the other shoe to drop, and the waiting's the hardest. How about you?"

"I'm not the one with the problem."

"Then why would you install a heavy-duty security system?" He pulled over to the side of the road.

Lauren made a production of looking at her watch. "We're going to be late."

"Why, Lauren? I can't imagine you're one of those paranoid women who looks under the bed before climbing into it. There has to be a reason."

She took a deep breath. She wasn't surprised he figured it out. "I came home from work one night and something about the house made me think someone had been there." She didn't have to look at him to sense his interest. She looked up. "Nothing was taken and nothing was out of order, except for a perfume bottle top left on my dresser."

"And you hadn't worn that perfume that day."

She nodded. "I told Detective Peterson about it. End of story."

Josh took a deep breath. "She's found a new outlet. You."

"There's no guarantee it was the same person," she protested.

"And there's no guarantee it wasn't." He touched her cheek with the back of his fingers. "Please be careful, Lauren."

"Don't worry, I fully intend to."

He still wasn't convinced, but he knew he had to take her word.

Lauren knew she wasn't going to tell Josh just how she felt about all that. That she didn't sleep as soundly as she used to. And that she kept her gun within easy reach. She knew she wouldn't hesitate shooting anyone who dared to break in while she was there.

"It's really getting to you now, isn't it?" she asked.

"I'm not used to having someone know my movements more intimately than even I do," Josh admitted.

"Probably another term for it would be male frustration over something they can't control. I wonder if more men are stalked by women or vice versa."

"I don't know. It used to be you only heard about men stalking women, but I've heard of more and more men becoming the victims nowadays." He chuckled, but there was no humor in the sound. "I guess you could call it another strike for women's lib."

She nodded. "Rumor has it you're very active in women's issues—domestic violence, rape. That you even successfully prosecuted a date rape case some years ago before it became such a hot issue. That's not an easy crime to convict, and back then it was even harder than it is now."

"It was easy to convict when the attacker had a less than desirable background like this kid had. He liked to date girls who didn't have a strong family life and might be known to have low self-esteem. He scared them out of filing charges by saying no one would believe them and then convinced them it was actually something they'd brought on themselves. Except one time, he chose a girl who refused to be scared off," he said grimly. "She took a lot of flack from him and his family and their high-priced lawyer and they tried to paint a pretty dirty picture of her, but she refused to back down from any of the slime they threw at her. She said he deserved everything he could get. Unfortunately, the judge only gave him community service, but his past caught up with him.''

She stared, unseeing, out the window. "I hope a woman finally had enough and shot him."

He shook his head. "He'd have been better off had he been shot. Instead, he died of AIDS about eighteen months ago. All of his known victims were contacted with the news, and so far, only two have tested positive."

Lauren sighed. "No wonder so many people talk about the darker side of justice."

She sat back in the seat, taking covert glances at Josh as they traveled down the freeway. Since her divorce, she'd deliberately kept herself away from the opposite sex because she knew she was still working things out in her mind. Except Josh was proving to be a different breed of man than she'd met in the past, and she felt something about him she never did about Ron, her ex-husband. She still wasn't sure if it was the dawning of sexual interest, or something more complex. And with what was going on in his life and what she'd heard about his social past, so to speak, she also wasn't sure he was the kind of man she'd even consider getting involved with.

She still wondered what the real story behind the man was. So far, all she'd heard was rumors as to why a hotshot prosecutor was working in an out-of-the-way area where chance of advancement was minimal and headline-grabbing cases very few and far between. But then, considering she was there to lick her wounds after her divorce and to rethink her life, she knew she had no reason to question him without inviting questions on his part.

Josh was also taking stock of Lauren. She was dressed more casually today than the other times he'd seen her, with her hair pulled back in a French braid and tan wool pants, a green-and-cream–print shirt under the green blazer. He wasn't about to tell her he'd done a little discreet checking on her, but the reports he received on her were surprisingly sparse, containing things he already knew. She was divorced, and she was gaining an excellent reputation in forensics medicine. He used to think there wasn't a woman on earth who could completely fascinate him. Now he learned there was. He couldn't help but wonder if it didn't have to do with his feeling that there was a darker side to Lauren Hunter. The trouble was, he would be the first to admit his life wasn't exactly ready for what could be a big change when there was so much turmoil going on. He only hoped there would be a chance to find out, once everything settled down.

The rest of the drive was spent in silence, punctuated only by Lauren's directions the closer they got to the Los Angeles city limits.

"Turn left at the next signal," she directed, suddenly realizing how close they were to their destination.

"Pretty humble digs, for a doctor with her credentials," he commented, when she directed him to a small medical complex not far from the county courthouse.

"Dana likes to keep a low profile, which is why she shies away from the ultramodern medical buildings where a patient's fee pays the rent," Lauren explained, as Josh helped her out of the car and they crossed the parking lot toward the sprawling one-story building. "She also works a lot with the police and fire departments with burnout cases, so this is more accessible for them."

A stocky man wearing jeans and denim jacket stared at her for a moment before quickly crossing in Lauren's path, forcing her to stop short. "Well, if it isn't the Queen Butcher herself," he greeted her. "How ya' doing, Laur?"

Her smile froze on her lips. "Hello, Mark, still working Vice?"

"Nothing but. Still screwing up a cop's case with your so-called 'expert testimony'?" He flicked a glance in Josh's direction and quickly dismissed him as any kind of threat.

"Mark had a murder case he was positive was airtight. Unfortunately, it turned out not to be after I performed the autopsy on a man he'd shot, convinced he was the killer; he only turned out to be a poor soul who happened to be in the wrong place at the wrong time." Lauren didn't take her eyes off the man's sneering features as she related the facts to Josh. "Internal Affairs took over from there."

Mark leaned forward and snarled in her face, the smell of beer heavy on his breath. "All you had to do was erase one little line and no one would have known the difference, but you were too self-righteous to do that, weren't you? You refused to help out one of your husband's friends."

"Mark, this gentleman is an assistant district attorney for the County of Riverside. Are you sure you want to say anything more about tampering with evidence? I'm sure he'd love to hear all about it, so he can get ahold of his colleagues here." Her pleasant tone was steel-coated.

He reared back. "The boss always said you were a grade-A bitch when you were in your doctor mode and how he was better off without you after everything that happened. No wonder you're running around with an assistant DA."

"You know what, Mark? I could really care less what he thinks about me. We have an appointment to keep. Don't expect me to say it's been nice seeing you." She pushed past him.

"Lady, you've got some interesting friends," Josh drawled, following Lauren down the narrow hallway. "So tell me, what does he do for kicks? Terrorize hookers for freebies, or does he just beat up kids when he's had an off day?"

"He's been known for that and more, but nothing's ever been proven, which is why the bastard's still on the force." She stopped at a door and opened it. A buzzer sounded discreetly from within the next room. Lauren dropped into a chair and immediately picked up a magazine. The jerky way she flipped through the pages told Josh how much the encounter had angered her.

He walked around the waiting room, noticing the lack of a desk for any front-office personnel. "No receptionist?"

"Dana's work is all by appointment, and even that's only part time, since she still consults with various government agencies so much." She didn't look up from the article she pretended to read.

Josh turned when the inner door opened. His jaw nearly dropped to the floor. The woman walking out was definitely not his idea of a psychiatrist.

"Lauren, my dear, you've achieved the impossible. You've somehow managed to find a reincarnation of the Marlboro Man." Dana's low voice was pure sex on the hoof as she studied Josh from head to toe. "Why can't I get that lucky?"

Lauren laughed as she accepted the other woman's hug. "Probably because there's no such thing as a Marlboro Woman." She looked over her shoulder at Josh. "Dana, this is Josh Brandon. Josh, Dana Sinclair."

"Dr. Sinclair." He held out his hand.

Dana's smile was movie-star white. "Forget about the doctor part. If I was hung up on titles, I'd be *in* therapy instead of giving it. Come on in." She stepped back to allow them to enter.

Josh was still in shock at meeting Dana, who was tall, with blond hair in loose waves to her shoulders, drop-dead bright blue eyes, a figure meant to be admired by all men, and a voice that fairly smoked. Her soft gray knit dress was businesslike, but her figure gave the word "professional" a whole new meaning.

"Have a seat." Dana waved a languid hand toward a couch against the wall. She bent over at the waist, rummaging through the varied colored file folders on her desk, until a soft "ah" of triumph escaped her lips. She held up a dark blue folder. "Here we are." She dropped into a chair next to the couch and opened the folder as she crossed her legs. "I'd offer you coffee, but Lauren would only warn you that no one can make horrible coffee like I can, and besides, I'm too eager to go over this case with you." She opened the folder and looked up. "Have there been any more instances since I received this?"

Josh shook his head. "Surprisingly, it's been real quiet. You'd almost think she's gone on vacation or she's found someone new."

"Oh, no, I sincerely doubt she's disappeared from your life." She spoke with a confidence that was almost jarring. She reached into a drawer and pulled out a pair of reading glasses which she slipped on. "I studied the police reports and your personal notes about the incidents with great care. Working up a suspect profile takes in the incidents, the kind of person the victim is, and a lot of little things people might not even think about."

"That doesn't say much about how we can find her," he groused.

"Science doesn't always have all the answers," she countered. "What I did find interesting was the mention of the flowers she left you each time." She pulled out a sheet of paper. "Since they all differed, I have a hunch they carry a great deal of significance in all this."

"How?"

"Flowers are known to have a language all their own." Dana passed him the sheet of paper. "What I've done here is list the flowers in the order you received them, along with their meaning. I noticed the first time flowers were sent to your office, they were daffodils wrapped in ferns. Daffodils mean *regard,* and ferns mean *fascination.* She was letting you know right away she was entranced with you. Then, the first time she left flowers in your house, she chose jonquils."

He nodded, still stunned by the idea the flowers could be telling him how she felt about him. "Someone familiar with plants said they were out of season, so she must have gone to a great deal of trouble to get them. I didn't see any significance in them."

Dana nodded. "She did go to a lot of trouble. She wanted them because of their meaning; jonquils mean *please return my affection.*"

"She hoped he'd understand the meaning and therefore, automatically know she'd sent them, even though she never gave her name," Lauren murmured. "She felt he should just know."

"That's right. She's probably convinced he's known her identity from the beginning and isn't revealing it for one reason or another. She might even assume he's doing it to protect her."

Josh scanned the list. "What you're saying is that she's sending a message with the flowers along with everything else she's done."

Dana nodded. "You have to admit that people who break into your house normally don't clean it as she does. Which also says she's familiar enough with your schedule that she doesn't worry about you walking in and catching her cleaning your bathroom. What bothers me is that the messages are now starting to turn very negative. It might be she's upset because you haven't publicly acknowledged her. Or she's even hoped you would have privately approached her by now to tell her you return her affection. Which is why, whenever she learns you're seeing someone, she sees it as a betrayal of her love and she feels the need to thrust that person out of your life. In the beginning, she was happy enough pulling juvenile pranks, such as destroying rose bushes, vandalizing cars, or throwing paint on people's houses. I have an idea it's going to get much worse."

"The night of the district attorney's retirement party, I came out and found a long key scratch on the side of my car," Lauren suddenly spoke up. "I didn't think anything of it then. And I also had a feeling that someone who hated me a great deal was watching me that night."

Josh had a grim look on his face. "So did I."

Dana looked from one to the other. "Obviously the lady sensed something between the two of you. Did you go there together?"

"We met for the first time there."

The doctor scribbled a note in the margin of the paper on her lap. "Umm, very interesting. She probably observed the two of you meeting and put her own interpretation on it."

"Stop making those umm sounds and saying those idiotic psychiatrist words!" Lauren snapped, sitting forward. "Why can't you spell it out like normal people?"

"This, coming from the person who just loves to throw out medical terms that no one without an advanced degree in Latin could understand."

"Time out!" Josh held up his hands. "Can we just put this battle of the doctors on hold and get back to discussing the deadly lady in my life?"

Both women turned to him, but it was Dana who answered. "It's very easy, Josh. To make it short and sweet, she's growing more unstable with each confrontation." She pulled several typewritten pages out of the folder. "This will explain the profile I worked up on her. I'd say she's white, mid- to late thirties, single, and has a higher than normal intelligence, which can account for her ability to slip in and out of your houses without being noticed, bypass alarms, and such. I'd also hazard a guess that the only relationship she's had is in her mind. Ten-to-one she's never been married and pretty much keeps to herself. She's very cunning in concealing her true nature because she couldn't handle anyone knowing what she's really like. She has a great deal of patience, which, unfortunately, could be running out, because now when she invades your territory she destroys something instead of bestowing her idea of a labor of love. She feels you've hurt her, so she wants to hurt you back, even though, in her mind, she's doing nothing more dangerous than seeking your love."

"Dana, this is crazy. You're saying she's dangerous, yet she's not really dangerous," Lauren questioned. "Which is it?"

"Both, and it isn't crazy. She sees Josh as an estranged lover she wants to seduce back to her. And we're talking about someone who knows Josh pretty well," Dana explained, pulling another sheet of paper out of the folder. "I looked over the list of women you know and/or work with that I asked you to compile." She arched an eyebrow. "Impressive, if I do say so."

Lauren shifted in her chair as she listened to Dana's subtle teasing as she ran down the names of women Josh wrote down. What she heard sounded too much like her ex-husband's favorite hobby, second to his guns, during their marriage. If there was a willing woman around, Ron wanted her.

She would be the first to admit she didn't know a lot about Josh. It wasn't as if they worked together or saw each other on a daily basis, so she knew she couldn't prejudge him. She reminded herself she was here purely as a colleague ready to help someone in trouble. Not to mention she'd somehow been pulled into this situation whether she'd wanted to be or not. She wondered why she'd allowed him to do it to her when she was doing so well to rebuilding her life from the ashes it'd once been.

"Did she enter any of the other women's houses, or just Lauren's?" Hearing her name spoken out loud brought her attention back.

Josh shook his head. "As far as we know, she's only been in Lauren's. Kevin talked to some of the others and asked about any strange incidents that occurred during the time we saw each other. They all said the same thing—that at the time, they didn't view anything that happened as any more than teen vandalism.

It was usually paint thrown against front doors or on their cars. One had her prize rose bushes destroyed. Most of them never thought to connect it with me until Kevin spoke to them."

"Most?"

"One mentioned that she noticed the little pranks stopped right after we broke up." His face reddened. "She said she even thought I might have had something to do with it."

Dana tapped her pen against her lips. "And now she's decided to invade her rival's territory. Which means she sees you in a very threatening light, Lauren."

"She has no reason to."

"She doesn't have to." Dana waved her hands in punctuation as she continued talking. "This is a woman who believes what she wants to, what she perceives as her own version of the truth. She broke into your house because she wanted to prove she could get in there anytime she wanted to. She wanted to walk in your territory, touch your things. I wouldn't be surprised if she tried on some of your clothes," she clucked, when Lauren grimaced at the idea, "maybe even fooled around with your makeup. I'd even say she walked out of there wearing your perfume. She didn't leave the top off the bottle accidentally. It was cold and deliberate. She wanted you to know she'd been there. And I'm afraid to say she'll probably be back." She gazed at her friend with sympathy.

"Not without tripping up the security system I had installed."

Dana shook her head. "How many times has she gotten into Josh's house, no matter how many times he's changed the locks and put in a new security system? This is one smart lady. She has the kind of knowledge many don't have, and she uses it to her advantage."

"Are you saying this woman could be in law enforcement, or perhaps work in the courthouse?" Josh asked. "Someone I work with, perhaps on a daily basis? I know I've started feeling a little paranoid about some of the women I see at work, but I don't want to think they would go to these lengths."

"It's a proven fact that just because someone carries a badge doesn't mean they're trustworthy. And she knows too much about your schedule to be a perfect stranger. Not unless she doesn't need to work and can follow you practically twenty-four hours a day. Just remember that things seem to be picking up. I don't want you to be surprised if she suddenly declares her love for you and insists you don't see any other women. It could get to the point where she might get even more upset than now if she so much as *sees* you talking to another woman, no matter how innocent it really is. She wants to think of you as her own private property, and woe to anyone who trespasses." She dropped the sheets back into the folder and closed it. "I wrote up a more concise and official report that I'll send on to Detective Peterson, and I have a copy of it here for your use. I hope you'll keep me apprised of any new episodes. And I suggest you be very careful," she advised her friend. "Some flowers are deadly."

"I'll brush up on my botany and not accept any flowers sent to the office or home."

Dana handed Josh a manila envelope. "There's still a lot we don't know about stalkers. New cases crop up daily all over the country. And I'm hearing about more cases involving children, which makes me sick to my stomach. We don't always know what causes them to fixate on certain people, what they hope to gain from it, or what causes it in the beginning. Unfortunately, it sometimes takes violence to bring them to light. At least, now you have the law on your side. It was much scarier when nothing could be done."

"It's a small comfort when you can't even find her," Josh grumbled.

"But you know enough to be careful, and that's what counts," She shook her head. "Many cases have ended in tragedy. A young woman of twenty dated a young man once. He saw more into it than she did. He kept calling; she kept telling him she was seeing someone else and it was getting serious. He didn't believe her and kept calling and sending her gifts which she always refused to accept. She even got a restraining order. Six months later, he walked into the church during her wedding ceremony and shot the groom and then himself. Just before he shot himself, he told her he wanted her to live with the knowledge it wouldn't have happened if she had loved him."

Lauren closed her eyes. "Death may be my business, but it still doesn't make it any easier," she whispered.

"I believe in stating worst-case scenarios so you'll stay alert," Dana said. "Good luck, Josh. And if you ever have any questions, call me." She reached out and pulled Lauren into a friendly hug, then leaned back to study her. "You look good. No dark shadows. Sleeping all right? No more nasties?" she murmured, then smiled at Lauren's answering nod. "I'm glad you're doing so well. Who knows? Maybe someday I'll decide to travel out to the toolies and see what the back of the beyond looks like."

Lauren hugged her back. "You do that."

"I can't thank you enough for your help." Josh held out his hand.

"Lauren will tell you I like nothing more than a

good challenge." Dana smiled, taking his hand. "And I can already see this one could prove interesting. If it's possible, I'd like to meet and talk with the lady when she's caught." She held up a hand. "Notice I said 'when,' not 'if,' because I'm basically a positive person. I also think she chose the wrong guy for her erotic fixation and it will ultimately cause her downfall. But I would still like to talk to her."

"I'll see what I can do when the time comes."

As they walked out of the building and crossed the parking lot, Josh noticed it had grown dark. He automatically moved closer to Lauren as they approached his car. He had her remain a few steps back while he quickly checked it over. He paused before unlocking the passenger door for her.

"The southbound traffic's going to be a bitch for the next couple hours. Why don't we look for someplace to have dinner before we battle the freeway?"

Lauren thought for a moment and checked her watch. "There's a pretty good place where Dana and I used to meet for dinner about four blocks from here. At this hour, it shouldn't be too busy. We can discuss what Dana told us while it's still fresh in our minds without having to worry about being overheard."

"Sounds fine."

"Shit." Josh pulled at a slip of paper tucked under the windshield wiper on the driver's side. "I can't believe they thought they could issue a parking ticket. There are no laws posted in this lot."

"Mark must have gotten one of the patrolmen to do this." Lauren took the parking ticket out of his hand and crumpled it into a ball. "His nasty idea of a joke." She clearly didn't find it funny.

He suddenly grinned as he took the ticket back and

pocketed it. "Then it's a good thing I have connections at the courthouse."

Her laughter didn't hold any humor. "Around here, you'll need more than that."

Ironically, as they got into Josh's car, they couldn't stop themselves from covertly glancing around as if expecting to find themselves under observation. And not necessarily by the police.

Chapter Seven

"I can't believe what crazy turns this situation has taken in the past few months. I'm beginning to think I'm living in a nightmare." Josh had waited to speak until they'd given their order to the waitress and she'd left them alone. He picked up his coffee cup she had just filled and drank deeply of the much-needed caffeine. If he wasn't driving, he would have wanted a double Scotch.

"Is it so crazy?" Lauren countered, wrapping her hands around her cup to warm her fingers. "How many stories about stalkers do we read in the news almost every day? They've practically become a regular feature on television talk shows. Your own lady love would probably make the front page in town if you hadn't used your connections to keep it quiet. Although I'd think it would be to your advantage to bring it out in the open. For all we know, someone could have information about her. Maybe she's done it before with another man who didn't want to say anything, but who might be willing to come forward if he discovers he's not the only one."

"There might not be anyone else."

"There's an old saying about never knowing until

you try. What would it hurt to announce to the press there's a woman out there who's fixated on the assistant DA?"

He shook his head. "We had our reasons for keeping the reports unofficial. Kevin has had to do some pretty fast tap dancing to keep his activities out of the eyes of the press. When it looked as if this woman was more than just the shy type who refused to sign her name on the cards, the DA, the police chief, Kevin, and myself discussed the case at length. We took into account that with the town growing the way it was, we couldn't afford this kind of publicity. Industry is starting to move out of the big city and into outlying areas, and several large manufacturing firms are looking at property on the city outskirts. We knew we had to keep it quiet as possible."

Lauren could understand his reasoning, even if she didn't completely agree with it.

"And if she becomes dangerous? What then? What if she finally loses her hold on reality and goes after you or the woman you're seeing, this time, with intent to kill?"

Josh reared back from her low-voiced fury. He didn't think twice in retaliating. "Since we're talking about my neck here, I don't see why you should worry."

She shook her head. "Since I happen to be with you at the moment and since my house has been broken into, I believe I have a great deal to worry about. Now I begin to wonder if she wasn't the one who scratched my car that night at the retirement party."

Even as the anger flared between them, so did something more elemental. Josh stared at Lauren and wondered if she felt the same sparks he did. For a moment, he wasn't sure whether to strangle her for forcing the issue, or kiss her. The latter seemed a lot more pleasant.

"Let me tell you something. I'd like nothing more than to know who to look out for." He automatically lowered his voice as he leaned across the table. "You have no idea what it's like to wonder if the woman who's been making your life hell is one of the secretaries or clerks working in your office, or if you should worry she's the receptionist at your dentist's office or someone you just happened to pass on the street one day and all you did was pick up a dropped package for her and she took it the wrong way." Angry frustration at the situation ran through his words. "I ask myself if she's someone I've known for a long time or someone I might have only said a few words to at some point. I go home from work wondering if I'll walk in to find she's washed all the dishes, waxed the furniture, and changed the sheets, or if she's torn up the room," he muttered.

"She does your housework and laundry while she ruins the surface of my dresser top with my most expensive perfume," Lauren murmured on a wry note. "How unfair!"

He didn't waste any time in shooting back at her. "This is not a joking matter."

"You're right, it's not. You should hear some of the estimates I received to refinish the dresser." She held up her hands in surrender. "All right, I'll stop. But the stories I've read and heard about stalkers say that if they break in, they take something personal; they don't clean the house. This woman has a very strong fixation about you, and it seems conceivable. I bet if you took a very careful inventory of your house you'd find something missing. Probably a piece of clothing."

Josh eyed her. "You seem to know a lot about investigative procedures."

"I was married to a cop. You hear so much that it's natural to learn all sorts of things."

He didn't miss her bitterness. "Bad?"

She raised her head so he couldn't miss the "back off" written in her expression. "Bad enough."

He leaned back in his chair. "You know, Lauren, I'd like to get to know you better, but you seem to keep putting up these walls if I ask a question that might be considered the least bit personal."

"I didn't realize wanting to keep my private life private was a crime. What part of 'none of your business' didn't you understand?"

"Lauren, I'm not the enemy here. Obviously, running into that friend of your ex-husband's upset you, but why take it out on me?"

"Running into Mark has nothing to do with it, although my day would have been considerably brighter if I could have run over him while driving a tank." She toyed with her fork so she wouldn't have to look at him. "Let me make this clear: it was a marriage that shouldn't have happened. We got married for all the wrong reasons and divorced for all the right ones. It was a time I don't care to discuss. Especially when the man asking doesn't seem to like to talk about himself very much."

"I've told you before, there's not much to say."

"That's not what the gossips say."

His dark eyes turned cold. "I've never believed in gossip, since it's a proven fact gossip isn't all that reliable. It's bad enough we haven't been able to contain the talk about my secret admirer, what with her sending me flowers every week. Since it began, I've tended to keep things to myself even more than usual," he said finally. "I only hope it hasn't been too noticeable. Gossip is pretty typical around there. I'm surprised I didn't find out about you sooner. I was involved in an important case at the time, but I usually hear what's going on."

"All you had to do was read your office memos you would have known before you met me at the retirement party. The local paper even wrote up a brief article about my taking over. All about a woman working in a man's world, and so on."

"I don't have the time to do more than keep up with my caseload, and there's times I feel as if I need more hours in a day just for that." He automatically glanced over his shoulder as if sensing something was wrong.

"I doubt she's followed us here." She still kept her voice low. "We both were very careful in keeping today's appointment quiet."

He still couldn't stop glancing quickly over his other shoulder. None of the other patrons in the restaurant looked familiar, but he knew that didn't mean anything. "You never said how you got out of the office without them wondering."

"I told them I was meeting with a colleague in San Diego. Personally, I didn't think it was any of their business where I was going and what I was doing, but Pete kept demanding to know how he could contact me if a problem came up." She shook her head in disgust. "He's not into taking any responsibility."

"It's probably because Harvey refused to give him any and tended to treat him like an idiot. I always had the feeling that Pete's lack of self-esteem was due to that more than anything else."

Lauren shook her head. "And, unfortunately, I probably treat him the same way. I'm surprised he's remained in the field with that kind of negative supervision."

"Harvey just refused to give him a chance, and I think he hoped for it when Harvey's health forced him to retire. And then you came along. Although it wouldn't matter, because everyone knew Pete wasn't ready to take over. Top professionals are hard to lure out here, since most people prefer the bigger cities. The trouble is, the salaries, naturally, aren't as high and advancement isn't as fast nor as satisfying as what they can get in the city."

"It doesn't seem to have bothered you." Lauren glanced up when the waitress set down her plate.

"I like out-of-the-way places where I can do my own thing. A judge in LA would slap me with a contempt charge if I showed up in jeans and not wearing a tie. Instead, it's part of my charm." He leaned back as the waitress moved to his side of the table to set his plate in front of him. "Besides, I don't need the high-profile cases to make a name for myself. I'm happy just being a small-town country lawyer making sure the bad guys stay in jail for a long time."

She concentrated on cutting up her steak. "Why do you think this woman has chosen a small-town country lawyer?"

Josh shook his head, showing the frustration he'd been feeling all along. "Beats the hell out of me. Dana's suggestion that it has to do with my involvement with battered women sounds pretty logical, since I give a lot of talks and conduct seminars on how to protect yourself in the courts and what to expect when dealing with the police. Admittedly, nowadays, the abusive spouse is automatically locked up if the cops are called, but that still doesn't mean the other party is safe when their abuser is released." He studied her bent head. "Lauren, did he ever abuse you?"

Her head shot up. "Abuse me? Ron knew if he ever tried it he'd find himself turned into filets. Besides, physical punishment wasn't his style. He enjoyed women too much to beat them up."

He didn't need to meet her level gaze to know what he'd read there.

"Did he like to flaunt them?"

She took several deep breaths to rid herself of the roaring in her ears. "Not now, please?" she barely whispered, as she picked up her utensils with extra care and concentrated on food she no longer had an appetite for.

"It seems we all have our own little form of hell, doesn't it?"

An hour later, Lauren stared out the car window at the landscape speeding past them but didn't bother looking to find anything beyond the darkness. She was relieved Josh had finally dropped the subject about her marriage and divorce. The last thing she wanted to do was reveal a piece of her past she preferred no one know. She already knew that part of her life wasn't something Ron wanted to get around, and all documentation had been destroyed. Not exactly a legal procedure, but something Ron had insisted on doing. More for his benefit than hers, she'd always thought. The only gossip known about her was that she was divorced from a cop, which was nothing new, since the divorce rate among policemen was high.

As cars flashed past them, she couldn't help but wonder if one of them held Josh's unwelcome admirer. Could she have seen Josh leave the building and decide to follow him? How difficult would it have been for her to keep up with them on the freeway? Traffic hadn't been heavy until they'd reached the outskirts of Los Angeles, and traffic was always heavy around the courthouse. Had she come into the restaurant where they had dinner and sat at a table nearby, watching them? Had she noticed the electricity that ran between them? Even Lauren was stunned by the sparks they generated and feeling shook-up. As a few more erotic pictures started to enter her mind, she quickly banished them by mentally reciting the names of the bones in the foot. Since there were so many, she knew it would take a while.

"What did you say?" His question brought her back to the present.

"Nothing important," she lied. Few people would understand how relaxing it was to recite the names of the bones in the foot. "I'm just figuring out my shopping list. I tend to stay out of grocery stores until there's nothing in the cupboards and I'll starve unless I refill them."

"You always speak Latin when you make up your list?"

"It makes it more interesting." She turned and leaned over to turn on the radio, fiddling with the dial until she found a golden oldies station.

"No good ole shit-kickin', boot-stompin' country western?"

"Not if you want to keep me as a passenger."

"Oh, I think I want to keep you."

That was when Lauren decided staying one step ahead of Josh might not be so easy, after all.

* * *

She was growing impatient as the day wore on and there was no word about either of them. She knew they were together. She could feel it. That story about his deciding to take the rest of the day off and her telling her staff she was going to San Diego to see a friend was all bullshit. She knew it was!

She went to his house first, but couldn't find any clues to tell her where he might have gone. She only prayed she was wrong for once and he was alone.

Her house was a little more difficult to get into because of the alarm system, but not impossible. All she learned there was that the boxes were now emptied and the rooms looked more lived in. The gun was in the same place, the *Playgirl* was a more recent issue, and she took the time to scan the files in Lauren's computer. Articles for medical and forensic journals, household records that were so complete she couldn't resist running them off on the laser printer to see what else she could learn about her. There were even a few games on it. She looked over the desk calendar and swore because nothing was written down for that day. Wouldn't meeting a friend benefit a notation on a personal calendar?

In the end, she flipped a mental coin and decided to stake out Lauren's house. She felt more comfortable hiding out around there because Lauren's house was set well back from the road and on high ground. The only entrance was a winding driveway. It gave the occupant a great deal of privacy because of trees planted along the road which provided a form of protection. She parked her car along a side road up from Lauren's house and settled back to wait. They would have to show up sooner or later. She wasn't even going to think how she would feel if they decided to spend the night at his house. She was growing much too tired of his seeing all these other women, and if he didn't stop soon, she knew she would have to do something about it. It had worked with Celia, years ago. It would work this time, too.

As she waited, she toyed with a strand of hair that had worked loose from her ponytail and played her favorite game. Josh had finally realized how right they were together. She saw them sharing that huge bed of his for the wildest, most incredible sex known to man. With the car windows rolled up tightly and no houses in close proximity, no one could hear her cries as her fingers and sexual visions brought her to a climax.

"You going to get mad if I say you look tired?" Josh swung the car around the corner when they reached Lauren's road.

"No reason to when it's true." She stifled a yawn. "I was up late last night working on an article that's due in a few weeks. Then I was up early this morning to go to aerobics class."

"I'm of the old school of running."

"As a doctor, I'd like to warn you, it can be bad for the knees."

He grinned. "Good thing I have strong knees. The only thing I've ever had to worry about is skinned knees when I don't look where I'm going on a new path." He turned up her driveway to the front door. "Part of your security measures?" He nodded toward the floodlights visible from the rear of the house and a strong light burning by the front door.

"They come on at dusk. While I have neighbors, they aren't exactly close enough to talk over the back fence, so I figured the lights might be a good deterrent." She rummaged through her purse until she found her keys.

"Lauren." Josh placed his hand on hers to stop her from getting out of the car. "I'd better go in with you."

She laughed. "Is this a new line?"

"No, just a safety measure."

"I have a state-of-the-art alarm system." Still, she allowed him to help her out of the car and walk her to the front door. Lauren unlocked the door and the moment she was inside, punched in the code to deactivate the alarm. "I forgot to do this a couple nights ago. I found out just how loud it is at 2 A.M.," she explained, turning back around. The look on his face told her everything. She wet her lips with her tongue. "Josh, while my marriage wasn't great, the divorce still left a few wounds that haven't completely healed yet." She suddenly laughed. "Not to mention, you presently have a few problems with your own private life. Let's not get into something that could only hurt us both."

He half turned and flipped off the entryway overhead light. With the front door partially closed, their faces were shadowed by the darkness.

"If I thought it would do any good, I'd try to change your mind," he said quietly. "But it would only make matters worse, wouldn't it?" He didn't bother to wait for an answer. "Stay here." He moved around her and quickly but thoroughly looked into each room. When he returned, he stopped long enough to trail the back of his fingers down her cheek. "Good night, Lauren. Maybe we can settle this between us when the other business is over." He closed the door behind him. It took a few seconds for Lauren to recover and activate the alarm.

She walked slowly down the hallway, stopping only when she noticed the red light on her answering machine blinking. She walked in and depressed the button, listening to the muted whir of the tape rewinding.

"Did you honestly think I wouldn't know the two of you went off together, Laurie dear?" The whispered voice struck a dark chord. "You don't like being called Laurie, do you? No one with the snooty-bitch name of Lauren would. Then I think that's exactly what I'll call you until I can give you a more appropriate name." Her voice turned harsh. "Did you tell Josh all the dirty details behind your divorce, Laurie? Or did the two of you find a motel room together for some down-and-dirty sex? No, I don't think you did, because if you had, he wouldn't have wanted you, would he?"

Shaking so violently she couldn't stand, Lauren dropped into the chair next to her desk as she listened to the insidious voice bring up memories she had buried months ago.

"Josh isn't a man to take things lightly, Laurie," the taunting voice continued. "But I can make it very easy for you. Just leave him alone and give him back to me and I'll forget all about it. I promise. And Laurie, I always keep my promises." Her demonic laughter whipped across Lauren's frayed nerves just before the click indicated the answering machine had cut her off.

Lauren sat in the chair for several more minutes before she could get up and leave the room. By the time she reached her bedroom, she felt more composed and positive she could handle anything that came her way. Until she found her favorite lipstick left on her nightstand when she knew very well she had put it away that morning. While she wanted to toss the case into the wastebasket—she doubted she could ever wear it again, even if she bought herself another tube—she followed the procedure she knew would be required by Kevin. She dug out a small paper bag in the kitchen and pulled on a latex glove before picking up the case, dropping it into the bag and folding the top down, taping it shut and writing her initials across the tape.

By then, her body shook with a soul-shattering fury instead of fear of the woman coming back.

"Who does she think she is?" she gritted, spinning around to see what else she would find out of place. "Does she honestly think any man is worth putting a person through hell? Does she honestly think *I'm* going to put up with her insane pranks?"

The minute she'd said it, she wanted to take it back. Even carelessly calling the person crazy was proof that her subconscious considered the woman not of her right mind. And there were too many people not of their right mind who could be considered dangerous.

She experienced a sudden burst of furious energy that she needed to get rid of before she could even think of resting. Working like a fired-up machine, she thoroughly cleaned her bedroom, including changing the sheets—she wasn't taking any chances that the woman had lain in her bed—before stumbling into the shower. The last thing she did before going to bed was to make sure her handgun was loaded and within easy reach.

The moment Josh stepped into his house, he was repelled by the heavy scent of the familiar perfume in the air. Swearing under his breath, he made a check of each room, but found nothing out of order. This time, his bed was still unmade. When he checked his answering machine, he found the message light blinking. Fearing Lauren might have found something after he'd left, he quickly punched the button, ready to run back out the minute he found out what was going on.

"Darling, I know you were with the Hunter bitch today. You have to understand she isn't for you." The unfamiliar, yet familiar, voice breathed through the speaker and left his blood running cold. "Besides, there's things about her you don't know that would change your mind about her. But she and I have made a deal. She stops trying to take you away from me and I won't give away her dirty little secret. I'll see you soon. Good night, lover."

Josh first thought was to call Lauren and warn her they must not have been as discreet in leaving town as they'd hoped, but he hesitated. What if it was only a ploy and she'd never tried to contact Lauren today? No, he'd wait and give Lauren a call in the morning.

He popped the tape out and inserted a new one before dropping the used one into a Ziploc plastic bag that he tossed into his briefcase, along with the file folder of notes Dana had given him. He'd hoped to look them over that evening before going to bed. Right now, he wasn't sure he wanted even that kind of contact with her.

"I hope she realizes she's costing me a small fortune in answering machine tapes."

Chapter Eight

"How do you feel about getting bad news in the middle of the night?"

Lauren looked up from the notes she'd taken at a crime scene not long ago. Considering it was four o'clock in the morning and she'd had less than two hours sleep, thanks to her frenetic housecleaning, which had done little to calm her raging fury, she looked remarkably fresh compared to Gail. The policewoman wore a tight black leather miniskirt and gold Lurex tube top with a black sheer long-sleeved top over that. Her makeup was smeared and she looked like a hooker who'd had a hard night.

"I got a call to go out and pronounce a death about one o'clock this morning. I just left the crime scene a half-hour ago, and will have the pleasure of beginning my day with the post." She stretched her arms over her head, then dropped them. She gestured toward the coffeepot. "It's been a while since I've been called out in the middle of the night and I'm feeling it. Want some coffee? It's guaranteed strong enough to float an aircraft carrier."

"I'd rather have four weeks' worth of sleep instead of a stronger caffeine buzz, but I don't think that will be possible just now." Gail poured herself a cup and dropped into a chair. She reached down to slip off her high heels. She winced as she flexed and pointed her toes. "I'm surprised more hookers aren't cripples, wearing torture devices like these instruments they call shoes." She held up her shoes, the deadly looking three-inch spike heels pointed upward. "Give me Reebok any day."

"We were brought up to believe that wearing them made our legs look sexier. They wear them because it makes their legs look sexier. Naturally, it's men who spout all that nasty propaganda." Lauren refilled her coffee cup. "So what's the problem that's going to make me rant and rave and scream?"

"Your victim is missing."

Her smile froze. "That's funny. I thought you said the victim is missing. Since I'd pronounced him dead, I can't imagine a medical miracle where he got up and walked away."

Gail looked chagrined at having to repeat her bad news. "I did just say that, and no, he didn't decide to come back from the dead."

Lauren sipped her coffee in hopes the caffeine would allow her brain to function at a normal rate. She could already feel the buzz traveling through her veins. She figured she'd be bouncing off the ceiling by noon. "No offense, Gail, but why are you the one bringing me that lovely piece of news?"

"Because it's my case and because I figured if you decided to throw a tantrum you'd prefer to throw it in front of another woman, instead of one of those macho ingrates who would just start spouting crap about what can you expect when women suffer from PMS and all."

Lauren played with a loose strand of her hair. "Yes,

men can be scum, can't they? So before I start yelling and screaming about the lost body, although I don't know why I should bother, since it means one less post to worry about, why don't you give me an idea where he might be?"

By now, Gail just looked disgusted. "I wish I knew. Paul and Kirk left the scene around the same time you did and they haven't been heard from. I talked to your lovely diener. I swear, Lauren, he reminds me of Peter Lorre." She wrinkled her nose as she mentioned the clerk in charge of the morgue. "But he hasn't heard from them either. I swear, things always go nuts when the moon is full."

"It usually *does* bring out the crazies," Lauren agreed, settling back in her chair. "You can stop worrying. I'm not going to lose my temper and I'm not going to worry about it. I'm too tired to worry much about anything." She stifled a yawn.

"Driving down to San Diego and back in one day can be pretty tiring. I'm surprised you wouldn't want to stay the night and come home in the morning."

Lauren looked at her sharply for a second, but there was nothing in Gail's expression to indicate she was being sarcastic. At least, she now knew that her cover story had gotten out and seemed to be accepted. And it showed just how quick the grapevine was. "I was able to miss most of the traffic by driving back after the rush hour, so it wasn't too bad. The trouble is, I got to bed real late and ended up with barely a couple hours of sleep."

"For someone who only had a little sleep, you look pretty good to me." Gail grimaced as she raked her fingers through her hair. "I'm afraid to look in the mirror for fear of scaring myself and breaking the glass. What's your secret for looking human?"

"A couple of tricks I learned when I was an intern from one of the nurses whose sister is an actress. One, you wash your face with icy water." She laughed at Gail's horrified expression. "Second, you use a pearl-colored moisturizing base under the foundation. At least, no matter how tired you are inside, you don't look it." She grabbed the phone and punched out a number. "This is Dr. Hunter. Do me a favor and put out an APB for Kirk, Paul, and one passenger." She paused. "Yes, I know it's a full moon. Yes, I know things always go weird this time of the month and a missing coroner's wagon kind of goes at the bottom of a long list. So let me put it this way: if you don't want me to sprout fangs and go looking for fresh blood, namely yours, you'll track them down and tell them to get back here right away. Otherwise, I'll have to come up there and pick someone out to take the victim's place for the first morning post. And remember, I don't carry anesthesia down here." She slammed the phone down. "Don't tell me. Harvey never minded if they took their time getting back on a slow night."

Gail shrugged. "He did tend to go a little easy on them."

"Then they're going to find out the hard way that I'm not Harvey." Lauren tossed her notes into a file folder and attached a label to it.

"I think they're already getting that idea." Gail stifled a yawn. "Do you know Mitzi Roberts?"

Lauren thought for a moment and shook her head. "The name doesn't ring a bell, but I'm still meeting people around here."

"She works as a clerk in the public defender's office," the policewoman explained. "She went through a bad marriage with an abusive husband and finally got up the courage to divorce him about a year ago.

She would have had a lot of problems with that if it hadn't been for Josh helping her out."

Lauren's interest was instantly caught, but she silently warned herself to be cautious. "I've heard he's heavily involved in those issues. I think that's very admirable."

"He's involved because he grew up watching his father abusing his mother and he's always regretted not being able to help her."

Another question answered. Lauren wondered what other private details Gail knew about Josh and why she was bothered by the idea when she'd told Josh just hours ago that she didn't need a man in her life. She idly picked at a chip on her desk's surface.

"Why are you telling me about Mitzi?"

"There's rumors that she's seriously hoping about making him her son's stepfather. Not only that, but she pretty much assumes Josh would have gone along with it if you hadn't come along and dazzled him."

For just a brief moment, the phone message came back to Lauren. She made a mental note to seek out the woman and find a way to listen to her voice to find out if it would sound familiar.

She shook her head, laughing as if she found the idea incredible. "People love to make unbelievable assumptions around here, don't they? He took me out to dinner because he lost a bet and I made him pay up."

Gail leaned over, surprise written all over her face. "Really? You have no interest in one of the hottest guys we've had here in a long time?"

Lauren nodded. "Is gossip so rare around here that if somebody sees us out together they automatically assume something hot and heavy?"

"It has been quiet lately," she agreed. "And while you can't consider Josh a womanizer per se, he does make sure not to be with one woman for too long, so they can't get any ideas. Although we all thought for a while that Carol Lawson, who worked for a marketing research firm, was going to be the one to change his mind. Now she's seeing one of the executives in her company. I guess she didn't like Josh having to break dates at the last minute." Gail plucked at a hole in her black fishnet hosiery. "I am going to be so glad I won't have to wear these things any longer. I can't understand why they were so popular to wear back in the late sixties. I always feel as if I have some disfiguring rash on my legs." She laughed, then suddenly said, "I heard you're divorced."

"Nowadays, who isn't?"

Gail looked up. "You were married to a cop, weren't you?"

Lauren nodded warily, wondering where the questioning was going.

"Drugs, alcohol, other women, or abuse?"

It took a moment for Lauren to realize Gail was asking the reason behind the divorce. "None of the above. We discovered that we functioned better without each other than as a couple," she said.

"No affairs on either side?" Gail winced. "Sorry, I guess questioning about things that are really not my business is a habit."

"I'm not embarrassed. I just don't feel the need to talk about a dead issue. As far as I'm concerned, it's over and there's no need to rehash old history." She smiled to take the sting out of her words.

"Sorry about sounding nosy. As I said, I guess it's part of my nature."

"No offense taken." Lauren started when the phone rang. "Dr. Hunter." She listened to the caller, rolled her eyes then gave Gail a thumbs-up. "Kirk and Paul just showed up. They said something about taking a detour that turned out to be a dead end." She stood up. "I think I'd better make sure they didn't pick up a new passenger along the way."

"Think I'll have time for some sleep before you post the guy?" Gail asked.

"Sure. There's a cot in the supply room just off Sophie's office you can use," Lauren offered. "I'll wake you up when I'm ready."

"Thanks, I'll take you up on that." Gail suddenly grinned. "Just do me a favor and remember I'm only sleeping and not one of your guests, so to speak."

Lauren pulled a elastic band out of her desk drawer and pulled her hair up in a loose ponytail as she walked to the door. "I'll try."

"Hey, Lauren?" Gail turned around with her arms uplifted to her hair. "Some people think you're a cold fish because of that 'touch me not' attitude you like to put out. I don't think you're so bad."

Lauren smiled. "Old habits die hard. Forensic pathologists aren't too popular because in a lot of instances, our word is considered law. After a while, you get used to being the bad guy to a lot of lawyers, and sometimes, even the cops. Go take your nap. Use the shower if you'd like. I keep toiletries in there for when I have to be here for an extended time." With a quick wave of the hand, she was gone.

Gail looked around the office, noting the difference from when Harvey had been in charge. The file cabinets weren't bursting with scattered papers. Files were piled neatly in the out and in trays; everywhere she looked she found papers, file folders reports, all in order.

"I bet she drives Sophie absolutely nuts."

* * *

"Whoever stabbed him wanted to make sure he was dead," Lauren announced, pulling off her latex gloves and tossing them away. Pete remained next to the corpse stitching up the Y-shaped incision. "There were twenty-seven wounds, twenty of them deep, which says the person either had a lot of strength or a lot of anger. The knife had a serrated edge which didn't give any clean cuts, and some of the wounds are spaced so closely together that his stomach came out looking like a piece of raw hamburger, so it was difficult to gauge the last time he'd eaten or even what he'd eaten. There were also shallow cuts on his hands, as if he'd tried to defend himself, and a deeper cut on his left palm, as if he'd tried to take the knife away from the killer. No skin under his nails, but I did find a few fibers I'll send over to the lab, along with blood samples. Although I have a hunch the only blood on him was his own."

Gail scribbled her notes. "Could a woman have done this?"

"Sure, and she wouldn't have to be a bodybuilder to accomplish it, either. I'd say the knife used was razor sharp because these are all clean cuts." She pressed the heels of her hands against her spine and bowed her back to relieve the muscle strain from bending over for an extended length of time. "I guess someone with his history has more than his share of enemies."

Gail nodded. The expression she directed toward the autopsy table was filled with disgust. "His share of enemies could have us digging for the next twenty years. Personally, I don't know why we don't give the person a medal for giving us one less piece of slime to worry about. I fought like crazy to get into Homicide, and wouldn't you know I'd end up with this for my first case?" She indicated her clothing. "I'm just glad I can finally get out of these things. I only went down there last night dressed like 'one of the girls' to get some information. Instead, I trip over him."

"Well, thanks for the business," Lauren teased. She glanced up at the clock and groaned at the hour. "I'm going to change and get some breakfast. Want to join me?"

Gail shook her head. "I've got to get back to the station and write up my report. Then I'm going home and burning these clothes. From now on, I intend to start wearing something a little more appropriate. Thanks for the info." She waved her notebook.

"Anytime."

Gail paused before she left. "Maybe you and I could have dinner sometime?"

Lauren's face lit up. "I'd like that."

"I'll see what my schedule will be like in the next week or so."

"Cozy with cops, cozy with DAs," Pete muttered from where he'd just finished his task.

Lauren spun around. "You have anything to say, Pete?"

He looked up, his ferret face gleaming with sweat under the harsh lights. "Coroners have to be objective."

"Yes, they do," she agreed. "And they also have to learn how to separate their professional lives from their personal ones so they can have a life at all."

"Like you do with Josh Brandon?"

Lauren guessed it took weariness combined the early morning hour for Pete to speak so openly.

She leaned against the stainless steel sink with her hands braced behind her. "So?"

"I should have been the one to take over here. Harvey promised me I'd get the job when he retired." He spoke with open hostility for the first time. "My qualifications are a hell of a lot better than yours. All you have are more fancy degrees than I do. They only took you because they wanted a forensics specialist." He spat out the words.

"Did he ever put his promise in writing for you? Did he say he submitted his recommendation?"

He was startled that she hadn't ripped right into him for his opening his big mouth. A saner voice told him she could probably write him up, although there were no witnesses to what he said.

She stared at the floor for several moments before lifting her head. "Pete, when you put your mind to it, you are an excellent second-in-command, but sometimes even experience doesn't hold enough weight. According to past performance reports, you refused to show any interest in the forensics side of pathology, which is badly needed here, and you have trouble dealing with crime scenes, especially the nasty ones. I threw up more times than I could count when I first went out to crime scenes. All you can do is pray your stomach will soon get the message. Start planning to attend some of the forensics seminars. Be willing to do more than your share. I had to do that and then some. At least, you don't have to worry about 'women shouldn't be doing these kind of things' speeches from the good old boys."

"Why are you being so helpful about all this?"

She exhaled a puff of air. "Because I figure if you want something bad enough you'll be willing to work for it. There's no guarantee I'll be staying here for the

next twenty or thirty years. And there's no guarantee
you'd want to stay if you could get in somewhere else.
I'm just saying if you're willing to try, I'll do what I
can."

Pete looked undecided, as if he was unsure she was
speaking the truth, but didn't want to ruin what could
be a good thing, either. "I'll think about it."

Lauren nodded and left, grateful he hadn't been
sullen about it. And wishing her day was already over.

"Come on, Josh, hear me out," the public defender
begged, dropping into the seat across from Josh as he
ate lunch. "Ricky Barlow is willing to plead guilty to
holding and give us the name of his dealer as a bonus."

He wasn't having any of it. He looked at his hamburger. "Larry, this is the second time Ricky's been
picked up for dealing. This time he was selling to an
eight-year-old. Forget it. I want him locked up for a
while."

The PD stared hungrily at Josh's fries. "Get real,
Josh, he won't even be in there that long and we both
know it."

"Not if we get Sawyer, who's a real hard-nose with
druggies. He believes in stressing rehab along with jail
time." Josh dipped a french fry in catsup and popped
it in his mouth. "Look, Larry, I know you're as
backed up as I am, but this is one I'm not willing to
deal on. That kid walked too many times when he was
a minor because his mother was in here crying a tale
how she needed him at home and the social worker
giving her sob story on how he needed to be out to
take care of his mother and brothers and sisters since
their dad had walked out on them eight years ago. All
he's managed to do is turn his fifteen-year-old sister

into a hooker and his twelve-year-old brother into a delivery boy. He's got an attitude I want to see cut down."

"Terrific, he'll be in there getting an advanced degree in dealing and picking up new contacts for when he gets out. Yeah, great way to keep the streets clean," Larry muttered, stuffing the file back in his briefcase and pulling out another one. "Okay, how about Ruiz? You handling him?"

Josh shook his head. "Sylvia is."

Larry almost buried his head inside his briefcase. "All right, what about—"

"Larry."

The public defender looked up, his expression almost glassy-eyed, so he didn't catch the grim reality in Josh's eyes.

"Larry, I am eating lunch here," Josh said slowly and distinctly. All slight trace of his slow drawl was gone as his eyes bored into the younger man's. "And for once, I'd like to enjoy my meal without a damn PD dropping in trying to cut a deal for another perp. I'm tired of popping Tums every chance I get, guzzling Maalox in between, and wondering if I'm going to end up with an ulcer. It's bad enough that I'm dealing with you guys who can't even keep your clients straight. Sawyer almost had a shit fit last week when Watson came running in five minutes late with a file for a different prisoner than the one he was defending. You want to deal, see me in my office, and if you dare interrupt my lunch again in hopes of cutting a deal, I'll make your life a living hell. Got it?"

Larry snapped shut his briefcase and stood up. "Okay, okay, you don't have to hit me over the head. You're going to have to learn to roll with it, old boy, or you'll end up under Dr. Hunter's knife instead of over her luscious bod." He made sure he was out of striking range before shooting off the last remark, and almost ran out of the cafeteria.

Several people chuckled at the man's quick escape. Josh's temper when he was crossed the wrong way was legend, and people made sure not to see that temper too often.

"No wonder no one wants to go up against you, Brandon," one of the other public defenders joked from across the room. "You scare the shit out of them when they just ask for an easy plea bargain!"

Muttering comments about the obscure sexual habits of public defenders, Josh piled his plate back on the tray, picked it up, and left. He'd toyed with the idea of stopping off to see if Lauren was in, but after Larry's crack back there, he decided against it. It appeared, while Lauren preferred they take it slow and easy, the gossip mill already had them in the midst of a hot-and-heavy affair. Not that he'd mind it if it was true.

For a brief moment, the scary thought hit him that if everyone else thought that, who wasn't to say a certain woman wouldn't think the same thing? He muttered a curse when his beeper sounded. He checked the number shown, didn't recognize it, and headed for the bank of public phones. As he heard the line on the other end ring, he idly scanned the passersby. The voice answering barely registered.

"Yes, this is Josh Brandon," he said matter-of-factly.

"I know that," the woman's voice was breathy and seemed to ooze pure sex. "How are you, Josh?"

He immediately straightened up. "I don't have time to talk, Heather."

"That I've been able to figure out, since you've never returned my phone calls."

He turned around to face the wall. This was the last conversation he wanted to have in a public place, even on the phone.

"It was all said six months ago."

"I was PMSing. I didn't know what I was saying."

Josh lowered his voice, praying no one would overhear him. "Your idea of fun and games differs greatly from mine. Why don't we just part as friends and be done with it?"

"I said I'm apologizing." Her sugar-sweet voice turned hard. "And I want us to get back together again."

"And I don't."

"I've been a perfect lady about this, Josh, but I don't take rejection lightly. You remember that." The sound of the phone slammed down vibrated in his ear.

Josh barely hesitated before putting a call into Kevin and asking him to do some checking on Heather's whereabouts.

"Will do," the detective promised. "No wonder they had those sayings about a woman scorned."

"Right now, I'm going to hope that she's the one. She's got some pretty strange ideas, so I wouldn't be surprised," Josh said grimly.

"Nowadays, nothing surprises me."

She had walked up to a group she knew and sat with them during lunch. She'd deliberately chosen to eat with these people because their table was so close to Josh's she could almost reach out and touch him. She could even swear she smelled his aftershave. And she could listen to him while Larry tried to cut a deal for another one of his creepy clients who relied on the public defender's office to get them off. She was so proud of Josh not giving in to that bastard Larry, but then, Josh wouldn't do that. Except her joy was short-lived when she heard Larry mention the bitch's name. Did people honestly think Josh would want a woman like her? So many men talked about Lauren, about her looks and the way she'd handled herself in a couple of recent cases she'd had to testify for. What made her so special that the men practically panted when they talked about her? It was the same when she had to listen to men talk about Celia as if she was the only woman in the world. She stared at the salad she suddenly didn't want.

She knew she was considered pretty, but she couldn't remember the last time a man had told her so or even commented about her looks. She wished Lauren would soon turn into old news because she was sick and tired of hearing about her!

Lauren better remember she had made a deal with her. That she'd promised to stay away from Josh. And she would stay away from him. Because if she didn't . . .

Chapter Nine

"When I find the culprit who did this despicable thing, I swear I will string him up by his toes! I'll dissect that human rat and then cut him into tiny pieces!"

Blind in her fury, Lauren walked right into a heavy object and found her feet starting to slide out from under her.

"Whoa!" A pair of hands shot out and grabbed her arms to keep her from falling. His fingers slid against the polished cotton of her blue surgical scrubs. "You're not carrying any sharp instruments, are you?" Josh's gaze traveled over her disheveled form.

She blew a stray strand of hair out of her eyes. "Norman is missing and the person who took him is going to end up in cold storage for a very long time."

"Norman? I don't recall anyone with that name. Is he new around here?"

Lauren took several deep breaths to calm her temper, but didn't get a chance to speak.

"Hey, Doc, this report's gotta be wrong!" Unshaven, wearing a pair of tattered jeans and beat-up t-shirt, he looked more like a homeless person than a homicide detective. Only the gold badge clipped to his waistband lent credence to his position.

"Now, where have I heard that before?" Josh murmured.

Lauren shot him a warning look before turning around. "What part of my report is supposed to be wrong, Detective Evans?"

He skidded to a stop, nodded at Josh, and turned to Lauren. He flapped the report in her face. "You said the bullet that killed the guy came from a .357 Magnum. That can't be. The slime that shot him used a 9mm Luger."

She took it out of his hand and quickly scanned the pages to refresh her memory. "Oh yes, this one. I also found the two 9mm's in him that you wanted, but it was the .357 that tore up his lung that did the trick. He basically drowned in his own blood. I told your partner that when I performed the post, and that's what I wrote up."

The detective looked uneasily at Josh. "Could cause a problem, huh?"

"It means until you find the .357 we don't have a murder case; only a case of attempted murder, or maybe assault with a deadly weapon."

"Shit!" He slapped the report against his thigh. "Why didn't Warren tell me this when he got back from the post?"

"Why don't you ask him?" Lauren suggested. "Sorry, Detective, but I have enough problems of my own. Everything you need to know is in my report."

"Maybe he would take a kidnapping report as a courtesy. Although they do like to wait twenty-four hours." Josh murmured. He flinched when Lauren's heel stepped back solidly onto his toes. Even though she wore running shoes, she put all her weight back there.

"Detective Evans, if you're so concerned because

you don't receive the results right away, you might consider coming down and observing the post next time," Lauren suggested, with a hint of acid in her voice.

The man shook his head and walked out. "Great, he knows I hate the sight of blood. That's why he handles that end of the case. Son of a bitch."

"I still say you should have asked him to fill out a kidnapping report. He might have done it as a courtesy."

"Norman is my anatomical skeleton. My very own personal skeleton which I brought with me. One in as excellent condition as he was isn't always easy to come by, either! He is very valuable, not to mention practically a family heirloom in my eyes." Her head whipped around as if expecting to find the guilty party lurking nearby. "And someone took him!"

Josh fought to keep from bursting out in laughter. "Fine, call the police and file a missing skeleton report. There might be a waiting period even for him, though."

Her gaze glittered with warning lights as she snapped back to him. "This is not a joke, Joshua Brandon," she spoke each word slowly and distinctly. "Taking Norman meant that someone had to have gotten into my office when I wasn't around. Since there's no reason for anyone to go in there when I'm not in, I keep the door locked. Now do you understand why I'm furious?"

He ignored her sarcasm. "Come on." He grabbed her shoulders and spun her back around. "Let's check this out."

"There is nothing to check out." She picked up her pace to keep up with his longer strides as he headed for her office. "He's gone."

"The lock didn't look tampered with? No sign of forced entry? Signs of anything else taken?"

She shook her head. "I didn't check the file cabinets because I doubted there'd be anything in there anyone would want."

Josh halted at her office door, stopping her from unlocking the door so he could examine the lock first. "No scratches," he murmured.

She placed her hand on him as she looked over his shoulder. "No offense, but shouldn't a *real* police officer be doing that? Couldn't you be obscuring evidence? Smudging fingerprints?"

"Didn't you unlock the door in order to go in where you found out Norman was stolen?"

She groaned. "So probably the only fingerprints they'd find are mine."

He straightened up and took the key out of her hand, quickly unlocking it and pushing her inside, closing the door after them. "Where do you usually keep your old friend?"

"In the coat closet." She opened the narrow door. A stainless steel pole was braced against the back of the closet. She closed the door. "And yes, if there were fingerprints here, there wouldn't be anymore, because I opened it when I came in."

"Maybe somebody's pulling a practical joke on you. Someone might have put him down in one of the refrigerated units in hopes of giving someone a good scare. The crew always enjoys a good practical joke."

"While I enjoy a good practical joke and have participated in some winners in the past, I've never allowed Norman to be part of one for fear something would happen to him. I've had him since I was a resident in pathology." She flicked her fingers through a pile of file folders on her desk and shook her head.

"It doesn't look as if anything is missing. At least, they're all in the order I'd left them."

They stared at each other for several moments.

"You think it's her, don't you? She's invaded my house, so now she's invading my office. It's probably easier to get into than yours, since there's more activity in your area."

Josh pushed the closet door closed. "If your staff knows that Norman is off-limits, then I can't imagine they would take him. It doesn't leave too many other options, does it? By the way, where did you come up with the name Norman? Or was that the name he was born with?"

She shook her head. "I named him after Norman Bates. Tall, skinny. It fits, except he lacks the dark hair and boyish charm, and you won't find his mother in the cellar, unless you count me."

"Somehow it fits."

Lauren stared at the top button of Josh's white shirt that had been left undone. She wished she didn't have this overwhelming urge to unbutton it the rest of the way. She tried to tell herself it was hormones making her act a little crazy today.

"Spend the morning in court?" she asked.

"An arraignment. How did you know?"

She crossed her arms in front of her chest and eyed him from head to toe. She noticed his unruly thick hair was even tamed more than usual. "Dress shirt, no tie. I'd say this is your own personal dress code for court dates." She uncrossed her arms and idly picked at a bloodstain on the front of her shirt.

He stared down at the top of her head. "Lauren."

Her body stiffened at the low tone. "Don't, Josh."

"Why?"

"You know why." She straightened up, walked

around her desk to her chair, and dropped into it. She doubted he knew her favorite defensive maneuver was to use her desk and cocky manner as a shield.

He leaned over the desk with his hands braced against the edge. "Bullshit. You're not the only one to go through a bad marriage and divorce, Lauren, and I think that's nothing more than an excuse."

"Don't let your overwhelming male ego get in the way."

"I don't think it's male ego saying there's a mutual interest between us. So what's wrong with our seeing each other after hours?"

She looked up. "It could be considered conflict of interest."

"I can't imagine that would be a problem. I think you're the type who would be stringent in keeping your professional and personal lives separate." He deliberately paused. "Or does your refusal to see me have to do with your promise to the nightmare lady to stay away from me?" Only a slight tightening of her facial muscles told him he'd hit it right on the mark. "She told me what she did, Lauren. Don't let her rule your life."

Nothing in her expression gave her away as she stared up at him. "You're the one with the problem, Josh—not me. Right now, I have a lot of work ahead of me to whip this department into shape. From what I've heard, you have a heavy-duty case pending. If there's something I can do to help you with your stalker, I'll do it. But don't ask anything of me that I can't give. And right now, romance is at the very bottom of my list."

He straightened up and walked to the door. Before he opened it, he looked back. "There's more to it, isn't there? What does she have on you, Lauren? What terrible secret is she using to keep you under tabs? In fact, what if I called someone in LA and asked about you? What would I find out?"

Lauren sat frozen to her chair long after Josh left with his questions hanging in the air.

"Hopefully, you won't call up there and find out," she whispered, once she was able to function again.

Josh's encounter with Lauren left him in a nasty temper for the rest of the day, and it escalated as he tore into an unsuspecting police officer whom he cornered in the courthouse after things went bad in court.

"Do you realize this case has to be thrown out because of your stupidity?" he growled, staring the man down.

The officer, a man in his late twenties, gulped. "Mr. Brandon, I swear—"

"That doesn't do diddly." He loomed over the shorter man. "Let me make this perfectly clear, Officer. You didn't properly mirandize the suspect, so the judge had no choice but to throw the case out. We're talking about a felony case that should have been open and shut, with that guy doing some hard time. Now he's walking because you didn't think." He looked as if he wanted to do physical harm to the man before he just shook his head and stalked off.

"Next time, let him go in there and try to hold down a guy who's loony tunes on PCP and see if he can do any better," the officer muttered to his partner, who had quite a few more years of experience in the field.

"He has and he did," the other man replied with the same disgust Josh had displayed. "Let me give you a piece of advice, Jefferys. Don't screw up again where

Mr. Brandon is involved, or next time he'll ream your ass but good."

His mouth dropped in disbelief. "What would you call what he just did?"

"I'd say you were lucky it wasn't worse." He walked off, leaving the officer to fend off curious stares and muttered comments. Josh's temper where botched arrests were concerned were well known in the courthouse.

"Josh!" Mitzi ran to catch up with him before he left the courthouse. She laughed as she finally reached him. "Are you in a hurry or what? Sorry your case went sour."

"Just another episode in a bad day." He shifted his briefcase from one hand to the other. "What can I do for you?"

"It's Brian. He's been having problems in school, and I thought talking to another male might help."

He hesitated. "Mitzi, what about your dad talking to him? I mean, Brian doesn't know me from Adam. Why would he open up to me?"

"Well, I talk about you all the time. He knows who you are and how much help you've been protecting us from Steve. I thought you could come over for dinner maybe tomorrow night or the night after," she quickly tacked on. "Maybe he'd talk to you where he won't talk to me."

Josh felt that rock and a hard place closing in fast. "I don't think that would be a good idea, Mitzi. If Brian needs a male figure, he needs one he can count on, not just someone his mom knows from work."

The hopeful light faded from her eyes. "I don't consider you just someone from work, Josh. I mean, I know my life hasn't exactly been normal lately, but . . ."

He held up his hand. The last thing he wanted was for her to say something she'd only regret later. "Mitzi, you are a very gutsy lady and I care about what happens to you because after what you've gone through, you deserve the very best. I only hope you find it."

She immediately realized he was offering her a graceful way out. "Maybe you're right about asking his grandfather to talk to him. My dad has been talking about taking Brian out kite flying on weekends or to a ballgame, but I was afraid he might take too much on. Maybe he feels he needs to do this." She took a deep breath. "He feels guilty that he didn't notice Steve's abuse sooner, and I was afraid he was trying to overcompensate. My mother died four years ago. So maybe I'll have him over for dinner instead." She rallied with a broad smile. "I hope you don't mind if I rescind the dinner invitation?"

Josh understood. "Not at all."

"I better get back." She suddenly looked uneasy as she started to walk away.

A thought suddenly occurred to him. "Mitzi?" She turned around with a questioning look. "Do you know anything about plants? I got one as a gift and I have no idea how to take care of it."

"What kind is it? Leafy, flowering? Indoor, outdoor?" she asked. "I love all kinds of plants. I have them all over the house. That was one of Steve's biggest complaints; that I spent too much time tending the indoor plants and the flowers out back in my garden."

He swallowed the nausea traveling up his throat. "Actually, I don't remember the exact name. I'll look on the tag and get back to you on it."

"Sure, look up the name and call me anytime,

Josh," she invited with a fleeting hopeful smile. "In fact, call if you just want to talk. You've certainly listened to me enough times that it's only fair I return the favor."

"Yeah, I'll call you about the plant," he muttered.

A strange look appeared in her eyes as she watched him. "The courthouse grapevine says you and the new coroner have a thing going. Are you sure that's safe?"

Josh only hoped none of his unease showed. "Hell, Mitzi, nowadays, dating anyone is considered a crapshoot. No offense to your sex. And while I know everyone's talking about me and Dr. Hunter, there's really nothing going on."

"I wasn't trying to pry. Just be careful," she advised, before walking away.

Josh stood there watching Mitzi until she was out of sight. He'd have to give Kevin a call as soon as he could get to a phone where he could guarantee he would not be overheard.

Lauren's mood hadn't improved by the time she got home that evening. She ate a sketchy dinner, then went into her office to go over an article she was writing for a medical journal. Except as she stared at the words, nothing made sense. She finally gave up and retired to a hot bubble bath and a book. She grew so immersed in the plot she almost dropped the book in the water when the phone rang. Silently praying it wasn't a call sending her out to a crime scene, she reached for her cordless phone that sat on the commode.

"Dr. Hunter," she said crisply.

"Remember your promise, Doctor, because you don't want me angry at you," the taunting voice whispered. "If you believe this is only an idle threat, there's ways to show you I keep my word."

Lauren hung up, then placed the phone on the floor with great care. She climbed out of the tub and had just wrapped a towel around her body when the phone rang again. This time she let it ring three times before she picked it up.

"Yes?"

"No hello? Not even a professional doctor's voice?"

She sat on the side of the tub before her legs collapsed under her. She'd never imagined that Josh's voice would be so welcome. She blurted it out before she could think twice. "She just called."

"What did she say?"

"Just the usual about staying away from you."

"You're lying, Lauren."

"Damn it, Josh, you're acting like a prosecutor bullying a defendant, and I don't appreciate your heavy-handed approach." She shut the phone off, then cursed again when it immediately rang. "What?"

"Don't you dare hang up on me."

She punched the off button with so much force she was surprised it didn't pop out. It rang again. By then she was past caring if it was Josh again or someone else. "Shit! Stop calling! It's bad enough I can't even slam the damn phone down to make a point!" She pulled in another breath to make another heated point when a sound on the other end stopped her. He was laughing! "This is not funny, Josh! Stop it!"

"You don't consider it funny that you're pissed off because you can't slam down your cordless phone? Personally, I consider it the best thing I've heard all day. Please, Lauren, don't hang up again. We need to talk." He paused as if figuring she'd hang up again.

When she didn't, he quickly continued. "Did Norman ever show up?"

"No." She reached for her robe and pulled it on around her. "I questioned everyone, but no one saw him or remembered anyone going into my office when I wasn't around. It's either a conspiracy on everyone's part, or they genuinely didn't know anything."

"Mitzi told me she's a big lover of plants. She also suggested I be careful. That came right after she mentioned your name," Josh told her. "I'm at Kevin Peterson's house right now. We're doing some brainstorming while he does a more extensive background check on her."

"She's the one you helped get out of an abusive marriage?"

"Yeah." Muffled sounds came though before he spoke in a lower voice. "Are you sure you're all right? The call didn't upset you too much?"

"I'm no more upset than I'd be if it was your run-of-the-mill obscene caller. I'm more ticked off than anything because I was in the tub feeling pretty relaxed before she called. And that mood is ruined!"

"Bath, huh? Did you use bubble bath? Want some company?"

"Don't be a pervert, Josh." She thought quickly. "If it will make you feel any better, we can meet for lunch tomorrow."

"Sounds good to me. Some nice out-of-the-way place?"

"Sounds even better." She deliberately made her voice husky and inviting, the kind that kept men panting for more. "And Josh? Why don't you bring Detective Peterson along? That way, if we're under observation, she'll think it's nothing more than a business meeting." She hung up before Josh could say anything more. She waited a few beats and when the phone remained silent, she breathed a sigh of relief.

Lauren had to admit Josh's phone call had accomplished one thing. She wasn't as jittery over the first call as she'd felt before.

"Now that you're finished talking dirty to the coroner, are you ready to tell me what happened?"

Josh turned back to Kevin. "She got another call. I don't remember saying anything dirty to her, either."

"It wasn't what you said, but what you implied, ole buddy. You want to get in the lady's pants real bad, admit it." The detective lit up a cigarette. "You've got one woman about ready to kill any woman you get near, and here you are, raring to get in trouble again. You've got a problem."

Josh settled back in the couch. "The problem is my feelings toward Lauren are more than just sexual. I admit I've played around more than I should have, but that's because I hadn't found anyone who kept my attention the way she does."

"She's kept your attention because you haven't met under normal circumstances. It's like a copy having to guard a beautiful woman for a long time or a prisoner becoming involved with his jailer," Kevin pointed out. "I'd wait and see how I felt once this whole mess is wrapped up."

"Someone stole her skeleton today."

"Ordinarily, I'd say something really asinine about that, but too many strange things have happened with the two of you." Kevin drained the last of his beer and headed for the kitchen. "Want another beer?"

Josh shook his head. "I don't want to risk getting stopped on the way home."

"Spend the night," Kevin invited, coming back with two more beer cans. "The guest room bed's made up and you won't have to worry about your lady friend calling you up in the middle of the night. If she called the doc, she's probably going to call you too."

"Except she'll think I'm at Lauren's."

He shook his head. "Knowing her, if she thought that, she'd head out for Lauren's house and not find your car. She might even be staking out Lauren's house right now." He held up a silencing hand before Josh could speak. "There's regular drive-bys, so don't worry too much." He handed him one of the beer cans. "Just drink and relax. You're getting too up-tight. I'll add the missing skeleton to the lady's list. At this rate, you could spend an entire morning in court just listening to the list of charges."

Josh popped the tab and drank deeply. "That's one morning I wouldn't feel was wasted."

She had a perfect view of Kevin Peterson's family room. The patio door vertical blinds had been conveniently left open so she could sit back in the shadows and watch Josh.

She was glad to see he was spending time with Kevin. Kevin was a very nice man. She already knew he was trying to find out who she was, but she wasn't worried. She had covered her tracks too well. She didn't think that made Kevin a bad detective, not when he was dealing with someone as clever as she was. She only wished he'd made it easier for her to access the file he'd compiled on her. She'd love to know what he thought about her. Oh well, maybe someday she'd let him know who she was. Maybe at his retirement dinner. Wouldn't that make a lovely retirement gift? Much better than a gold watch!

She sat back in the lawn chair she'd pulled off into the woods where she could sit undisturbed and lovingly studied Josh's every gesture as he talked to Kevin. She made note of the dark green polo shirt he wore with his jeans. Watched the way his hands moved as he talked and imagined them on her. Her breathing deepened before she could pull herself back under control.

She wondered if Lauren had tracked him down to whine about the call she'd made to her earlier. Just as quickly, she dismissed the idea. After all, he was still here and not racing to Lauren's house, giving the bitch the sympathy she didn't deserve. Just as Celia always looked for sympathy anytime she tried one of her whorish stunts and failed. But she still lost in the end. Just as Lauren would lose. She just hoped her call had made her nervous. If it didn't, well, that was all right, too, because she never liked to leave anything to chance. She'd also made sure to leave Lauren another warning that was a little more tangible than a phone call. Too bad she didn't know how to rig up a hidden camera in Lauren's house. She only wished she could see Lauren's face tomorrow morning when she discovered the surprise she'd left her.

Chapter Ten

"It's about time you showed up here. Where the hell have you been?"

"Whatever happened to 'Good morning, Lord and Master Boss'?" Josh walked past his secretary and into his office. He dropped his briefcase on his desk before walking around and falling into his chair.

"The day I say something that ridiculous is the day you'll have to put me away for strangling you for even suggesting I say it." Ginnie stopped short as she surveyed his gray features and bloodshot eyes. "You look like hell."

He thought of the untold amounts of beer he'd consumed at Kevin's house last night, then had a hazy recollection of falling into bed still clothed. He didn't even want to think about when Sharon, Kevin's wife, informed them she would not tolerate hangovers even as he tried to ease his way out of the house. With time running against him, he realized there was no chance of going home first and taking a quick shower. He opted to stop at his health club and use the shower there, grateful he kept a change of clothing in the car.

"Yeah, well, you ought to look at the world from my end." He rummaged through his desk, found a bottle of aspirin, and tossed four in his mouth. He made a face as he crunched down on the tablets.

"I called you at home, called your car phone, and left messages at the police station, sheriff's station, and anywhere else I could think of," Ginnie said, looming over him. "I should have thought of trying some of the bars."

Josh closed his eyes in hopes that not looking at her would drown out her voice. It didn't work. "Kevin and I spent the night brainstorming, all right? What can be so important that you played bloodhound?"

The charged silence brought one eye open. He looked up, noticing that Ginnie's furious expression wasn't her usual one. This wasn't the expression that told him he was late and she was mad he hadn't called in to tell her; this was something much more serious. He quickly swallowed the pasty mass in his mouth, certain that granules were sticking all along the sides of his throat. A sinking feeling hit his still sensitive stomach. "It's about Lauren, isn't it? What happened to her?"

"Detective Peterson called about a half-hour ago and he sounded the way you look. He was at the emergency room, taking Dr. Hunter's report. All he would say was that she'd had an accident and he thought you should know." Ginnie stepped back before Josh could mow her down as he bolted out of the room. As he passed her, she grabbed his arm. "Calm down, Josh, or you won't do her or yourself any good."

"Not until I know what happened to her."

She glanced around and lowered her voice. "We both know her troubles are tied up with yours. You're going to have to be very careful. This isn't the case of some jokester showing up in a hearse at a company party."

Josh looked down at the woman he believed was an extension of himself. "Thanks for your concern, Ginnie. You know what to say if anyone calls in for me."

"I've already said something unavoidable came up. Just be grateful you didn't have to go to court today. I doubt you could have gotten out of that."

"Don't bet on it." He was gone before she could say another word.

Josh had no recollection of driving to the hospital. He parked the car haphazardly, cutting off another driver for a space close to the emergency room door, and ran inside.

"I'm Assistant District Attorney Brandon," he told a clerk at the desk. "Detective Peterson is here with a Dr. Hunter."

"Wait over there and I'll have someone with you in a minute."

Josh leaned across the counter. "Look, miss, we're talking about a crime, and I need to be present. So I suggest you tell me where they are. *Now.*"

She shot him a look filled with dislike before checking a clipboard. "Go on through, they're near the back."

Josh hit the door with his palm, walking swiftly through, glancing through cracks in the curtains surrounding each gurney. As he reached the rear of the large room, he heard Kevin's low voice and Lauren's, huskier than ever. He whipped the curtain aside and stepped into the closed-off area.

"My God." He stepped forward with his hand outstretched to touch her face, then quickly pulled back as he saw her problem. He settled for putting his hands on her shoulders. He whipped around to Kevin.

"What the hell happened?" He turned his gaze back to Lauren, taking in skin that looked raw to the touch, some of it bleeding in parts. Ointment shone on her skin.

Kevin grimaced. "The doc, here, was scrubbing her face with a facial cream this morning and soon found out her skin was stinging like crazy. She said she looked in the mirror and saw that there was spots of blood all over the skin and it was bright. She kinda blanked out after that. A neighbor heard her screaming and came running. She called 911 the minute she saw her. You got to admit she's got a good pair of lungs if the neighbor could hear her, considering the distance between those houses."

"It hurt so much," Lauren whispered, as Josh gently pulled her toward him, careful not to touch her tortured face with even his shirt front. He dreaded even the soft cotton abrading her skin.

"There was ground glass in her face cream, along with some kind of caustic agent that must have burned like hell when it touched her skin. We won't know what it was until we get the report back from the lab. The crime scene crew is going over her house right now," the detective explained. "The doctor who treated her said she basically got a chemical peel for free. He said there shouldn't be any scarring, but it's going to feel real sensitive for a while."

"He also said I better not plan on tanning this summer. I reminded him I'm a doctor, aware of the hazards of too much sun, and he just laughed and said he might be a doctor, but that hasn't stopped him from smoking three packs a day. Personally, I didn't find it very funny." Lauren swayed slightly. "They gave me something for the pain," she mumbled. "I hate sedatives. They always make me feel weird." She pressed her hand against his chest. "Not too close, please. My face feels as if I've had a massive sunburn and I don't want anything touching it." Her eyes kept closing. "She said she was going to give me something to remember, so I wouldn't forget my promise. You know, there is one word I really hate used in conjunction with women, but it fits her. She's a very sick bitch." She swayed backward this time. Josh carefully eased her down until she lay on the pillow.

He gestured for Kevin to step outside the cubicle. "Sick isn't the word. What kind of person does something this disgusting?" He glanced past the curtain, reassured to see her eyes still closed as she gave in to the sedative.

"Someone who hoped her little trick would make the doc so ugly you wouldn't want her anymore, that's what kind." Kevin flipped his notebook shut and pushed it into the back pocket of his jeans. "When I went out back this morning, I discovered one of our lawn chairs was missing. I did a little snooping and finally found it just past the trees. Whoever sat there had a good view of the family room last night." He waited a beat. "How much you wanna bet she was out there watching us?"

Josh shook his head. The anger he felt inside had completely obliterated his hangover. "That's not a bet I'd take." He glanced between the curtains to make sure Lauren was asleep. "Lauren talked about a promise she was supposed to keep and the woman said something about it to me. I have an idea it has to do with something back in LA. Anyone up there you could ask without making any waves?"

"Yeah, I'll see what I can find, but she's not going to like us messing in her business."

"Tough. I'm not going to allow this woman to rule

either of our lives. Besides, maybe it might give us a clue."

"Let's not get too optimistic, okay?" Kevin twisted his neck from one side to the other. He slipped his sunglasses on to cover his bloodshot eyes. "Has anyone told you today you look like shit?"

"Only Ginnie and about twenty others. Not that you look all that great yourself."

"Next time we brainstorm, let's stick with Cokes. I'm too old for all-night beer marathons to still be able to function the next day. Besides, Sharon said if I pull that stunt again she's going to make my life hell for the next year, and believe me, she can do it."

Josh looked up when a man wearing a white lab coat approached them.

"This is Dr. O'Neill," Kevin told Josh, before turning to the doctor to explain. "Assistant District Attorney Brandon has an interest in Dr. Hunter's case."

The men shook hands.

"I'm going to keep her overnight," he said, "just to make sure there won't be any signs of infection. Dr. Hunter told me the jar of cleansing cream wasn't new and she honestly didn't feel it was the act of a sick individual who somehow contaminated a bunch of jars of face cream. But I can't imagine this to be an isolated incident."

"We'll definitely be checking into this, Doc," Kevin assured him.

"What do you think the caustic agent was?" Josh asked.

The doctor shrugged. "Hard to say. Luckily, it wasn't anything strong enough to eat at the skin and cause irreparable harm." He was so engrossed in his discourse he didn't notice Josh's wince.

* * *

Lauren was positive she was fighting her way through miles of cotton batting while a sharp smell stung her nostrils. When she tried to turn over, she discovered a sharp pain along the side of her head and reflexively groaned.

"Hey, don't try too fast," a man's voice murmured.

"Water," she croaked.

He placed one hand under her head, carefully lifting her up as he held a glass to her lips. She drank greedily until he took it away.

"You have to be careful so you don't get sick."

"Josh?"

"Yeah, how do you feel?"

She still hadn't opened her eyes. "As if I just woke up with an incredible hangover."

He chuckled. "That's something I can relate to."

Lauren's mouth started to curve upward until tiny pinpoints of pain stopped her motion. "Why would she do such a disgusting thing?" She sounded as if she was going to cry.

"Honey, you can't cry. It will only hurt more."

It took her a moment to compose herself. She slowly opened her eyes. The room was dark, save for a night light in one corner and a strip of light from the partially opened door. "What time is it?"

He leaned over the bed, resting an arm by her pillow. "About nine. You've caught up on any sleep you've missed in the past week."

"Believe me, I'd have picked a more interesting place to rest up at than here." She mentally checked out the rest of her body. "Aren't visiting hours over?"

"Not if you've got connections. Besides, I told them I wasn't leaving here until I knew you were all right."

He brushed her bangs from her forehead. "The doctor said if you're hungry, you can have something light to eat."

"Are you kidding? Have you ever eaten hospital food?" She turned her head as she groped for the bed controls. Josh found it first and raised the head portion a bit.

"Better?" he asked.

She nodded. "I hate sedatives."

"I know. They make you feel weird."

"They make me feel out of control. And I always wake up feeling horrible."

"Sounds as if you have experience with them."

Lauren stiffened. "Why would you say that?"

He searched her face for clues, but by now she'd closed up against him again. "It probably has something to do with your saying you've had them before."

She carefully shifted her body and was grateful to find her brain could still function enough to interact with the rest of her. She lifted her hand and held her splayed fingers a fraction above her face. "It feels as if it's been encased in cement."

"The nurse put more ointment on it earlier. You were so out of it you didn't wake up. Although, considering how it might have felt, maybe you were better off," he explained. He carefully sat on the side of the bed and took her hand in his. He picked up her water glass and held it out to her.

She gratefully downed more water for her dry throat. She breathed deeply once through. "Any word on what was in the cream?"

"Not yet. Kevin put a rush on it at the lab, and hopefully, we'll know by morning, but you never can tell. It could take a few days, maybe a week, depending how rare a substance it is."

"Gee, Counselor, I could have told you that." She started to make a face, then quickly reconsidered. The stuffed cotton feeling from the sedative was finally clearing from her system. "It looks like I'm going to have to remember not to move my face too much for the next few days." She fiddled with the lightweight blanket covering her as she groped for the call button. "Now, if you'd be good enough to leave the room, I'm going to call the nurse and sign myself out of this place."

"That wouldn't be a good idea, Lauren." He moved the call button out of her reach.

"Why not?"

"Because right now, you're pumped full of pills and you couldn't walk more than two steps without falling on your face. You can barely sit up in bed as it is."

"I'm a doctor and am very aware of my capabilities." She started to reach for the cord only to have him pull it further from her reach. "Josh, if you do not give me that cord, I swear I will scream this place down."

He wasn't the least bit intimidated. "Considering the shape your face is in, I doubt you could do it. As for your being a doctor, you're a doctor who deals with people who couldn't move if they wanted to. So I don't think anyone would care to listen to your opinion of your condition. Besides, you look as if you're going to fall back asleep any minute if you'd just give yourself half a chance." He placed the cord on the bedside table, still out of her reach. "You're going to stay here tonight, where you'll be safe and have the chance to recover." He wrapped his hands around hers. "Lauren, what happened to you is proof she's starting to get out of control. You can't afford to take any chances. I'd like you to stay here until Kevin and I can figure out some precautions."

"I'm not going to hide away like a frightened animal, Josh. If she wants to come after me, let her. Let her come out in the open, where we can see what we're dealing with."

He shook his head.

Lauren struggled to sit up. "Do you have a better idea how to catch her?"

He ran his fingers through his hair. "Damn it, you know I don't! That doesn't mean you have to do anything stupid. What's so wrong with your staying here, relaxing, and letting them pamper you for a while?"

"Tell me, Counselor, when was the last time you were a patient in the hospital?"

"I had my tonsils out when I was nine. It was great. All the ice cream I could eat."

"Adults aren't that lucky. The food is usually worse than what you would be served on an airplane, they believe anything soft and runny is perfect for anyone, and they wake you up in the morning to take your temperature. I can do all that at home without some ghoul of a nurse smiling at me."

"Look who's talking about ghouls."

Lauren wasn't going to get by without a bit of grumbling. "It isn't fair to tease me when I'm in a bad mood and can't move my face very much."

Josh took note of her weariness. "Go back to sleep. No one's going to get to you here."

"Not that I'm worried, Counselor, but you can't order round-the-clock protection." Her eyes kept drifting shut. "Call Dana. She'll have some answers for you."

Seeing that she'd fallen back asleep, Josh eased off the bed and hooked his foot around the leg of the nearby visitor's chair and pulled it toward him. He settled back in it with his legs stretched out in front of him, crossed at the ankles.

He watched the sleeping woman, wishing he could figure out what was going on in his head. And cursed life for giving him Lauren, then almost snatching her away from him before he could fully figure out what was happening. But he had an idea he was going to make sure they were around together for a good long time.

"So she's striking back."

Josh shifted the receiver from one ear to the other so he could hear better. He hated using a public phone as it was, because he didn't want to be overheard, but he didn't want to use Lauren's room phone because he didn't want her to overhear him.

"In spades. What now?"

The psychiatrist's end was silent for a moment. "I wouldn't be surprised if she lies low for a while. She probably figures she has Lauren scared out of her mind and she'll want to relax and savor her triumph. After all, the stunt she pulled was directed at what she probably sees as Lauren's vanity, her face. The thing is, Lauren's one of the least vain people I know. But this woman is too blind in her sickness to bother to care. I wouldn't be surprised if she returns her focus to you next." A faint hum over the line seemed loud in Josh's ear. "Will Lauren be released today? Silly question, she'll sign herself out if they don't let her go. She hates hospitals," she murmured more to herself. "Tell her I'll call her tonight. And watch your step, Josh."

"Would you be effective in advising Lauren she needs round-the-clock protection?"

She laughed. "You might as well tell her to leave town. She'll only tell you what you can do with that suggestion. Lauren makes a mule look mild, compared to her own stubborn streak. But I will tell you something—if this woman strikes at Lauren again, she's going to find herself with a very angry woman on her hands. Lauren's temper is slow to burn, but when it ignites, watch out."

"That's it? That's my advice?" He pounded his fist against the wall, then quickly backed off when a nurse passing him flashed him a reproving look.

"Be grateful I'm not charging you for this, because believe me, I don't come cheap. If Detective Peterson has any questions, tell him to give me a call. I have a patient coming in five minutes. I'd say your waiting period has shortened by a great deal."

Josh muttered several curses as he next called his secretary for messages.

"If I were you, I'd call Her Highness first," Ginnie advised. "She's only called here six times and she's downright furious with you."

"Since she got her check, I don't know what she can bitch about, but I'll find out." With a resigned sigh, he punched in his ex-wife's number next, only to learn that she was staying with friends in California. That was one coincidence he didn't appreciate, and he quickly got the number.

"It's about time you called," Stephanie's cold voice assaulted his ears.

He wasn't about to waste any sensibilities on her. "Look, Stephanie, a colleague was badly injured, and time is something I don't have. What do you want?"

"I want you to call off your needless investigation."

"What are you talking about?"

"You know very well what I'm talking about. I

couldn't believe you were investigating my movements. We're divorced, thank God, and there is no reason for you to find out any part of my life. I suggest you stop it immediately or pay the consequences." She didn't bother to wait for a reply as she slammed down her phone.

"Thanks, Kevin, you're checking all bets," he breathed, as he walked away from the phones.

"No."

"Be reasonable, Doc," Kevin pleaded from the narrow counter he perched on while Josh took the one visitor's chair. "This broad wants you bad. You can't stay in your house alone. You should be under constant observation for your own protection. Or maybe take a vacation."

"I just started working there, remember?"

"Considering everything, I don't think you'd have to worry about having your vacation request denied."

Lauren turned to Josh. "Did you call Dana, as I asked you to?"

He nodded. "First thing this morning."

"What did she recommend I do?"

Josh shifted uncomfortably. "She's worried about the woman, yes, but she says she knows you well enough that you're not going to go into hiding. And she'll call you tonight."

Lauren nodded, as if expecting to hear exactly that. "I guess that settles that, doesn't it?"

"It seems the lab was able to figure out that powder pretty quick. One of the techs said they felt really stupid, since they figured it would be something pretty sophisticated and it turned out to be something you can get in the grocery store." Kevin pulled his notebook out of his pocket and flipped the pages back. "It was your run-of-the-mill flea powder in the cream. They figure you had an allergic reaction to it, so I guess it's a good thing you're not a dog or you'd have real problems." His attempt at humor fell flat.

"I told Dr. O'Neill either he could discharge me or I'd sign myself out, so I can leave anytime," Lauren said.

"Fine, I give up. We'll leave while you get dressed, and then I'll drive you home." Josh shot her a look that was filled with as much stubbornness as her own. "Don't fight me on this one."

"Don't worry, I don't intend to." She swung her legs over to the side of the bed. "Now, out."

"No wonder they say docs are the worst patients," Kevin told Josh as they left the room. "I'll send a patrol car out to her house and have it wait there until you show up."

"Good."

Lauren was grateful her skin didn't burn as much today, thanks to the ointment, but it still felt ultrasensitive. She flinched when the lightweight fabric of her sweater brushed against her face as she slipped her sweater on over her head and quickly pulled on her jeans.

Once the paperwork was dispensed with, Josh walked alongside Lauren glumly seated in a wheelchair.

"You won't fight me on this," the nurse told her.

"And you wonder why I don't like hospitals," Lauren told Josh.

"You might want to have the security people back

out to look at your system," Josh said, as he drove to her house.

She opened her window and breathed in the crisp, late morning air to clear out the disinfectant smell she always associated with, and hated about, hospitals.

"I'll do it first thing."

"Would you be willing to settle for a driver to and from the morgue?"

She kept pulling in lungfuls of air even as she felt a bit lightheaded. "Even though she hasn't tried anything with a car?"

"There's always a first time."

"I'll concede on that point, as long as it isn't Pete or Sophie behind the wheel."

"Damn gracious of you to give in on something."

She would have smiled if she'd dared. "I can be damn gracious when I want to."

When Josh passed the patrol car parked conspicuously in front of Lauren's car, the driver looked at Josh and nodded that everything was all right.

It wasn't until Josh unlocked the front door and pushed it open that Lauren started to feel uneasy. She hesitated for a moment, then quickly walked inside, moving through each room, grateful Josh was right behind her. She was glad to see someone had thought to turn off her coffee maker and dumped the contents in the sink.

"Mrs. Turner is going to have a fit when she sees the mess." She nodded toward the black fingerprint powder covering every surface. "And I suppose nothing was found."

"Not a thing, but we can always hope."

It wasn't until she moved closer to her bedroom that she felt the heaviness in her chest, constricting her breathing, suffocating her. Her stride slowed with each step she took. She thought of her unmade bed with her nightgown still thrown across the surface. Her makeup was scattered across the bathroom counter. She vowed to pick up a different cleanser as soon as possible. She'd never be able to use that brand again. And the glass canister she kept cotton balls in was probably still in pieces on the bathroom floor from when she'd spun around as the powder had burned her skin. She swallowed the nausea searing the back of her throat. She jumped when a pair of hands landed on her shoulders.

"Are you all right?" Josh's rumbling voice was comforting in her ear.

"Yes. No. I'm not sure. All of the above. It's just that I hadn't had a chance to put anything away yesterday, so this room will look worse." She finally reached her bedroom. And froze the moment she stepped in the doorway.

The bed was made up and the furniture shone with polish that left a faint lemon scent in the air. She hurried into the bathroom and moaned a soft keening sound.

The broken canister had been swept up and the pieces deposited in the wastebasket. The counter was cleared of her cosmetics and the surface wiped clean. Even the mirror was wiped clean of the spots of blood. She knew her jar of cleanser would have been taken for evidence, but to find another jar sitting on the counter was too much.

The final insult was the small white card propped against the new glass canister holding cotton balls.

Welcome home, Lauren. I'm sorry I wasn't able to do more for you. By the way, did you realize you need to have your birth control pills refilled? You really should be more careful with important things like that.

Lauren felt so shattered by the note, she did the only thing she could. She retreated to a hazy world where she didn't hear Josh's loud curses as he guided her out of the room and back to the living room. She was so lost in her own world she didn't hear him open the front door and yell for the officers. By then, she didn't care what happened.

Chapter Eleven

"The card is preprinted. There's no guarantee we can find out where she bought it, but we'll give it a shot. Too bad she couldn't have had the courtesy to sign her name. A good, strong hint would have been nice about now," Kevin told Josh in a low voice as they stood in one corner of the room. Both men stared at Lauren, who was curled up in a chair. Her arms were wrapped around her body, although the room was overly warm, with all the extra body heat coming from the lab technicians walking in and out as they searched for nonexistent evidence in the bedroom and bathroom. "She was also obviously the one who turned off the coffee maker and dumped the pot. Some of the men are canvassing the neighborhood to see if anyone noticed a car parked near the house, but that's a pretty slim chance, since no one's seen anything before. What happened to the nosy neighbors who practically memorize license plate numbers if a car looks out of place?"

"They're out working to afford the house payments." Josh's face was lined with the frustration that grew more each time. "Did anyone drive by my place and check it out?"

Kevin nodded. "And went in. There's nothing out

of order over there; your wardrobe's still in one piece and a faint layer of dust is on the furniture. Probably because she spent so much time here. It also might mean she doesn't know you spent the night at the hospital. We should try to keep that as quiet as possible."

"That's not going to be all that easy if she works at the courthouse. There's no such thing as a private life around there."

"Maybe not, but we don't have to let all the details out." Kevin inclined his head in the direction of the bedroom. "The report I'm filing is calling this a simple B & E, and we're assuming the perp was probably scared off by a neighbor's dog or something before anything was taken. Hopefully, no one will check the report too closely and learn the houses are too far away for a dog to be bothered by more than a low-flying plane."

Josh lowered his voice. "I heard from Stephanie. She's not too happy with being investigated."

Kevin grinned. "Considering she's been in this vicinity around the times of the break-ins, I don't blame her. She could take one of the top slots as main suspect if we don't come up with anything to counter it."

"Good, maybe I wouldn't have to pay her alimony then."

"Hey, Sarge." One of the patrolmen stood in the doorway.

Kevin walked over, then went outside with the officer. Josh moved back to Lauren and hunkered down on his heels next to her chair.

"You doing okay?" He touched her hand with his fingertips, surprised to find it ice cold to the touch. He picked it up, rubbing the skin gently to restore the circulation.

"I know that once I'm over the shock I will be very angry about all of this," she spoke slowly and distinctly, turning her head. Shock had left shadows under her eyes and etched faint lines around her mouth. "It's bad enough she came in here with the intent to hurt me. But to come back and deliberately clean up the disaster she caused is more than any sane person should bear. How could she be so blatant?"

He kept rubbing her hand until it felt warmer, then took hold of her other one to do the same. "She wants to keep you unnerved."

"Then she should be very proud of herself, because I don't think it will take much more to start me screaming. Look at this." She held out her free hand. "It wobbles so much, you'd think I was having the caffeine shakes." She took several deep breaths that shuddered throughout her body. "I'd kill for a cigarette right about now."

Josh stood up. "You have any brandy in the house?"

"In the cabinet over the refrigerator, but I'd rather have Irish Cream. Brandy gives me a headache, and I think I've had enough headaches to last me for a very long time."

Josh nodded and disappeared into the kitchen. Lauren closed her eyes and rested her head against the back of the chair. She found the faint sounds of his moving around the kitchen punctuated by faint curses as glasses clinked together.

"I couldn't find the glasses you probably use for this, so hope you don't mind this."

She opened her eyes to find a juice glass in front of her. She smiled faintly as she accepted the glass. "It tastes the same no matter what it's in." She started to sip the rich liquor, then changed her mind and downed it the way she would have drunk whiskey. "It's almost as good as a cigarette."

"Don't you think it might be a good idea to have something to eat now?"

"Not at all." She handed him the empty glass. "More, please, and would you fill it a bit higher next time? Say, to the brim. After all, I'm not driving anywhere, so it isn't going to matter how much I have."

"Lauren, I don't think—"

"I don't care what you think, Josh. This woman has invaded my home more than once. She's gone through my clothing, my makeup, everything a woman considers private. She's as good as raped me." She pushed the glass at him again. "I haven't taken any pain pills because I don't need them. All I'm suffering is mild discomfort, which aspirin will more than take care of. So, please fill the glass up; in fact, just get a taller glass, because I fully intend to get bombed tonight."

"Maybe I'll get lucky and it won't take much to put you out." Josh returned to the kitchen. Before he refilled her drink, he checked the refrigerator, only to discover Lauren's idea of cooking was far more involved than his own. He settled for slicing cheese and finding crackers.

"I thought you might like something with your drink." He set the plate on her lap. "You didn't get any lunch." He glanced at his watch.

Another part of reality hit her. She grabbed his wrist and turned it so she could read the time. "Oh, Josh, your office! You've spent the day with me when you should have been at the office."

"I called Ginnie before we left the hospital. If anything major came up, she would have called me here." He topped a cracker with a slice of cheese and handed it to her. "Here, I slaved over a hot churn to make this for you."

"Churns make butter, not cheese."

"Whatever. But it made you smile, didn't it?"

Lauren placed her palm against his cheek. "We're a pretty sorry pair, aren't we? You have a woman who wants you so badly she'll hurt anyone who gets in her way. And when I moved out here, the last thing I wanted was to get involved with a man."

"I thought we couldn't get involved."

"Gossip already has us lumped together." She held a cheese-topped cracker to his mouth, smiling slightly when he bit down. Smiling even more when he polished off the cracker with a second bite. She sipped her drink. "Don't take this the wrong way, Counselor, but I don't want to be alone tonight."

"Good, because I'd already planned to stay."

"You think she's going to try again, now that she probably knows her surprise didn't work, don't you?" she asked softly.

He knew better than to try to lay a story on her. "Dana figures she's going to lie low for a while and savor her success. Since she knows more about this subject than I do, I'm sure she's right, but there's always a first time when an expert is wrong." He looked around the room. "The couch looks pretty comfortable, and even better than that, it's long enough."

"I have a guest room where you should be more than comfortable." She stood up, forcing him to step back. "I'm going to change. Why don't you call and have a pizza delivered. I keep flyers in the drawer by the phone. I like anything but anchovies or olives."

"Mushroom, extra cheese?"

"Even better."

Josh waited, watching Lauren walk slowly down the hall. She hesitated for a moment before stepping into her room. He could understand her reluctance to enter it, after what had happened. He moved to the kitchen, found one that looked promising, and called the order in.

"They said it would be about a half-hour," he called out.

"Fine, then I think I'll take a shower, too. There's nothing worse than a hospital smell."

Josh settled back in the living room to watch television. When the phone rang, he stared at the receiver for a moment, unsure whether to answer.

"Dr. Hunter's residence," he spoke crisply.

"Josh? It's Gail. I just heard what happened to Lauren. Is she all right? But then, how can she be, if she goes home to find another nasty surprise? Why is all of this happening to her? She's new in town. She couldn't have had time to tick anyone off."

He breathed a silent sigh of relief. For a second he'd feared it was the woman calling to check on Lauren. He wouldn't put it past her fiendish sense of humor. "She's fine, except for feeling a little hassled from all that's happened. She's in the shower right now. Do you want me to give her a message?"

"No, I'll call her tomorrow, when she might feel more like herself. Just please tell her I called—and if she starts feeling spooked and wants company tonight, to feel free to give me a call."

Josh opened his mouth to tell her she wouldn't need to worry about Lauren tonight, but something held him back. He silently called himself a classic paranoid and merely said, "I'll let her know, Gail. Thanks for calling."

Lauren came out dressed in a robe, her wet hair

slicked back from her face. The redness from the powder reaction had faded to a dark pink, and the many cuts across the skin didn't look so obvious now. She dropped into the chair she'd been sitting in before and began towel-drying her hair.

"I thought women didn't like to be seen without makeup." Josh lowered the sound on the television.

"After everything else that's happened, I doubt the real me could scare you away."

"Gail called to see how you were doing. She said she'd call you tomorrow."

Satisfied her hair was dry enough, Lauren set the towel to one side. She rested her arms on her knees as she leaned slightly forward, watching Josh carefully. "What else did she say?"

Josh wondered if she was starting to have the same suspicions he was. "Just that."

"But something about her call left you feeling a little uneasy, didn't it? She said something you didn't like."

He gave her his best prosecutor's stare, which usually had people cowering. "Don't push it, Lauren." The staring contest lasted longer than it ever had for him. He had to give her points on that score. "Fine, if you have to know, she also offered to come over and spend the night, if you wanted company. She said to go ahead and call her. I told her I'd tell you."

"Amazing, how quickly you forgot to pass that part of the message on. Didn't you let her know I already had a sleepover guest?"

He shook his head. "I didn't think it was any of her business."

"Are you sure it was that, or don't you trust her?"

Josh leaned forward and picked up the glass dish on the coffee table, examining it from every angle. "Fancy ashtray?"

"The day I quit smoking, I threw out all my ashtrays. And since then, I don't keep any reminders around the house. I want you to answer my question, Josh. What about Gail suddenly bothers you?"

"She bothers me the same way every woman I know and/or have worked with now bothers me. I can't help wondering if she's the one and what will happen next." He set the dish back down. "Kevin sent a couple of men over to my place to check it out and it seems all right. In fact, after we eat, I should take a run over there tonight and pick up a change of clothing."

Faint lines of distress appeared across her forehead for a second before suddenly disappearing. "Fine. I'll give Dana a call, then. That way I won't have to wait for her call." She froze for a moment when the doorbell rang.

Josh jumped up and headed for the door. He took a quick peek through the peephole before opening it. He paid the delivery boy and carried the flat pizza box into the kitchen. Cabinet doors rattled as he searched for plates and glasses.

"You want some Coke with yours?"

"I guess so, since Irish Cream doesn't go with Italian food." Lauren sat on the floor by the coffee table, which she'd cleared off. "There's some placemats in the drawer by the silverware drawer that I use out here," she told him, when he'd brought in their drinks.

When she took her first bite, she savored the tangy flavors. "You know, for some reason, I always considered pizza comfort food. Right after my divorce, anytime I felt depressed, I ordered a large pizza. What I couldn't finish that night I'd have for breakfast the next morning. I was convinced that pizza and chocolate kept me sane during that period." She wound a string of cheese around her finger and stuck it in her mouth.

Josh wasn't sure whether it was safe to speak, since anytime he'd brought up her divorce before, she'd backed off. He waited and hoped.

Lauren looked off in the distance, as if something important was written on the walls. "Ron is one of the top detectives in the city. He can look at a crime scene and get a feel for what happened in such a way that it's no surprise he has a high arrest rate. He never took his work home and he never brooded on a case that baffled him. In fact, the challenging ones always seemed to act as a tranquilizer. He merely assumed the answer would occur to him one day. He could handle anything that came his way. The fact that he needed other women was just an extension of his true self and he saw no harm in it." She idly picked a mushroom off her slice of pizza and popped it in her mouth. "He was your cold, analytical cop until the night I was attacked, about two years ago." She looked up to gauge his response.

"Robbed, beaten, what? The whole mugging routine?" He was afraid to to voice the question that haunted him.

She shook her head. "Oh, I was beaten and robbed, but I was also raped. The man was one of Ron's arrests that walked on a technicality. One of the first times he'd screwed up. It also didn't help that the man had to spend three days in the hospital because of injuries. Ron's story was that he went after him with a pipe, so Ron had to defend himself. I guess since he knew he would lose if he went back up against Ron, he chose me instead. He caught me in the parking lot when I was leaving the morgue late one night." She touched her nose. "My nose was broken, so was one cheekbone, the usual cuts and bruises."

Josh hissed several curses. "Did Ron catch up with him again?"

"They told him he couldn't have anything to do with the case. I was unconscious when I was taken to the emergency room and had no idea what was going on for a good twenty-four hours," she said, speaking in a far-off voice. "But I heard how Ron went absolutely crazy when he got the news and screamed he'd kill the bastard. Someone had gotten a good look, so it wasn't long before he was picked up. They brought mug shots into the hospital and I picked him out with no trouble. Charges were filed, the case went to court, and he went to jail. End of story." She held her hands out, palms up.

"No, it's not. It might be the end of the story for a rapist, but it doesn't end there for the rape victim. Did you get counseling?"

For the first time, anger shone in her eyes. "I'm a doctor, Josh. I knew exactly what to do. Yes, I got counseling. Dana found someone for me. She said she couldn't treat me, since we're friends and she didn't feel she had the experience to give me the right kind of help. I joined a support group, listened to more horror stories than I could count, and began the climb back up to normality."

Josh was certain he could see it coming. "But Ron couldn't handle it, could he?"

She took a deep breath. She continued picking mushroom pieces off the pizza surface and popping them in her mouth. "His idea of handling it was to ignore the fact that I'd been raped. You see, if I wasn't raped, then he hadn't screwed up the arrest, which made it all one tidy little circle." She tore tiny pieces off her slice and chewed them. "Then he decided it must have been my fault. That I was wearing something too sexy, or I said something provocative to the man. Luckily, I was logical enough to realize what he believed was ridiculous, or I probably would have turned into a frightened little mouse. Instead, I heard how my work clothing was too sexy. That I shouldn't work all those crazy hours because they would attract the nuts. He called the coroner's office at odd hours to make sure I was there because he decided I was having an affair."

"Something easier to handle than the truth," Josh said softly.

Lauren nodded. "Much easier. I first tried ignoring him, figuring he'd eventually realize how wrong he was. Instead, he filed for divorce. Word got around it was because I'd turned into a nymphomaniac after the rape and he couldn't handle it." She uttered a short laugh. "My work clothing, sexy? You've seen me in my surgical greens. Would you honestly call them sexy?"

He didn't hesitate in his answer. "To be honest, yes, I call those baggy greens sexy, but that's because I find you sexy and whatever you wear looks sexy on you. If you're asking me if I think you deliberately wear provocative clothing to entice men, no. Did you ever stop to think Ron might not have been able to handle the rape because he was powerless to stop your being hurt? That if he hadn't screwed up the arrest, it wouldn't have happened?"

"I think if it hadn't been that, Ron would have found another reason. He wanted to divorce me before I got fed up and threw him out. We both knew it was coming. He just acted on it first."

"Except he left you during your time of need. He

wasn't there during your recovery, so he was labeled the bastard anyway," he guessed.

"Ron learned that the hard way. I finished up a research project and put out the word I was looking for another position. When I heard about this one, I knew it was what I needed and grabbed it." Without being aware of what she was doing, she raised her robe's zipper until the high collar curled down over her throat. "Ron was free to screw every woman he came in contact with, which I'm sure he has, and I can finally sleep without the nightmares, I can walk across a parking lot at night without having a panic attack, and I can deal with live men in close quarters. I never had any problem if they were dead." She began working on her second slice of pizza. Josh figured it was easier than having to look at him and see his reaction to her story.

He studied his hands clasped in front of him, the fingers tightening around each other. And wondered how it would feel to throttle the slime that had attacked Lauren. "Had you started dating before you moved out here?"

She shook her head. The drying hair dropped across her cheek, hiding her expression from him. "At the time, I felt more comfortable keeping track of my research. No demands, no having to keep a smile on my face if I didn't feel all that cheerful. As far as I was concerned, that was the best therapy I could get." She slowly raised her head and met his gaze head-on. "And somehow she found out the whole sorry story. Or at least, the story Ron wanted the others to believe; especially that he discovered I was having an affair."

"It's natural she'd figure you wouldn't want me to know all the dirty details and you'd back off and she'd have me all to herself again."

"Exactly." She gestured toward his plate. "I'm sorry. I talked so much you didn't get to eat your food. If that's cold, you can warm it up in the microwave."

He took a bite. "I'm so used to cold pizza I wouldn't know what to do if it was hot."

Lauren watched him demolish several pieces while his brain seemed to pick and choose tidbits.

"If she does know, then we can be fairly certain that she has police and/or courthouse connections," he said finally, pushing his plate to one side.

She stared at the almost empty box. "Wonderful, it only took you seven pieces to figure that out, when I could have told you that for a fact long ago."

"Oh?"

She nodded. "She knows too much about you to be someone you might only see where you shop for groceries or at the dry cleaners or maybe the drugstore. This might be a smaller city than Los Angeles, but it's still a city. She would need the right kinds of contacts to find out anything that wouldn't be readily available to her."

"Kevin and I thought of that almost at the beginning, but nothing panned out."

Lauren smiled. "That's because you're not a woman."

"Meaning?"

"Meaning, you've been doing this all wrong. A man can't know a woman's mind, but a woman can." She moved her legs until she sat cross-legged, her robe draped over her bare legs. "And I won't apologize for sounding sexist, either. You men do it all the time and you never apologize."

Josh started grinning.

She looked at him, unsure of what had prompted it. "What?"

"You did a hell of a great job of surviving, Doc. Something tells me this lady better watch it if she's going to mess around with you anymore, because she could end up the loser."

Lauren took a deep breath. The fear she'd felt when she'd discovered her cleaned-up bedroom and bathroom had disappeared. The sorrow she'd felt over the loss of her former life was also gone.

"Damn right she will."

"Amazing, how you moved out there because it would give you plenty of peace and quiet, and instead, you end up part of the focus of your typical fatal attraction stalker," Dana said. "You were better off back here in crime-filled LA, sweetie. At least the cops there know a little better to handle that kind of situation."

Lauren switched the phone to her other shoulder. Josh had just left for his house to pick up a change of clothing, and Lauren had immediately called her friend. "As far as I'm concerned, she's playing the opposite of a matchmaker, except that she seems convinced Josh and I have something going."

"He's a hell of a lot more man than Ron ever was."

"Come on, Dana, you never make such a quick decision about a person. And since you're using your 'I know I'm right' voice, I'd enjoy knowing what made you decide that about him." Lauren tried to ignore the quiet surrounding her and wished she didn't feel like such a coward.

"Lauren, Josh and I were on the phone for a good hour and a half last night. He was alternately furious and sick over what happened to you."

"I don't know why he should be." She ran her finger across her dresser's surface and idly realized the woman was a better housekeeper than her own cleaning lady. "She's going after me, too. It seems like it's not just all her."

"Simple, he sees it as all his fault. He feels that if he hadn't taken you out to dinner that first time, this wouldn't have started. And his little playmate from hell might not have fixated on you, too. I told him that was a load of shit. This woman needs victims to blame for his not loving her and you were just the next in line."

Lauren held the receiver in place with her chin as she pulled a pair of pajamas out of the dresser. "This sounds as if you've been doing a little more studying of her."

"She needs Josh to send little gifts to, to choose the flowers for, to admire from afar, but she needs a rival to focus her hate on," Dana told her. "And you're very convenient."

"Dana, you are not making me feel safe."

"I'm a shrink, sweetie, I have to keep you feeling insecure, so you keep coming back to me. How else can I make the payments on my Maserati and condo?"

"You drive a '57 Thunderbird and you held a mortgage-burning party four years ago. All I'm asking is some suggestions on what to do now. How to handle this before I go completely insane and you have to lock me away in that padded room where I'll be given finger paints for therapy."

"Lauren, what I'm going to tell you has to stay strictly off the record because no doctor in his right mind would advise this." Dana used her crisp doctor's voice. "Keep your gun loaded and handy, and if she ever gets angry enough to go after you face to face, don't be afraid to use it on her. It may be the only way she can be stopped."

Lauren threw up her hands. She'd forgotten about her friend's bloodthirsty nature. "That's not the kind of advice I was looking for!"

"All right, then do yourself a favor and don't let that man get away, even if he is a lawyer and we both know what I think of that breed since Karen moved out last year. You *have* told him what happened to you, didn't you?"

"Yes, I did, and he took it very well. But I only told him tonight, so he may change his mind after he has a chance to think about it and realize what a mess I am."

"I don't think so. He doesn't seem the type to back out of a problem the way Ron did. If he was, he would have left town the minute his problem with this woman started. No, just do as Dr. Dana says and grab onto him and hang on tight. After our talk, something tells me he's going to be around you for a long time."

After Lauren hung up, she sat on the bed, listening to the faint sounds a silent house was prone to make at night. She used to enjoy this time to herself, when all was quiet and she could plan the next day. She always relished the solitude and quiet.

Not anymore.

Chapter Twelve

"I put clean towels in the bathroom for you," Lauren told Josh.

She was bleary-eyed from their decision to stay up late and watch the Creature Feature movie marathon on cable. But at the time she welcomed the diversion, since she still felt too nervous to go to bed just yet. She suspected Josh sensed that and suggested the movies to help her relax. Now she felt so relaxed she wanted only to crawl into bed and sleep. As she looked up at his face, with its features too rugged to be considered classically handsome, and listened to his lazy drawl, with that hint of Texas, she came to realize what a comfort he'd been to her the past few days. And what he'd come to mean. For a woman who was determined to keep all men at arms' length, she was doing a pretty sorry job of keeping him at arms' length. Probably because that was the last place she wanted him to be.

"Don't worry, I'm pretty good at making myself at home," he assured her. "You go on and get to bed before you fall down."

She laid her hand on his arm. "Thank you, Josh. Knowing you're here will make it easier for me to sleep." She stood up on her toes and kissed him on the cheek. Before she could draw back, he turned his head and caught her mouth.

His kiss didn't demand or even ask. It was meant to show her he cared, and she took it as such. His arms wrapped around her, giving her another form of protection with his body warmth. Even then, he never asked for more than she wanted to give at the time. In the back of her mind, Lauren wondered whatever had made her think she could easily dismiss him. When she finally pulled away, her breathing was more than a little erratic. She stepped back.

"Good night, Josh."

He remained in the bedroom doorway until she entered her own room and didn't speak until she began to close her door.

"Still think this is something we can just turn off at will, Lauren?"

She didn't bother to reply and just closed her door. But then, Josh didn't expect her to say anything. Not when she knew he spoke the truth.

Past experience should have warned Lauren that sleep wouldn't be easy that night. Even with Josh sleeping down the hall, she felt the shadows in her room closing in on her. She disregarded the sleeping pills the doctor had prescribed when she'd left the hospital because she hated the way she felt when she woke up. Her previous success with relaxation techniques Dana had once taught her was nonexistent tonight. All she could do was lie on her back, stare at the ceiling, and feel convinced that every tiny sound she heard was someone breaking into the house. Only her self-imposed order to remain calm kept her from reaching for her gun and probably making a fool of herself.

"Think of something else, Lauren." Her quiet voice seemed to bounce off the walls. "Think about what will be waiting for you in your office when you return. No, on second thought, don't. That will only upset you more."

She finally gave up and climbed out of bed, pulling on her robe as she headed for the door.

The door to the guest room was ajar, and one peek inside told her what she needed to know.

"Can't sleep?" Josh's quiet voice reached out to her.

"I was tired until I turned out the light."

He sat up, plumping up the pillows behind him. "Come on in and pull up a piece of the bed."

She pushed the door open wider and walked in. The faint light shining through the parted curtains allowed her to easily find the bed and sit on the end.

"After the rape, I had trouble sleeping with the lights off. I couldn't even take a shower without having the bathroom door open and sometimes even the shower door open. I was willing to clean up the mess because my peace of mind was worth it. I always parked under a light post, a security guard always walked me out to my car after dark, and drive-bys were increased when Ron was on duty. But after a while, I started to forget to keep the shower door open or I'd automatically close the bedroom door at night. I didn't overreact if a man accidentally touched me and I learned to live again. Right now, I feel as if it's happening all over again, except it's a member of my own sex who's doing this to me. There's something very wrong about that."

"There's something wrong about the whole situation." He held out an arm. "Come 'ere."

Lauren slid across the bed and curled up against his

side with her head on his shoulder. She idly wondered if he wore anything to bed.

"Why are you so gung-ho on women's issues?"

"You mean you didn't hear all the stories?"

"Of course, but I'd rather hear your version."

Josh settled back more securely against the pillows, pulling Lauren closer to him. "It's a typical story about a kid who grew up watching his dad knock his mom around the nights he was drunk and knock her around nights he wasn't drunk because he'd already spent all the money on booze. I hated him for it. The first time I tried to stop him I was about six and I ended up with a broken finger." He ignored her shocked gasp. "Each time I fought him, he broke something else, until I got big enough to fight back and break a few of his bones. He ran out on us when I was fourteen. I considered it one of the best days of my life, because I figured if he'd stuck around I'd have killed him." The ringing conviction in his voice told Lauren he still felt that way. "I was willing to quit school and take care of my mom, but she was more determined I'd get a decent education. She cleaned houses and offices and I hated her doing it, so I raised more than my share of hell because it was the only way I could handle it."

"What an ungrateful son you were!"

He grinned. "Yeah, well, Mom had a better way of putting it. One night she picked me up at the police station; some friends and I were picked up for vandalizing the grade school. She kept talking about how she didn't want to see me turn into my old man and that she wanted me to have more and to have a chance to get out of the town. Small, dead-end towns in Texas don't have a lot of business opportunities. Then she broke down and cried. You know, I could have handled her yelling at me, hitting me, anything, but I couldn't handle her tears. I promised I'd never do anything to make her cry again. I concentrated on my studies, got a scholarship, and chose law school because it was a challenge and I needed that."

She punched him in the arm. "You should have been ashamed of yourself, vandalizing a grade school."

"Don't worry, they didn't let us get off that easy. The four of us had to paint all the classrooms, which took a hell of a lot of weekends."

"Poor baby," she cooed, rubbing his arm with the same mock sympathy.

"Yeah, right."

Lauren snuggled down further in Josh's arms as he pushed the pillows down a bit.

"Do you think life will ever return to normal for us?"

"Maybe this is supposed to be normal for us. Maybe we were thrown into the Twilight Zone and will have to figure out some deep, dark secret before we can get out of it."

"Then I hope we can figure it out real soon." She half rolled on her side and moved in closer, absently looping an arm across his waist. Within moments, her body was relaxed in a deep sleep.

Josh lay awake for a long time after Lauren fell asleep. He kept his senses tuned to their surroundings, listening for the faintest sound that didn't belong. He looked down at Lauren sleeping in his arms and lowered his head to press a light kiss against her forehead after carefully brushing her bangs to one side. He usually didn't feel comfortable sleeping with a woman throughout the night, although he was never crass enough to climb out of bed and head for home unless he had an excellent excuse. Early morning appointments were usually the best. Except he'd already decided sleeping with Lauren was something he could easily get used to. At the same time, a chance to do more than just sleep with her interested him even more.

Two o'clock in the morning. The lights were out inside the house and his car was still parked in the bitch's driveway. What did she do to convince him to stay? Did she whine that she didn't want to be alone or act like the typical helpless female who had to have him around? By playing on his sympathy, she probably easily seduced him into her bed. For a moment, she thought of switching on her car engine and ramming the vehicle through the side of the house. But she knew it wouldn't make her feel better unless she was able to hit Lauren.

She suddenly snickered. She probably had to keep the lights off so he didn't have to look at her marred face.

She considered mixing glass bits into the cleansing cream pure genius. She had gotten the idea one evening while watching a movie on TV set in an ancient Middle Eastern harem where an enemy was given tea with ground glass mixed in as an added ingredient. She didn't want to go that far. Not if Lauren was willing to listen to reason and leave Josh alone. She tapped her fingers against the steering wheel in movements that grew more agitated by the moment. Except it appeared Lauren didn't want to listen to reason. What was she going to have to do to convince Lauren she was better off staying away from Josh? She knew plenty of men who were panting to have sex with her.

She didn't need to have Josh on her list of conquests, too.

She kept staring at the darkened house until she was glassy-eyed. Lauren didn't need Josh, but *she* did. He could save her, she knew he could. From the beginning she knew he was perfect for her. She just didn't have a good enough chance to prove to him how perfect she was for him. Lauren't hadn't given her that chance, just as Celia hadn't given her her chance long ago. Why couldn't Lauren just go away? Just as Celia finally had. Just thinking of Josh started to calm her down. She ran her fingertips along the V-neckline of her sweater, then brushed her knuckles across the swell of her breasts, touching herself the way Josh touched her. She lost herself in a haze of imaginary memories as she continued stroking herself into a frenzy. Only a tiny speck of sanity kept her from screaming Josh's name when she climaxed.

Josh discovered two things when he woke up. He was alone in the bed and the smell of brewing coffee was in the room.

He knew before he did anything else he had to make sure Lauren was all right. He quickly pulled on jeans and a t-shirt and headed for the kitchen. Dressed in a bulky terry robe that somehow looked sexy on her, her hair pulled up in a loose topknot, Lauren was standing at the counter, beating eggs in a small bowl.

"Don't worry about serving me breakfast in bed. I was never much for room service."

"Good, because I hadn't planned to." She looked over her shoulder and angled her chin toward the coffee maker. "Help yourself. I'm making French toast. If you don't like it, you're on your own."

He poured his coffee, took several sips, and went on to pull plates out of the cabinet and silverware out of the drawer.

"I may not be a good cook, but I can set a mean table." He found placemats in another drawer and set everything up, including pouring juice. "How are you feeling this morning? Any tenderness or extra sensitivity in your skin?"

"No, but it does itch because of all the scabs." She lightly touched her face. "I look as if I have a rare skin disease."

"Naw, more like a good case of the chickenpox or measles. Think of it as a good reason to stay home for a few days and catch up on your reading." He gave in to his first instinct and placed his hands on her shoulders, turned her around, and kissed her. The light good morning kiss soon lengthened to much more as Josh pulled Lauren closer against him. He wrapped one hand against the back of her head as he slipped his tongue between her parted lips.

"Wow," he whispered, when he finally came up for air. His hands still cradled her face, his fingers tangled in her hair. "If that's what happens when we share one of those easygoing good morning kisses, what's going to happen when we finally pull out all the stops?" He winced when he saw the red streaks his morning beard had left on her face. He offered her a silent apology, not stopping to think how it must have felt, then remembered she hadn't bothered to complain.

Lauren smiled as she retied her robe's sash. She hadn't even been aware Josh had loosened it during their kiss. No wonder he looked as awestruck by it as she felt. At the same time, she felt more relaxed than she had in the last few days. "If we're lucky, someone will call out the fire department." She turned back to the bowl of egg mixture and added vanilla powder and cinnamon before dipping in two slices of bread and dropping them in the frying pan. "I already put the syrup in the microwave. You want to zap it for about ninety seconds, please? I already cooked up some bacon and left it warming in the oven. Why don't you get it out and put it on the table, too?" She dropped two more slices into the frying pan. "This will be ready in a couple of minutes."

Josh took the time to drop a kiss on top of her head before complying with her request.

"Do you know you snore?" Lauren waited until Josh had taken his first bite before dropping her bomb.

He almost choked as he hurriedly swallowed his food. "No wonder I woke up alone."

"You woke up alone because I decided it was a better idea to get up rather than wake you up." She stirred her coffee, although she hadn't added anything to it. "I still feel as if we're moving too fast in the face of circumstances that aren't present in most dating situations." She carefully set her spoon down. "I also walked through the house and looked out the windows because I felt she was out there."

"Damn, did you see anything?" He helped himself to a third and fourth slice of French toast. "Even a car you don't think belonged around here?"

She shook her head. "You can barely see the street from the house. But I felt a stronger pull when I went into living room. I was careful to look between the folds in the drapes. Although one thing was strange. A neighbor two doors over usually has his floodlights on all night whether he's home or not, and they weren't on last night."

"I'll ask Kevin to have someone check it out." Josh glanced at the clock. "I don't like it, but I have to go.

I didn't think to bring any clothes for court, and I have to get home and change first."

"I'm sure if I looked through a couple of boxes I might be able to find one of Ron's old ties."

He got up and walked around the table to kiss her. "Bite your tongue. Better yet, let me bite it for you." He settled for a gentle nibble. "There will be someone around here all the time. I won't be available, but you can get a message to me through Ginnie. I check in with her during recess and lunch."

"Josh, you're starting to sound like a mother hen." She turned him around and gave him a slight push. "Please, don't do this."

"Sorry, for a guy who prides himself on his objective stance and ability to keep a discreet distance, I'm doing a pretty lousy job." He rubbed his jaw. "Okay, I promise to do better. I'd better get my stuff together."

Even then, Josh didn't hurry as he walked out the door, after giving Lauren a light kiss. He was afraid to further abrade her skin.

"I'll call you later."

"Just go. I'll be fine. I intend to finish an article that's due next week and maybe even watch a few soap operas. There was one particular one I watched a few years ago when I had to stay home. I'm sure I can catch up on the plot in no time. Go, before you show up late for court. Why give the judge any more ammunition than your lack of a tie?"

Lauren deliberately stayed in the kitchen after Josh left. She found the familiar tasks of washing dishes and putting them away calmed her fears that someone was still out there watching her. Except every time she reminded herself that the person out there was a good guy, was the police officer Kevin had sent to guard her, she had trouble feeling better. In an act of desperation, she even switched on the radio and found a station playing golden oldies. The loud music wasn't sufficient, but she found it better than the charged silence she felt hovering over the house.

"I don't care if the patrol car didn't see anything. Lauren felt it, and I have to trust her judgment on this," Josh spoke into his car phone to Kevin while racing through early morning traffic and keeping an eye on the rearview mirror for any black-and-white that might not like his excessive speed. A prosecuting attorney stopped for speeding wasn't exactly good news.

"Hey, I believe in the doc's hunches, same as you, Josh, but there weren't any cars that didn't belong out there, and no one saw anything out of the ordinary last night," the detective argued.

"Not even a house that is normally illuminated by floodlights and wasn't last night? Tell me that isn't a little strange, Kevin."

"I'll get someone to check it out this morning. Josh," his tone warned that a lecture was coming, "you're getting too emotionally involved in this. I know you're seeing the doc as more than another victim. If this crazy broad after you is associated with the courthouse, she'll somehow find out you spent the night there last night. That doesn't look too good for either of you. Especially after you went rushing over to the hospital the minute you heard about what happened to her."

Josh turned onto his street and made a quick turn up his driveway. "Lauren could have been severely injured because of me, Kevin. Even if we weren't involved, I would have gone over there to make sure she was all right."

"You know what I'm hearing, Josh? I'm hearing you say that the two of you are involved now. Shit, Brandon, haven't you learned to keep those pants zipped?"

"So help me, Kevin, if you try to make Lauren sound like an easy lay one more time, I'm going to break every bone in your body. I'm furious with this whole situation, and I want to see it settled fast. I've got to go." He cut off Kevin's sputters and raced out of the car and into the house with the intent to shower and dress at record speed.

Josh didn't look right or left as he entered the bathroom and switched on the shower. He made record time showering and only nicked himself a couple of times when he shaved.

It wasn't until he returned to his bedroom that the musky fragrance hit him. With the drapes drawn shut, the room was so dark he could barely see. He crossed the room and jerked the cord so savagely it almost broke in his grip.

The early morning light spilled across his bed first. The artfully planned display before his eyes was even more gruesome because of its intent. Josh had been present at grisly crime scenes before, but nothing had ever turned his stomach as much as the insane spectacle before him.

He didn't waste any time in calling Kevin again.

"If you're calling to tell me you've been acting like a shit for your attitude, don't bother. I already know you're one," the detective said, the minute he got on the line.

"Get over here fast," Josh said without preamble, keeping his back to the bed. He wasn't sure he could look at it again with out getting violently ill. "I have to leave now or I'll be late for court. I want to know if you find anything."

"Our crazy lady?"

"In spades."

"What did she leave this time."

"Kevin, it's enough to turn your stomach. You'll find it in the bedroom. Just let me know what you find."

After he hung up, Josh forced himself to turn around and stare at the macabre display set up on the bed.

A skeleton with the spaghetti straps of a turquoise silk nightgown draped over its shoulders reclined under the covers with the sheet top neatly folded down over the comforter, the blindly staring skull placed in the middle of the pillow. One bony hand rested upward, the fingers curved, as if gesturing for someone to come forward. The final blow was a honey-blond wig almost identical to the color of Lauren's own hair placed on top of the skull and carefully arranged in a style similar to hers.

Chapter Thirteen

I can sense her presence. I feel she's nearby, watching me. She's probably sitting out there, planning her next move. What will she do next? Pull out a gun and get it over with, once and for all? Put us both out of our misery?

Josh's surroundings receded until he was positive he and the unknown watcher were the only ones in the universe. He forced himself to sit back in the chair, silently tapping his pen against the table's edge, trying to look as if he was listening intently to the defense attorney's opening statement.

He wished he could turn around and see if there was a woman sitting in the back of the courtroom who just might have that insane look in her eye. The trouble was, he wondered if she really was in the courtroom watching him and he was picking up her unstable vibrations, or if he had finally lost his own sanity and was turning paranoid in the bargain. He could see it now. He'd be sitting in court, awaiting the judge's verdict whether he should be committed to the local funny farm or not. He just knew the judges would toss a coin to see who would get the pleasure of putting him away.

"Mr. Brandon, are you with us this morning, or did you merely project your physical self here to make an appearance until your brain was ready to be awakened?"

His head snapped up. "I've been right here all along, Your Honor. Body and brain." He winced as the courtroom audience chuckled and the judge's expression indicated she didn't find him amusing.

Sylvia Greene, a no-nonsense lady with fifteen years on the bench, gave him what many called her stern schoolteacher's look. "I'm sure we'd find out differently if I were to ask you what Ms. Taylor just said," she said, which only furthered her resemblance to a teacher. "However, I'll only ask that you look a little more alert this morning. It would make me feel so much more secure to know you're hanging on to Ms. Taylor's every word, just as we all are."

Josh shifted in his chair. "Anything to ease your mind, Your Honor."

Her benign smile disappeared as quickly as it appeared. "Good."

Josh leaned over to whisper in his assistant's ear. "Do me a favor and when you get a chance, scan the room and see if there's anyone looking out of place."

The young man looked confused. "Out of place how?"

"As in foaming at the mouth, purple face, crazy-looking eyes, I don't know what. I just want to know if there's a woman sitting back there staring holes into my back," he snapped.

He nodded and after a moment, casually turned around. He turned back and scribbled on the pad in front of him.

All I see are the usual courtroom groupies and em-

*ployees. No foaming, no colorful faces. It's always been
hard for me to tell the crazies from the normal ones.*

Josh scanned the lines and nodded as if the man had
written a profound statement. Except he didn't feel
reassured, because he was positive he could smell Obsession in the air. But since more than half the occu-
pants of the room were women, it was a better than
even chance that one or more of them was wearing the
fragrance. Hell, for all he knew, the judge even wore it.

"So, if Mr. Brandon gives us his approval, we will
recess for lunch until two."

"Damn," he murmured under his breath. "I've got
to get my mind back on track or I'll ending up losing
this case big time."

"That's only if you're lucky," his assistant muttered, hurrying out of the courtroom as if fearing he
would be tarred with the same brush.

Josh pushed his papers into his briefcase, equally
eager to get out.

"I'm so glad 'the professor' is after you and not me
this time, Josh," defense attorney Carole Taylor sang
under her breath as she passed him. "Keep it up. Then
I'll have no problem winning this case."

"Up yours, Taylor." He was hot on her heels when
he saw Kevin standing near the doorway.

"You're so concise, Brandon. I do wish I had your
way with words," she retorted, before disappearing
down the hallway.

By now, Josh was past noticing anything but the
grim features etched on Kevin's face as the detective
stood by the open doorway. He hadn't been gone from
Lauren's house all that long. Had the woman waited
until he'd left and gone in? Had she made sure Lauren
couldn't recover from her next attack? Fear sent boiling nausea crawling up his throat.

"What happened? Is Lauren all right?"

Kevin gestured for Josh to sit down. He waited until he sank into a chair before giving his report.

"Your skinny bed partner was positively identified as Norman, the doc's missing skeleton. She also identified the nightgown as one of hers. She checked her drawer and found it missing. We're not sure where the wig was bought, but we're checking it out. There aren't that many local places that sell them, so we should run into a piece of luck there. The doc had a surprise visitor sometime after you left. The officer who went to her door to let her know he was there so she wouldn't get spooked if she saw someone on the property found a bunch of tansy on the doorstep."

"Tansy? What the hell is that? It sounds like something a witch would use to cast a spell." That's all he needed. A witch behind all this.

Kevin scanned his notes. "Yeah, it does, doesn't it? It seems it's some kind of weedy plant. I guess it's like an herb. According to a flower language experts I called, it means *I declare war on you*. I'd say she's letting the doc know that what's happened before is nothing compared to what's gonna happen."

"Joshua."

The voice that usually sounded like pure sex was strident and harsh as it echoed in the hallway. The woman walking toward them captured every man's eye. Whether it had to do with the heavy mane of silvery blond curls or the bright blue eyes or the voluptuous figure encased in a cobalt-blue dress or the three-inch spike heels that gave her walk that extra wiggle or all of the above, she was definitely a woman created for man.

"Shit," Josh muttered.

"Heather," Kevin clarified.

The woman walked up to Josh. "I told you I don't like people hanging up on me." Her eyes, usually limpid, shot with killing sparks. "Don't do it again or you will be very sorry." She stared at him for a long moment, then turned and walked away.

"Did you check her out?" Josh watched her exit, as did all the men around them.

"She likes to collect odd plants and she was away from home the nights and days in question," Kevin replied. "You didn't tell me she was a financial consultant. Hell, packed in that X-rated body is a computer mind." He heaved a heavy sigh. "Now, *that* is a woman who could raise a dead man." He gave a "what can I say" look when Josh glared at him. "We're still doing a little more checking. Especially since there was a story that she took a class in poisonous plants."

Josh shook his head. "No wonder I'm going crazy."

Unable to sit still, he jumped to his feet and spun around. He looked as if he was ready to put his fist through a wall.

"Do you have someone with Lauren right now?"

"Yes, and believe me, where she is right now she couldn't be safer."

Left hand wrapped over right, shoulders squared, legs slightly spread apart, think of it as doing nothing more dangerous than pointing your finger. Squeeze, don't jerk. And if you're lucky, you'll hit what you're aiming at.

Lauren was prepared for the recoil, but the bucking action still shook her body. At the moment, she was past caring about technique. She eyed the target, wished she could put a face on it, and kept squeezing the trigger until it clicked empty. She took off the ear protectors and left them hanging around the back of her neck as she pushed the button to bring the human outline target back to her.

"Not bad," Gail commented from behind. The policewoman had called that morning and Lauren was grateful to have her come over instead of having a stranger around the house.

Desperate to get out of the house, Lauren suggested they go by the shooting range so she could get some practice in, then stop somewhere for a late lunch.

Lauren wasn't as pleased with the results. "Not enough through the heart."

Gail unclipped the target so she could have a better look, then handed it to Lauren. "I'd sure hate to have you mad at me. You're too good with that thing."

"My ex had his faults, but he did make sure I knew how to use a gun and took me down to the shooting range on a regular basis. He said if I was going to pull out the gun, I was to make sure I didn't miss. Right now it's easy because I imagine I'm shooting at the idiot who took Norman."

"Naming your skeleton after Norman Bates is a pretty sick thing to do, Lauren."

"Not really. I know one pathologist who named his Freddie Krueger. Norman is very special to me, and now, because of this ridiculous case, he's evidence, and they don't know when I can have him back." She looked mad enough to pulverize the target with her bare hands. "I'm sure they're treating him like a joke in that property room. I just know it. They'll mishandle him and he'll end up in pieces. Not to mention what's probably happening to my nightgown down there." She rolled her eyes.

"True, we all know the real perverts are down there." Gail twirled her ear protectors around two fingers. "Talk to Kevin. Maybe he can do something to speed up the process."

"Good idea. I'll ask him. I just hate to think what will happen next." Someone standing near the entrance caught Lauren's attention. "I guess it's a sign of the times when you see more women here than men."

Gail turned around. She suddenly frowned. "That's true, although I don't remember ever seeing Mitzi here."

Lauren turned back to slap a new cartridge in her weapon. "Is Mitzi the redhead near the end? The one giving me a mild version of the evil eye?"

"Yes. She was the one I told you about, the one Josh gave advice and comfort to when she got out of an abusive marriage. I'd heard she'd applied for a gun permit when her husband tried to snatch their son out of school not long ago." Gail leaned over to confide, "I'd say she doesn't look too happy to see you. I don't know why she tries to consider Josh hers. He never gave her that indication, but don't let it worry you. I doubt she's the type to make a scene."

Lauren clipped on another target and sent it sailing down the lane. She took a quick look to her left, noticed the woman was still staring at her, and deliberately turned back, arranging the ear protectors in place. Gail stepped back.

"Maybe she's just surprised to see me still in one piece," she muttered, squeezing off each shot in quick succession. This time, her aim was a great deal more accurate.

"You were very lucky, you know."

Lauren looked up from the spinach salad she'd just finished. Gail sat across from her, looking at her with frank envy.

"If I'm considered lucky, the world is in a great deal of trouble."

Gail shook her head. "What I mean is, now don't take this the wrong way, but you should look as if you have all these pockmarks all over your face and it doesn't look any different than usual."

"I used a heavier coating of makeup to cover up the worst of them, so I wouldn't look as if something had erupted all over my face. I'm just glad the irritation from that flea powder went away. The ointment the doctor used on my face felt as if it was motor oil."

"I wouldn't worry. With looks like yours, no one would notice if you had a wart on the end of your nose." Gail made a face as she tugged on a ponytail that brushed the back of her neck. "With me, they'd notice the absolute worst."

"I doubt that." Lauren set her fork down. "Come on, give me some good gossip. Who have you been dating lately? Anyone I might know about, or someone you've kept under wraps?"

"A love life and my old schedule didn't work out, so I'm hoping to rectify that now. But good men around here are pretty scarce, so I'll probably have to go out of town to find somebody!" she laughed. "I'm real picky about the men I date. Not to mention that most of the ones I've met lately don't even seem to belong to the human race."

"They can't be that bad."

"You want to bet? You haven't seen some of the guys I've dated. I don't know what you're worried about. You've got Josh hanging on to your every word. The way he acts about you, he wouldn't see another woman if she stood naked in front of him. That's a lot of power for one woman to have. We all should be so lucky."

Lauren felt as if she could venture into unknown territory. "I don't consider it power." She took several sips of her iced tea as she tried to formulate her thoughts. This wasn't the first time Gail had made pointed comments about her looks. "I consider it more genetics. I have my father's coloring and my mother's build. They both freely admit my personality belongs to a past descendent because both have extremely weak stomachs and can't imagine being a doctor, much less a pathologist. My dad once made a mistake of looking through one of my infectious disease textbooks and he became convinced he had a skin ailment that had been last seen in Southeast Asia about eighty-five years ago. It took a lot of persuasive arguing for him to realize the truth." She smiled at the memory.

"Have you told your parents about what's going on?"

Lauren shook her head. "My mother had a slight stroke a little over a year ago. I didn't want to worry them more than necessary."

"Yes, I guess you wouldn't want to upset your parents." Gail looked toward the rear of the restaurant and stood up. "I'll be right back."

Lauren looked up and nodded when the waitress asked if she wanted more iced tea, then froze when she looked across the room and saw the woman she'd seen at the shooting range standing at the cashier's desk. After she paid her bill, she walked directly toward Lauren.

"Dr. Hunter, you wouldn't know me and who I am doesn't matter, but I've heard a lot of nice things about you," she said without preamble. "Josh Brandon seems like a really nice guy and he's a wonderful help to women in trouble, but he also has this black cloud following him, so to speak. Please, for your own sake, don't get any more involved with him. So many other women have had difficulties because of him. Don't let yourself be another victim in Josh's name." The minute she finished, she turned away.

"Wait a minute, if you don't know me, you shouldn't even care what happens to me. So why are you warning me?" Lauren demanded in a low voice.

She didn't bother to turn around. "Because the next time you might not be so lucky." She started to walk off.

"Why do you care about Josh?"

But her question went unanswered. Lauren reached for her glass but found her hand shaking so badly she was afraid to pick it up. She concentrated on breathing deeply, willing herself to calm down before Gail returned. She didn't want to be asked any questions she didn't care to answer at that moment.

"I swear men are behind the lousy lighting in women's bathrooms," Gail grumbled, sliding into her chair. "How can they expect you to put on lipstick when you can barely see the end of your nose!" She flashed an apologetic smile. "Sorry, I guess I'm going through PMS or something. I woke up this morning hating myself and I haven't been able to shake myself out of this ugly mood."

"Then I suggest we do something to take care of that." Lauren quickly finished her drink.

"Meaning."

"Meaning, shopping. New clothes, makeup, the whole thing. There's nothing better to cure the uglies than spending money on things that are absolutely not necessary, but which can make you feel much better just knowing you have them."

It wasn't until late that afternoon, when Gail

dropped her off after their marathon shopping trip, that Lauren realized she hadn't told Gail about Mitzi's warning. She wasn't sure if her oversight was deliberate or if she'd just plain forgot. But she felt a voice deep inside warn her to keep it to herself. She made the decision to not even tell Josh because she was afraid how he would react to what sounded to her like a less than subtle threat. As far as she was concerned, she'd experienced enough overt violence to last her a lifetime.

She learned Lauren was upset. Good. She learned Lauren was worried. Even better. Too bad she couldn't become so distraught that she felt she had to commit suicide. Wouldn't *that* send the right kind of message to any other slut who thought they could take Josh away from her! She wanted to laugh and dance as she thought of the ways Lauren could hurt herself. Just as Celia had hurt herself in the end.

She thought of driving by Lauren's house to see if Josh's car was there and decided against it, for now. No, now she would just sit here and think lovely thoughts—of Lauren out of her life for good.

"But first," she heaved the weary sigh of one who considered her next chore a exhausting one, "I must give Josh a call. Lauren didn't listen to me, and so, as much as I dislike doing this, I must punish her for ignoring my advice." She picked up her phone and tapped a number she'd committed to memory long ago. She smiled as Josh's drawl instructed the caller to leave a message. "Hello, darling," she whispered, in that husky voice she knew would drive him wild in bed. "You never heard the truth about Lauren, did you? The woman ignored her marriage vows by flaunting her affairs to her poor husband. She passed her work on to her assistants and went out looking for cheap sex. She's no better than a whore. Is that the kind of woman you want? The kind of woman you need? Look at Carol. She wanted you only because of your status. All she liked to talk about was how good you were in bed. And what about Celia?

"Dear, sweet, Celia," she spat out the name, "she was the worst of the lot. She thought she could give you what you needed, but she couldn't, could she? I'm the only one who can, Josh. I just wish you could realize that. The others have; that's why they won't see you anymore. And now, if you stop and realize I'm telling the truth about Lauren, you'll know how wrong for you she is. And then we can be together. I'll see you soon again, love. But don't worry. I left a surprise for you that I hope will encourage you to think of me. I hope you liked the one I left this morning. Turquoise is such a passionate color, isn't it?"

As she returned the phone to the cradle, she kept smiling at the newspaper photograph of Josh she'd carefully arranged in an ornate gold frame that she kept by her bedside.

She curled up against her bed pillows, comforted by the t-shirt she wore that was still imbued with Josh's scent, since she'd taken it from the hamper. The scent would soon be soaked up by her skin and the two scents blended. It was all so fitting. And very soon, he would be all hers.

Josh used the flat of his hand to shut off the answering machine and silence the seductive whisper that still echoed in his mind.

"To this day, I'll never understand what makes a

woman think she can force a man to love her, sight unseen." Kevin squatted down on his heels so he could better examine the crystal paperweight that had been placed by the telephone. It was the scene portrayed inside the paperweight that caught his attention. The tiny figurines of a woman making love to a man made the paperweight an erotic art object sooner than something purchased from an X-rated shop. "It looks like she's pulling out all the stops now for you. And as a result, she's getting careless. I doubt you could buy this at your corner card and gift store."

"Funny, that's what you said about the wig."

Kevin ignored his friend's sarcasm. He straightened up, wincing as his knees protested. "How did I know you could buy wigs through a catalog? And how did I know there were so many companies that made them? With the label cut out, it won't be easy to find out where it came from. The right kind of lab could tell us, by examining the hairs, what wig company it came from, and I'm checking into having that done. Until then, we're making calls just to see if we can get lucky. But they're all demanding we put our request in writing for names and addresses of anyone from this area ordering a blond wig."

"What I want to know is, who is this Celia?" Josh shook his head. "I've never known anyone by that name."

Kevin's eyes lit up. "Buddy, I think we just got our first clue."

"How easy will it be to find out who she is?"

"About as easy as this case has been so far, but I'll take anything I can get." He hesitated as if unsure whether to bring something up. "My contact got back to me. I don't know how to say this except straight out, and hope you don't go for my throat in the meantime.

"The doc was beaten and raped a couple years ago. Story has it that she came unhinged for a while, brought guys home, had sex marathons, and was even coming on to guys in her department. Her husband got so fed up with what she was doing that he kicked her out. Then she was told to resign or else. She bargained with her superiors to keep the story under wraps so she could go elsewhere. She knew enough people to latch onto here."

Josh experienced that now familiar red haze in front of his eyes. Right now, he wanted to do nothing more than beat the hell out of his best friend for saying such a thing. "Do you believe that shit?"

Kevin shrugged, which could have meant many things. He never believed in tipping his hand to anyone. "I only believe the truth when it hits me in the face, Josh. I'll say she doesn't look like your typical nympho, but who knows what being raped could do to a woman's thought processes." He refused to back down from Josh's warning glare.

Josh leaned forward, looking very dangerous as he ground out the words. "I've prosecuted enough rape cases that I can tell you the victims don't turn into raving nymphos because of it. If anything, they shun any form of physical contact, especially a man's touch. Which is why Lauren gives off that 'touch me not' manner to everyone she meets, especially members of the opposite sex. But then, maybe I've missed something and you've seen her throw herself at men. Which I doubt. The woman you're talking about isn't Lauren."

Kevin held his hands up in surrender. "Hey, don't shoot the messenger. I'm only repeating the story they gave me. I didn't say I believed it. Anybody can see Doc's got too much class to turn into a nympho, rape or no rape. I think they were just stringing me along. But I *did* get something a hell of a lot more interesting about her ex. It appears he likes to play around with teenage hookers. That one I'd believe a hell of a lot more. While he's considered a decent cop and has a number of commendations to prove it, he wouldn't receive any good conduct medals as a human being. And this is from his so-called friends."

"No wonder she got out of there if she put up with crap like that," Josh murmured, looking down and finding his fists clenched. "He deserves to be thrown out with the garbage."

Kevin reached into his jacket pocket and pulled out a tiny case. "I want you to start keeping this with you at all times from now on. If anything happens, all you'll have to do is push in the button on the side here and it will activate my beeper with a code that will alert me that you're in trouble. I've got one for the doc, too." He pushed in the side button, which immediately set off his beeper.

Josh took the case and examined it. "What's the range?"

"According to the guys who invented it, it should be far enough for our purposes. Call it a little bit of insurance. The doc asked for a special permit to carry her gun on her at all times."

He shook his head. "We both know she won't get it, because that could mean it would be concealed."

"She's only asking for one until the woman is caught, and it's under consideration. After all that's happened, they're figuring it might not be a bad idea." Kevin watched Josh thread the case onto his belt loops. "But they want her to try this first."

"I'll give it to her tonight." Josh took the second case and tucked it into his shirt pocket. "While I admit I don't like the idea of private citizens carrying weapons since they're turned on them so frequently, I'm beginning to see why Lauren would want hers with her all the time. Who knows what will happen next?"

Distaste flashed across his features as he looked down at the paperweight, with its glittering snowflakes floating about the figures. A tiny brass plaque attached to the base was engraved in an ornate script with the words "The Eternal Lovers."

"I sure don't like the idea of her using the word 'eternal,'" Kevin said, carefully easing the paperweight into a box that wouldn't smudge any fingerprints, although he doubted the lab would find any. They hadn't before. He sealed it shut with several strips of Scotch tape and wrote his initials across it. "It has a final sound to me."

Eternal, as in forever.

Josh was never so glad as when the paperweight was put out of sight. He'd given up the hassle of changing his locks and changing the alarm codes. She seemed to find a way in anyway, so why should he bother? If he thought it would help, he'd just put out the welcome mat and wait around until she showed up.

"Yeah, I'm not too fond of the sound of it, either."

Chapter Fourteen

"Do you think she wanted you to think of the figures in the paperweight as the two of you?" Lauren walked out of the kitchen carrying a glass of white wine. On the way to the couch, she paused by the stereo to insert another batch of CDs in the carousel. Humming along with the music, she walked over to Josh, handed him the wine, and curled up on the couch next to him. She leaned back against his outstretched arm resting along the back of the couch. She tucked her bare feet up under her body, carefully draping her rose-colored tunic top over her knees.

"I wouldn't be surprised if that's what she meant." He downed half the wine, then offered his glass to her. "From the very beginning, she seems to have visualized us as estranged lovers. What I don't understand is her reference to a Celia. It doesn't make any sense. Which makes me think of Heather, since she soon didn't make a lick of sense." He frowned in thought. "Heather once mentioned playing some kind of sick game with a girl in college where they'd see who could score the most guys in a weekend." He twisted his face in an expression of distaste. "That's when I knew what a mistake she was."

"And here Heather sounds so cute and cuddly; like a kitten," she cooed. "I even heard that she used to call you all sorts of cutesy names."

"Yeah, a kitten with the morals of an alley cat." He shook his head. "It just sounds like the kind of sick joke she'd enjoy playing. Maybe Celia was that person in college."

"From what you said, it sounds as if she was so upset, she slipped up without realizing it. Maybe this will be your break. She just might do it again." She absently tapped the glass rim against her teeth as she mulled it over. "When all this first began, did you ever try to find out her identify so you could get in touch with her to find out why she was sending you notes and gifts? Explain to her that there couldn't be anything between you?" She peered at him over the rim of the glass as she sipped the tart liquid before handing it back to him.

He sighed as he recalled that time. "From the beginning, she never talked to me directly. She always confined her messages to my answering machine or sent typewritten notes. When the flowers and gifts started arriving on a regular basis, I put Ginnie on the trail. She's better than a bloodhound in finding out something, but even *she* couldn't come up with a name. The orders were paid in cash, and the person wasn't memorable. It wasn't long before the deliveries turned into a joke around the office. I got kidded about my secret admirer, and the women even worked up a dibs list as to who got the next delivery of flowers." He drank the rest of the wine, then studied the now empty glass. "I think whiskey would be better right about now. Wine doesn't numb the senses well enough."

She shook her head and settled back more firmly in his arms with the intention of not getting up again.

"Just as well, since you can't numb anything right about now. Besides, I can't drink whiskey because of the antibiotics I'm on."

"Then you shouldn't be drinking wine."

"Who's the doctor here?"

He leaned forward and set the glass on the coffee table. "Some doctor you are, if you think you can rationalize safely drinking wine while taking those pills, while you refuse to drink anything stronger."

"I never hear my patients complain about my methods."

"How can they? They're dead!" He started to laugh, suddenly feeling more relaxed than he had in a long time.

He cradled her more closely in his arms as he idly combed his fingers through her hair, watching the way the lamplight highlighted the tawny strands to gold, dark blond, and ash shades. A faint scent of lemon from her shampoo clung to his fingers. It wasn't the first time he wondered how a battle-weary guy on the wrong side of forty got so lucky as to find someone as special as Lauren was. He wasn't about to question it too closely for fear something would turn horribly wrong and she'd disappear from his life just when he'd discovered how much he wanted having her in it.

"When this is all over, what would you say about going off somewhere quiet and remote for a few days where we can just kick back and be ourselves?"

She tilted her head to look at him better. "What, and go crazy with boredom because we'd have nothing to do?"

He nuzzled her ear as he whispered, "I'm sure if we put our heads together, we could come up with something to keep the excitement level pretty high."

"Yes, I'm sure you could."

He rested his chin on top of her head as he twisted to wrap his arms around her. "I thought it might be nice if we got out of town for a while and found an out-of-the-way place where we wouldn't have to worry about phone messages or uninvited visitors."

"A place on the beach," Lauren said promptly. "I want to fall asleep hearing the ocean in the background."

"I'll find us one. Just don't count on doing a lot of sleeping."

They sat together for several moments, content to listen to the music in silence.

"I'm going back to work tomorrow," Lauren said in a low voice. She spoke quickly to forestall Josh's protests. "I can't hide away, Josh. I did too much of it before, and it only left me afraid of my own shadow before I began to fight back. She's never tried anything there."

"What do you call stealing Norman? I'd say we have pretty strong proof that she was the one who took him."

"I think that was more a show of power. She wanted to show me she could get into my office anytime she wanted to without being seen. She strays into our territory because she thinks it gives her an edge. It's as if she likes us to know she can go through our personal things any time she wants to. I'll be fine working in the morgue. I can't imagine she would want to go in there too often. There's plenty of days when *I'm* not too happy about going in there." She wiggled out of his arms and turned around to face him. "So far, you and I have been able to carry on our lives pretty much as usual. That means my going back to work so I can prove to her she hasn't won."

"And here I'd thought about taking a leave of ab-

sence. I hoped things might calm down if I wasn't
around the courthouse so much."

"Considering the workload you carry, you'd go
crazy within a few days if you didn't have anything to
do. Besides, I don't think that would help." She softened her voice. She didn't want to explain to him that
there were times when she felt as if his unseen admirer
could hear everything they said. As if she knew what
was going on before even Lauren and Josh did. "We'll
just go on as if she doesn't matter."

He reached for her, laughing when she edged her
way backward. "As far as I'm concerned, she doesn't
matter. So why don't you come on back over here and
we'll discuss the proper way to dissect a frog."

"If you want to talk about dissection, I can always
tell you about my first autopsy."

"Gory?"

She grinned. "The kind little boys go nuts over."

"Then I'm all ears."

Lauren grinned. "Good, because the victim'd had
his cut off, along with a few other parts of his anatomy
I'm sure he considered very important."

"Ouch."

"I'm sure he protested a lot more than that."

Josh stared at Lauren for several moments.

"What? Do I have something on my face?" She
started to lightly rub her chin, then crossed her eyes to
stare at her nose. "What's wrong?"

"You could have been badly scarred from all that
glass and caustic, yet you haven't seemed to worry
about it. In fact, all you've done is complain about
your face itching. People would think you're merely
getting over the chickenpox."

"I don't see any sense in worrying about something
that didn't happen," she said, dragging a throw pillow

onto her lap. "As it is, I doubt I thought about the consequences, even in the beginning. At that time, all I cared about was getting rid of the burning sensation because it was so strong. You're the second person to bring that up. Gail talked about that today, too."

Josh grew still. "Gail talked about it?"

She nodded. "She asked me about it when we went to lunch and later, when we went shopping, she brought it up again. She didn't seem to think she could have handled the whole situation very well if it had happened to her. I tried to tell her you never know what will happen until it does and there's no reason to worry about something that may never happen. And if it does, you just have to roll with it. I also think it has to do with growing up in an impossibly normal family. My mother was a statewide beauty queen when she was a senior in college, and my dad was a star college athlete. They believed what was important was what was inside a person, not what they looked like on the outside."

"So you're saying I must have something pretty good inside me, since I don't have anything else to recommend me?"

She couldn't resist teasing him then. "I guess I did think of you as some aging cowboy who should have been riding the trails as a Texas Ranger instead of spending his days indoors, even if he was a prosecutor. But I figured I'd give you a chance anyway."

"Aging cowboy?" He advanced on her with the intention of getting even.

"With all that gray in your hair, how could I think otherwise?" She laughed so loud there was no doubt Josh wasn't frightening her. She scrambled backward over the side of the couch and continued backing away from him. "Now Josh, just remember that you're bigger than I am, so anything you're thinking of doing wouldn't be fair."

"You're one to talk about fair. You're the one with the evil mind, not to mention easy access to quite a few sharp medical instruments, and you are accusing *me* of being unfair? Tell me another story, Doctor."

Figuring on faking him out, Lauren feinted to the left, then quickly reversed to the right, except Josh guessed her move and tackled her. She shrieked, more with laughter than fear, as they rolled on the floor until they ended up with Josh sprawled on top of her.

"Josh, I can't breathe! You have to let me up."

"First you have to admit I won this round."

She shook her head. "You won only in your imagination." She pushed against his chest. "Let me up, Josh."

He shifted his body so his legs straddled hers. "Naw, I think I like you this way." He lowered his head. While he initiated their kiss, he allowed Lauren to control it. At first she seemed to want it soft and cuddly, with light, teasing touches. But it wasn't long before it changed as they each wanted more. Josh nibbled on silky soft skin while whispering in her ear equally teasing and outrageous ideas.

Lauren wasn't sure if it was something she heard, or a flicker of movement in front of the patio door caught in the corner of her eye. She froze and dug her nails into his arms. Keeping her expression that of a woman only interested in what was happening, she raised her head to whisper in his ear.

"I could be wrong, but I'd swear I saw something, or someone, go past the patio door."

Josh quashed his first inclination to jump up and investigate. He cradled her head against his shoulder so he could look as if he was doing nothing more than whispering sweet nothings in her ear.

"Don't look around or say anything. Act as if nothing's wrong." He made a point of nibbling her earlobe. "If she's out there, let's give her a show she won't forget for a long time."

"Don't expect me to give her too much of a show, darling." She did some nibbling back. "I prefer a little privacy when I indulge my wilder side. Besides," she breathed in his ear, "isn't what we're doing a bit dangerous? What if she doesn't like what she sees and decides to do something about it?"

"Then maybe we'll get a chance to find out just who is behind all this." He wrapped his arms around her and rolled until they were further from the patio door and the partially drawn drapes. He hoped he could angle his body where he could reach the beeper. "I'm going to try to reach the alert button for Kevin."

"What if it's all in my imagination?"

"I'd rather have a false alarm than do nothing and have her out there playing peeping Thomasina." He made sure to keep his back to the door.

Lauren kept her eyes half closed, trying to look as if all her attention was for Josh while she was really trying to catch a glimpse of something, anything, outside. The trouble was, Josh's wandering hands were making it difficult for her to concentrate on anything else but him. At the same time, anger was growing inside at the woman for doing this to her and to Josh. She tamped it down before it erupted. Wouldn't she enjoy watching Lauren begin a fight with Josh that, in a way, she'd initiated?

She sensed more than saw his hand reach the plastic case at his belt.

"No." She quickly covered his hand. "She's gone. I

can sense it." She moved out of his arms and quickly crossed the room to close the drapes all the way. "This is ridiculous. I'm afraid I'll soon start jumping at shadows; that I'll be always looking over my shoulder anytime I'm out in public. If that happens, I wouldn't be surprised if I turned into a nervous wreck. I don't like this feeling, Josh." With a quick look over her shoulder at the securely closed drapes, she moved away from the door. "See, I do it in my own home. Not anymore, Josh. We have to fight this. We have to start fighting her with everything we've got."

Josh grasped her hand and pulled her down on the floor beside him. "Kevin and I have thought of that but couldn't come up with a good enough idea we thought would work. Do you have an idea?"

"Of sorts. There's only one way to do this, and that's by sheer gall. We literally smoke her out. We spend all our free time together, make sure there's plenty of gossip about us circulating that she'll be sure to hear. Mainly do anything and everything to force her out into the open."

He was shaking his head before she finished talking. "The last time she did something, you had ground glass in your face cream. Next time, it could end up in your food. No, I don't want you to take that chance."

"Too bad, Counselor, because I don't intend to allow her to rule my life any longer. The more I think about this, the angrier I get. What gives her the right to force us to change the way we live because of her whims? The only way we'll win this battle is to force her out into the open."

He rubbed his hand over his jaw, wincing as he thought about his heavy evening beard scratching Lauren's still sensitive skin. "Have you asked Dana about this?"

"No, but I know she'd agree."

"I'd still be interested in hearing her opinion."

She couldn't help but push a bit more. "And if she says it's a good idea?"

"Then we'll get together with Kevin and talk about it more. And only talk." He held up a hand. "Lauren, this woman is turning out to be more dangerous than we could have imagined. I'm not taking any chances."

She agreed to shelve the idea until talking to Dana, but she knew it wouldn't stop her from doing whatever she could do in the meantime. Something she decided not to mention to Josh.

"Dana holds her group meetings tonight, so I'll call her in the morning. For now, we'll play the parts expected of us. Why don't you find a good horror film on TV while I fix some popcorn? We'll share a nice, quiet evening." She picked up the wineglass on her way to the kitchen.

"That's not exactly what I had in mind for tonight," he called after her.

"Too bad, because you're lucky I don't tell you to go home."

"That's because I wouldn't go."

Why did that woman have to close the drapes? She wanted to throw a tantrum right then and there, but she'd always been careful not to leave any signs of her presence out here. The open back yard was perfect for her to blend in with the shadows in the rear. Not having neighbors behind Lauren's house helped even more. No one to get curious about someone lurking around.

The minute she drove past Lauren's house and saw Josh's car in the driveway, she sensed something was up. Seeing Lauren in those thin leggings and top that just skimmed her waist told her that she wore them to show off her body to Josh. Just as Celia used to wear skimpy clothing whenever a boy came to see her. Celia, who always got what she wanted. Lauren's just like Celia. They were now rolling on the floor like two animals in heat. She knew she would have seen even more if Lauren hadn't closed the drapes. They were probably having sex right there on the carpet. She could see Josh tearing off her clothes, and her tearing off his. A keening animal cry erupted from her throat before she could clap her hands over her mouth to stop it. She barely drew a breath as she waited to see if anyone had heard her.

"That bitch will pay for taking him from me." She stared at the closed drapes as if she could see right through them and watch them writhing on the floor, having the hot sex she was supposed to have with Josh. "She'll pay. Just as Celia paid."

"Would you please stop yawning!" Sophie dropped a typed report on Lauren's desk. "All you're doing is making me sleepy."

Lauren stifled another yawn as she skimmed the pages. She was pleased to see that Sophie had made use of the computer's spell-check program. She was even more pleased to see that Sophie had forgone the bubble gum today. While the secretary's attitude still bordered on insolent most days, she had worked on improving her office skills.

"Sorry, I had a late night." She quickly signed her name on the last page. "Didn't the detective in charge of this case ask if we'd let him know when the report was ready so he could pick it up?"

"I already called him." Sophie turned a bright red under Lauren's surprised gaze. "Well, he's kinda cute, and . . ." She looked off in the distance, too embarrassed to say anything more.

Lauren handed back the report. "Then why don't you take care of this for me? Tell him if he has any questions, he can call."

Sophie remained standing by the desk. "Is it true you and Mr. Brandon are having an affair?"

Well, she knew gossip traveled fast.

"We're friends, and we see each other."

"When he found out you were at the hospital, he left his office right away because he was so worried about you. After all, some old girlfriend of his broke into your house and put ground glass in your face cream." She wrinkled her nose.

Lauren leaned back in her chair and gestured for Sophie to sit down. "It seems the gossip chain has been having quite a time discussing what Mr. Brandon and I are supposedly doing. What else have they said?"

"I don't tell anyone anything!"

"Sophie, I never thought you had. You've never seemed the type to spread gossip. I'm just curious about what you've heard."

The young woman fidgeted. "You already know about Mr. Brandon's secret admirer. I mean, everybody knows about her. How he started getting flowers and stuff from her. Then she broke into his house a couple times and cleaned it up. Except the night of his birthday, when she tore up all his clothes because he was out with somebody. As if he'd know she was there or that he'd even want to see her. If I knew who the woman was, I'd tell her to get a life. Why bother with a guy who doesn't even know you're alive when there are so many other guys out there?" She rolled her eyes.

Lauren smiled. "Do you agree with what the others think? That she's associated with the courthouse?"

She thought the subtle up-and-down motion of Sophie's shoulders was meant to be a shrug.

"Beats me. But I could see where it could be. I mean, she knows nearly everything about him. I just don't know why she'd want to bother with him."

"Why not?"

"Well, he's so," she suddenly made a face, "so old! He's got to be around forty, and my dad's forty-three, and let me tell you, he's ancient. And he's not all that cute. And he's got sorta grayish hair and that moustache. Now, Ted Logan, the new lawyer they've got up in the DA's office, he's really cute. He just passed the bar a few months ago, and he drives this great car."

As she listened to her secretary's chatter, Lauren suddenly visualized gray hair and a rocking chair in her near future.

Sophie stopped when she heard the phone ringing. She hopped up. "I guess I'd better get back to my desk."

Lauren knew the moment she asked this question she was in trouble. "Sophie, where do you draw the line at where you consider a person old?"

She thought for a moment. "Oh, I guess twenty-eight, twenty-nine. I mean, when you turn thirty, your life is almost over, isn't it?" She hurried out and grabbed the phone. "Coroner's office."

"Terrific, my life was almost over a good five years ago."

"She's a kid, what would you expect her to say." Pete stood uncertainly in the doorway. "You got a minute?"

"Make it fast. It appears I'll be ready for the rest home soon."

He held up a brochure. "There's a weekend seminar here that looks interesting."

Lauren studied the titles of workshops offered. They all specialized in forensics medicine. Several she'd taken in the past and found very informative. "You're thinking of gaining a broader background in forensics?"

"The way the times are going, cities will need forensics pathologists more than run-of-the-mill pathologists, and I figure I should be ready."

"Good idea. Write up the request and I'll authorize the payment for your registration fees."

"That kind of thing was never figured in the department budget before."

"It will be now. Go fill it out. I also want you to start accompanying me to more crime scenes." She noticed the fleeting look of dismay on his face. "A lot of people have trouble handling them, Pete. You have to learn to distance yourself, not see the victims as people, just as another part of the scene. It's cold and ruthless, but it helps. Just be grateful you're not in LA or New York. Think what you'd have to deal with there." She handed him back the brochure.

Pete rolled it into a tube between his palms. He kept his head down as he talked. "It was pretty obvious I didn't want you here in the beginning. I guess I believed Harvey when he said I'd be replacing him. But I see what you can do and that you didn't hold my attitude against me, even when I acted like such an asshole, and I thank you for that. Most people would have gotten rid of me a long time ago."

Lauren flashed him a wicked grin. "Never that. If anything, I just would have practiced my Y-incision on you. That's usually enough to get an unruly assistant's attention."

Pete's grin was too shy to be full-fledged. While he finally learned to relax a bit around his boss and her easygoing way of working, he still hadn't gotten comfortable with the banter thrown around. He gave a jerky nod and started to leave.

"I heard you and Sophie talked about Josh. Funny, how the police think they can keep something like that quiet when everyone knows what's going on almost as soon as it happens. There's been talk about that woman for months now. When it went on so long that it started to seem weird, the cops tried to keep it under wraps, but secrets can't be kept around here. I don't know why they think someone wouldn't notice what was going on and talk about it. Josh is pretty popular around here. It's natural people would talk about what was happening. And then, for something so horrible to happen to you. Some women are almost afraid to even talk to Josh, in case this woman gets the wrong idea and goes after them."

She nodded. "I can understand that. Did anyone come up with an idea who it could be?"

"There's quite a few people who think it's Mitzi. She works in the PD's office. She's had what you could call a crush on Josh ever since he helped her file the restraining order against her ex-husband. I can't imagine her doing all the other stuff," he gestured toward her, "but don't some people say who you'd least expect is usually the one to watch out for? Maybe that's why Josh feels safe with you. You weren't around when this first started." His smile disappeared when he looked at her face.

While it had been healing nicely and she'd applied a light coating of makeup base that morning, the many tiny scabs were still visible. From the time she'd arrived early that morning, people had been teasing her with comments about odd rashes and asking if she realized she was a bit old to come down with chicken-pox. With a brief wave of the hand he was gone.

"Of course. The one you'd least expect," she murmured to herself, leaning back in her chair. As she mulled over Pete's words, she absently tapped her pen against the edge of her desk. She stared at the gray metal filing cabinet as if the answer might be found in there. She only wished she could be that lucky! "Terrific, that probably narrowed the list by one or two people."

Chapter Fifteen

"Do you realize how crazy you are even to *think* you can succeed with a dangerous stunt like that?" Dana shook a cigarette out of the pack, picked up her lighter, and quickly lit up. She looked around for an ashtray, then, ignoring Lauren's frown, pulled the saucer out from under her coffee cup and tapped her ashes into that.

"Is that a professional opinion or a personal one?" Lauren glared at Dana's cigarette, then at her friend. "If all you wanted to do was insult me, you could have done it just as well over the phone instead of driving all the way out here to do it. Then I wouldn't have to put up with your smoking."

"Yes, but I believe in giving my diagnosis face to face. Especially when I'm dealing with someone who's more stubborn than a mule."

Lauren should have known better than to contact Dana for advice. But she'd promised Josh she would run it by the psychiatrist first. The moment she told the psychiatrist her idea, Dana told her she wanted to think it over and would get back to her. Instead, she showed up on Lauren's doorstep that evening, saying this was something that needed to be discussed face to face instead of over the phone. Josh was already there and put in a call to Kevin, suggesting he come over to Lauren's house to offer his input on their plan.

"I guess we're all in agreement that this woman's mental health has taken a turn for the worse."

"I said it was obvious after her addition to your facial cleanser," Dana interjected.

Lauren wasn't about to give up the fight just yet. "Then maybe what she needs is one good push to force her out into the open."

"Yeah, and she might be so pissed off at you she'd have a gun on her the next time," Kevin spoke up. "What will you do then? Pull out your gun and have a showdown with her? We're still checking out Heather's and your ex's alibis, Josh. Some aren't washing at all."

"That wouldn't do any good, and we both know it." Lauren snatched Dana's cigarette out of her mouth and dropped it in Dana's coffee cup. "You know very well this is now a nonsmoking household."

"Are we feeling hostile tonight, Lauren?"

"I don't want to hear any psychobabble from you, Dana, or so help me, I'll show you what true hostility looks like. Why aren't you all listening to me?" She looked at each one. "Something has to be done, and it has to be done now."

"We've thought that from almost the beginning, Doc, but this lady is too smart for a trap," Kevin argued. "If she can sneak in and out of your houses without getting caught, she isn't going to walk into anything we set up."

"All right, then we handle it another way." She turned to her friend. "Tell me something, Dana. People want to believe Josh and I are having some hot-and-heavy affair. What I would like to know is, what if we have a public battle where I tell him I never want to see him again? There'd be a good chance she'd find out about or even be present to see it for herself. Do you think she'd leave me alone after she realizes I'm no longer having anything to do with him? She's done that with the others."

Dana shook her head. "I doubt it. The more that's happened along with her using another name instead of yours makes me think you've triggered some hidden memory of hers. Either you remind her of someone she hates a great deal, or she hates you for bringing back that old memory." She tapped out another cigarette and held it up. "If you take this one away from me, I promise I will drown you in your own coffee cup. Just because you've become a fanatical ex-smoker doesn't mean you have to make the rest of us suffer. If you don't like it, start smoking again and leave us smokers in peace."

"Ladies, please." Josh held his hands up to forestall the battle he could see coming. "Let's get back to the subject at hand." He grabbed Lauren's hand and pulled her down beside him onto the couch. When she tried to get up, he kept hold of her hand and refused to release it. "I can understand the frustration Lauren's feeling. She wants this whole damn thing over. I know I do. Maybe we're leery of her idea, but she could be right. Maybe the only way we can stop her is to force her hand and hopefully, bring her out into the open. The problem is, we don't know exactly how she'll react, or what methods she'd use. She's been so unpredictable every time she's struck against us, we can't even hazard a guess as to what she'd do next."

Dana quickly inserted, "Which shows how well she can mask her hostility when she's among others, so no one's ever gotten an idea how she really feels. It's only when she's alone that she allows her anger to fester and get out of control."

"Then it sounds as if we're in a Catch-22 position. We're damned if we do and damned if we don't do something," Kevin brought up. "Maybe we should just say the hell with it and let Lauren try out her idea. We could map out a plan that keeps them all safe, make sure there's a back up figured in."

Considering the serious conversation going on around them, Josh couldn't help smiling at Lauren shooting poisonous darts in Dana's direction as the psychiatrist pointedly lit up her cigarette and blew smoke rings in the air.

"Wait a minute," she hurriedly interrupted. "Didn't somebody once say the simplest plan is the easiest? All we do is go away for a weekend. We all know that word will get out about it."

"Especially if they hear that Lauren and I are getting real serious."

She looked at Josh. "That wasn't part of my plan."

"No, it's part of mine. You want to push her. That will do it."

"You two are nuts!" By now, Kevin was ready to retract his part of the plan. "We just want to smoke her out. Not have her go ballistic on you!"

"She considers Josh her property, and it appears she sees Lauren as a repeat of a previous threat, which makes her hatred for Lauren that much stronger. She won't let up."

"Celia," Lauren murmured. "I feel as if this Celia's the key in this."

"Exactly. I agree with Kevin that it's dangerous and needs to be handled carefully, but at the same time, what do you have to lose?"

"I don't think I want to get into that," Lauren said wryly. "How soon can we put this into effect?"

"Weekend after next?" Josh suggested. "I'll have Ginnie make the arrangements and tell her she won't have to be real discreet about it."

Lauren stopped him with a touch of her hand. "Better yet, I'll have Sophie make them. She doesn't mean to gossip, but she can't help herself. Word will be out in five minutes. Ginnie will be discreet because she'll feel the need to protect you. And she isn't known for gossiping, so some people would wonder why she started talking openly now. Sophie will announce to one and all I'm nuts to do it and they'll believe her."

"You're right, Sophie is the right one for this."

Kevin finished his beer. "Why do I feel we could be making a mistake?"

"Because you're a cop and you tend to look on the dark side of life."

Dana looked from one to the other. "When this is all over, I intend to hold a group therapy session, because we're all going to need it."

"I don't like leaving you tonight," Josh murmured, when Lauren walked with him out to his car more than an hour later. Kevin had left a few minutes before.

"Dana's here, so I'll be perfectly fine," she assured him. "She has a black belt in karate and is a better shot than most cops. No one in his right mind would dare mess with her."

"That's the problem. The person we're dealing with doesn't seem to be in her right mind." He looked around, but the moonless night didn't give him much chance to see anything. He was relieved to see the house across the street had its floodlights illuminating the area. One less hiding place to worry about.

"I don't think she's here tonight," Lauren said softly, not bothering to look around as he did.

"How do you know?"

"It's more a hunch than anything. If she decided to drive by here, she'd see Kevin's and Dana's cars in the driveway along with yours, so she wouldn't feel threatened. Hopefully, she went home and stayed there." She drew her sweater more closely around her. "Josh, go home."

"All right, I'll take the hint, although I doubt Dana would be shocked if I spent the night." His kiss started out light, but quickly turned into something a lot deeper. "Purely for protection."

"Josh, go home." Lauren's order wasn't as strong this time.

He unlocked his door and held it open as he turned back to her. "Call if you need me."

"I promise I will." She pushed him into the car. "Now go so I can hurry back inside before I turn into a popsicle. Just think you'll have all that peace and quiet and I'll get to listen to Dana's lecture that I must be crazy to think I can pull this off single handed. And we'll soon end up in those battles we had all through high school."

"Debate team?"

She nodded. "It left us pretty much evenly matched." She hesitated. "Josh, I know I stole your plan for us to go away later on, and I'm sorry for that. I started thinking about our going away for a few days and how it would affect her right now and I realized it could work in our favor."

He ran the back of his knuckles down her cheek. "Lauren, I'd be stupid to be mad at you moving things up a bit. You were right; she's had her way for far too long now. Either we start to fight back, or God knows how long it will take to catch her. In case you didn't notice, I didn't object to anything you said in there."

She managed a brief smile. "I'll have Sophie make the arrangements tomorrow and let you know."

"I bet Igor will be ecstatic to have the place to himself for a few days."

"Actually, Pete and I get along better now. Probably because I found out he just needed to have some direction and the assurance he wasn't going to be confined to doing routine posts. He's even decided to take some seminars on forensics pathology to broaden his experience. I was lucky. I had a wonderful mentor for several years. Maybe I'll be able to return the favor." She smiled. "I'm sorry, Josh, I'm now beyond freezing. Good night." She gave him a quick kiss on the lips and retreated before he tried to draw it out again. "No, we're dangerous enough without starting something out here where we can't finish it."

He had to grin at that. "I'll remember that." He climbed in his car. "Go in before I leave."

Lauren walked back to the door and stood just inside until Josh turned down the street.

"And you thought you were only friends," Dana drawled. "Still, he's a hundred percent better than Ron, he obviously cares a great deal for you, so I give my approval. Although, if the two of you are going away for an illicit weekend, I doubt you'd care if I did or not. Although I do hope you'll think safe sex."

Lauren closed the door and punched in the alarm code. "No jokes, Dana."

"Then you do have strong feelings for him."

The two women stopped in the kitchen for two glasses and a bottle of wine before they walked into the family room. Out of habit, Lauren checked to make sure the drapes were securely closed.

"Let's just say I've revised my opinion of the man." She poured wine into the two glasses and handed one to Dana. "I told him about the rape."

"Good. It's something you need to feel you can speak openly about. Obviously, it didn't frighten him off."

"He understood it's been rough for me to get over, and he's been patient, of sorts."

"So now you're ready to dive back into the battle of the sexes." Dana beamed as if Lauren was a precious child who'd done something spectacular. "It's about time." She held up her wineglass in a toast. "Now that I've assured myself that you're all right and most definitely in good hands, I'm going to head back to Los Angeles in the morning. I'm sorry, sweetie, but I don't know how you can survive out here in all this clean air. Honey, I can't breathe properly in anything but heavy-duty smog."

Lauren couldn't resist inserting, "It probably has something to do with all that smoking you do."

Dana's laughter stilled. "You must be very careful, Lauren. This woman has nothing to lose. I don't want to hear that you've ended up on your own autopsy table."

Lauren thought of the stainless steel table, the trays of instruments beside it, and suppressed a shudder. "Dana, with that kind of visualization, you should write murder mysteries."

"Better to write one than be part of one."

Lauren had trouble sleeping after Dana's voiced worries. Admittedly, she'd smoothly changed the subject and the two women stayed up late catching up on each other's news.

Even the knowledge that Dana was down the hall in the guest room and that a patrol car drove by on a regular basis didn't relax her enough to sleep. And then, when she did, dreams of glass flying through the air, endless perfume bottles dancing around her, and a woman's maniacal laughter piercing her ears disturbed what little sleep she could get.

Lauren called Sophie the first thing in the morning to say she'd be coming in late. She and Dana treated themselves to a leisurely breakfast out before Dana started her drive back to Los Angeles and Lauren drove on to work.

After parking the car, she sat there a moment, taking deep breaths until her heart rate slowed.

"All you have to do is stick with the plan. You can do it." Chanting the words like a protective mantra, she got out of her car and headed for her basement office.

"Detective Thomas called about the post on that hit-and-run. A Dr. Williams asked you to call him about a talk you agreed to give after the first of the year. And," Sophie frowned as she searched through the pink message slips, "somebody else called, but I don't remember who. I'll find it."

"Good idea." Lauren picked up the other message slips and walked into her office. When she reached the door, she snapped her fingers and turned as if she'd suddenly remembered something. "Oh, Sophie, could you do me a favor?" She pulled her Day Runner out of her briefcase and thumbed through it until she found the business card she wanted and quickly jotted down a phone number. "Would you call them and make a reservation for two for the weekend after next?

If it's available, I'd like bungalow number twelve."
She handed her the slip of paper.

Sophie nodded. "For two?"

"That's right."

"You and Mr. Brandon?"

Lauren gave her the kind of secretive smile she'd
seen other women use when they were considering
what some would call an illicit weekend. "We thought
we'd get away for a few days."

Sophie blew a small bubble. "Okay, but if you ask
me, this isn't a good idea, after all the stuff that's
happened to you guys."

"That's why the best thing we can do is get away. So
I'm sure you can understand it's something we really
don't want to get around." Lauren walked into her
office confident Sophie would openly question her
boss's lack of good sense.

Once she had the door closed, she grabbed the
phone and punched in Josh's number.

"Hi, Ginnie, it's Dr. Hunter. Is Josh around?" She
glanced through the messages, absently sorting them
into piles signifying *important, not so important, forget
altogether.*

"Not this morning. He's at a bail hearing right now
and he has a sentencing this afternoon. Do you want
him to call you back when he gets a chance?"

"Hm." Lauren looked down at her schedule. "We'd
probably end up missing each other because my day
looks pretty full, too. I'll talk to him tonight. Just tell
him I called, but not to worry. It's not anything important."

"When he calls in for messages, I'll let him know.
Dr. Hunter," the secretary lowered her voice. "You be
real careful, you hear? I already took care of what the
two of you wanted me to."

"Don't worry, Ginnie, I haven't cut myself during a post once, and I intend to keep that record."

"That's not what I mean and we both know it. I was here when the flowers and gifts arrived. And when women he'd see would call him and say they're weren't going to see him anymore. It wasn't until later on we found out it was because of that woman who's been following him. She's gotten out of hand. Especially since it's obvious the two of you are getting serious. You just be careful."

Lauren couldn't help but respond to the woman's sincerity. "Believe me, I intend to."

"You ready?" Pete stood in the doorway. He then noticed she still wore charcoal wool slacks and a blue blouse. "Guess not."

She looked up. "Sorry, Pete. I had to make a call. I'll change and be there in a minute."

Lauren went into the small area used as a dressing room. It wasn't until she pulled her surgical scrubs out of her locker and started to put them on that the faint odor hit her. Without any warning, she sneezed several times. Taking a chance, she sniffed and found that along with the sharp tang of disinfectant mingled with various chemicals, she detected the scent of perfume—a perfume she didn't wear because the few times she'd tried it, she'd always sneezed. *Obsession.*

She dug through a stacked pile of clean laundry for another pair that carried only the odor of detergent and faint starch. After she dressed, she pulled a can of Lysol spray out of the storage closet and sprayed the room with a heavy hand.

"If nothing else, she had the guts to pick the right perfume for her fun and games."

* * *

Lauren stood back from the table after searching the woman's body for anything to indicate it might have been a murder. Since she had been found dead in her apartment without a doctor in attendance, it was standard procedure for an autopsy to be performed.

Lauren rattled off the woman's name, age, height, weight, and other particulars as she worked.

"She's badly decomposed, which isn't going to help us much." She muttered, automatically wrinkling her nose against the gases escaping the body once it was opened. Even the vent sucking up air couldn't always take it all in.

"The liver is enlarged," Pete murmured, from the other side of the table.

She nodded. "Looks as if she had an alcohol problem. If we're lucky, the lab tests will bear our diagnosis out."

"I couldn't find anything under her fingernails to indicate she'd fought off an attacker. And there were no traces of semen found in her vagina or rectal area," Pete told her. "At least we can rule out rape."

Lauren nodded her approval. "I heard you had a crime scene to visit last night?"

"One gang fighting a rival one for their territory. The usual bullet and knife wounds. Three of them under sixteen, one of them with a bad case of acne," he finished with disgust. "Babies playing with guns. It's not right. They should have been worrying about their math homework or asking girls to the movies— not about who was going to shoot who." He weighed each organ, sliced samples for testing, and sealed them. "Sophie thinks you're nuts to go away with Brandon for a long weekend."

Lauren's hands stilled for a moment, then resumed their task. "She doesn't waste any time, does she?"

"Not her. She's never been able to keep secrets well. Oh, she doesn't talk about the posts. She thinks they're too disgusting. But when it comes to the living, breathing human beings around here, she considers us fair game. You should be glad you weren't here seven months ago, when she went on a health kick. She was always pushing vitamins and strange-looking herbs on us. We were all pretty grateful when she decided they were bad for her skin."

"And to think I worried it might be a little boring out here," she murmured.

"I don't think you've had that problem so far."

"So are you going to give a brotherly speech about how I should take myself out of the scene? That I'm only putting myself in more danger. That I really should reconsider having anything more to do with Josh Brandon until she's caught?"

He shook his head. "I decided a long time ago not to give anybody advice. That way, they can't blame me if they take it and I turn out to be wrong. But I can tell you that Sophie heard that Mitzi Collier is applying for a secretarial job that's opening up in the DA's office in a couple of months. She might be able to start sooner, if Josh agrees to let her take Ginnie's place while she's on vacation next month. That way, she can begin work sooner and be close to Josh. She may not be their only suspect, but she's still considered pretty strong, right along with the others."

"Considering her penchant for remaining unseen in the background, that would be a little too obvious, even for her, wouldn't it?"

"Some people have brass balls." He suddenly flushed. "So I've heard."

"Don't worry, I've been accused of much worse." She peeled off her latex gloves. "Until we have the lab reports back, we won't know for sure, but I'd say it's a good bet the lady died from alcohol poisoning, wouldn't you agree?"

"It sure seems that way." Pete hesitated as if unsure whether to say any more.

She didn't miss his expression. "What's wrong, Pete?"

"I know this sounds weird, but I could smell perfume in the locker room when I changed clothes this morning. And no one's been in there for the last couple of days except me. I don't remember you ever wearing that particular one and it's pretty distinctive, so I think I'd remember it. I had Sophie go in there and take a whiff. She said she doesn't wear anything like that."

"It's Obsession. Josh's little playmate from hell likes to wear it when she's making a statement. I guess she decided to leave me another fragrant reminder of her presence, as if I'd ever forget the little darling. I sprayed Lysol in there. The blend didn't turn out pleasant, but as far as I'm concerned, it's much better."

"I don't understand what's going on here with all this. Why is she going after you more than she went after the others Josh used to date?" He looked as confused as Lauren remembered once feeling. "You'd think she'd give up, cut her losses, and look around for another guy."

"It's been thought I resemble someone she knows and hates. Maybe she hopes she can get back at that person by getting to me. Hopefully, we'll be able to find out who she is."

Before it's too late hung unspoken between the two of them.

Chapter Sixteen

Did they honestly think they could keep their getaway a secret from her? Not when Lauren's idiotic little secretary has a mouth bigger than the Grand Canyon. Although it wasn't Sophie she'd heard it from. It was pure luck that Debbie, a friend of hers who worked in the crime lab, overheard Sophie telling several people at lunch about her boss and Josh Brandon. Her friend then happened to pass the news on to her when they ran into each other a few days later and stopped for a cup of coffee while they caught up on gossip.

"For two people who supposedly aren't involved, they're sure going about it the wrong way, wouldn't you say?" Debbie laughed. "You should have heard Sophie moan and wail about how she just knew something would happen to Lauren and she'd have to break in a new boss. As if she's all that important over there! If it wasn't for her City Hall connections, she'd have been out of there a long time ago."

"You're right, they're definitely going about it the wrong way," she replied, although her answer had an entirely different meaning than the first. "Who knows, maybe this is Dr. Hunter's way of letting people know

Josh is all hers and for everyone else to keep their dirty little hands off him."

Debbie looked at her strangely. "Are you all right?"

What did I say wrong? "Fine, why?"

"You just sounded, oh, kind of snappish, almost sarcastic, and that's not like you."

"I guess I'm more tired than I thought I was. Late night, last night."

She was relieved Debbie believed her explanation. Afraid she might inadvertently say too much that might give her away, she made a quick escape. There wasn't any reason just yet for them to know that Josh was really hers. They'd find out soon enough when Lauren was out of the picture, and she was very much in it.

The first thing she needed to do was find out where Lauren and Josh were going to spend the weekend. Knowing Sophie, it wouldn't be difficult to learn all the details. She wasn't sure if she would decide to drop in and see them, or if she would wait until they got back, but it wouldn't hurt to know, just in case.

Until then, well, perhaps she'd just keep to herself. Josh would expect her to come see him, so she wouldn't do it. He'd also expect her to strike at Lauren again, so she wouldn't do it. She wanted to laugh out loud with triumph. While she loved Josh dearly, she wished he wasn't so predictable. She'd have to show him just how much fun "unpredictable" could be.

"Sophie did her job even better than we thought," Lauren had told Josh that first evening, when they'd gone out for dinner after work. "I think everyone, including the trash collectors, know we have illicit weekend plans, and probably even where. Little do

they know I made the actual reservations we'll keep.
I'll cancel the ones Sophie made the day before we
leave." She nodded when the waitress asked if she
wanted black pepper on her salad and waited until she
left. "Although she did tell me several times she could
cancel the reservation at any time. She also told me she
has a cousin I might like to meet."

"Is his name Adrian?"

She had to think back to the conversation. "I think
that's what she said. Why? She told me he's a wonderful guy."

"Oh, he's perfect, if you enjoy health food, no meat,
not even fish; and astrology; and he has his own personal psychic, to make sure he doesn't make any mis-
takes. Word has it he even consults the woman when
he's unsure whether to leave the house or not."

"You're making all this up," Lauren accused, as she
tackled her salad with less vigor than she had before as
she thought about the medium-rare steak she'd ordered for the main course. "Sophie said he's very kind
and sensitive to a woman's feelings."

Josh nodded. "Isn't that how people usually de-
scribe blind dates when they're really pretty bad and
there's nothing positive to say about them? Isn't that
how *you* always described them?"

"I used to call them the kiss of death."

"It just goes to show that Sophie isn't really on the
ball concerning men. You'd know what I mean if
you'd ever seen her boyfriend."

Lauren shook her head. "No, I haven't been that
lucky."

Josh reached across the table and swiped a crouton
from her salad, popping it into his mouth. "No one's
sure what his real name is. He goes by 'Snake,' snarls
instead of talks, rides the typical Harley, and has the

usual number of tattoos, although I haven't had the pleasure of seeing him naked, thank God. Ten-to-one he has more than the ones decorating his arms and chest. He usually wears a denim vest without a shirt. He's an ancient twenty-five."

"I doubt she considers him all that ancient. She once described you as pretty old, though." She grinned at his pained wince. "Those old war wounds kicking up?"

"Thanks a lot, lady. And here I figured I was feeling younger every day."

"I wouldn't worry. She thinks thirty is close to retirement age. I'd love to be around for her thirtieth birthday and see how she handles it." Her smile dimmed a bit as the thought she might not be around then hit her hard. She knew the tenderness of her face would be a reminder slow to disappear.

He reached across the table with lightning speed and covered her hand with his. "Don't, Lauren. Don't even think it."

Her low-pitched laughter was filled with disbelief. "That's easier said than done, Josh. After all that's happened." She stopped and quickly shook her head. "She's so clever, what else can I think? She's won every round so far."

"And we can make sure she won't win any more of them. We're going to see the plan through just as we discussed, and afterward . . ."

"And afterward, life will go on as before? Too much has happened for us to believe that." She managed a brief smile as the waitress served them their meals. "What if she decides on the code 'If I can't have you, no one will'? What if she decides next time to cut you up, instead of your clothing? Or maybe put ground glass in your coffee?"

"Then it's a good thing I rarely make myself coffee at home." He threw up his hands at the look in her eyes. "All right, I admit I was against your plan in the beginning. Probably because I was afraid we would push her too much. Since last night, I've given it a lot of thought and have come to realize it's our only option if we hope to stop her soon."

She nodded a brief, mocking bow. "Spoken more like an attorney than a human being."

He took his time admiring the rose-colored dress that bared her shoulders. "I'll stay sane if I think like an attorney. Although the way you're dressed right now could cause a few problems."

"After a day looking like a drudge, it's always nice to wear something that doesn't have blood or disgusting body fluids on it." She instantly took pity on him. "Don't worry, I won't tell you what I did today."

"Thanks. After reading some of your reports, I already have an idea what you do, and dispensing with shoptalk during dinner sounds like a good idea."

Lauren reached across the table and snatched a bite of Josh's prime rib.

"I should have ordered that." Her smile froze on her lips. "We're being watched."

He resisted the urge to turn around. "Who?"

"Mitzi, that secretary who's dying to work in the DA's office. Especially dying to work for you. She's at a table near the bar." She started cutting her meat and continued smiling. "She keeps looking over this way."

"Maybe she isn't sure it's us."

"Josh, we're in a well-lit restaurant. She knows it's us, and she doesn't look happy. She's with a boy probably ten or eleven."

"Her son."

Lauren drank her wine, although she wasn't sure the

idea of alcohol slowing her reflexes was a good one. "Do you think she followed us?"

He shook his head. "It's a pretty popular place. Look how long we had to wait for our table, and we had reservations. Maybe it's better if you pretend you didn't see her. She'll have to come to us." He picked up the wine bottle and topped off both glasses. "So tell me, if we're not using the reservations Sophie made for us, where are we going?"

"Someplace just as nice, but not as accessible."

"Do I get to hear a name, or is it a secret?"

She smiled. "A secret, for now."

They had just declined dessert and opted for coffee when Lauren's attention was briefly diverted.

"Mitzi's coming over here."

He gave a barely perceptible nod. "Let's just play it by ear and see what happens."

"Josh. Dr. Hunter." Mitzi's smile was bright, although it wavered a bit when she looked at Lauren. "I told Brian we deserved a special night out, although I'm sure he'd have been happier with McDonald's or Carl's Jr. I just thought I'd come over and say hello. And to let you know I've started going to that support group for abused wives Gail oversees. They even have a group for the children and it's helped Brian see he isn't the only child going through this. We're going to make it," she finished, with a great deal of confidence.

"I'm glad, Mitzi. I also heard you applied for Kim's position, since she isn't coming back after she has her baby. I hope you realize working for Ted isn't all that easy. I've even heard he's worse than me."

"I thought a change of scenery would be good, since I've been a little too vocal when some of the sleazier clients get off. And I'm thinking of taking some night courses and work toward becoming a paralegal."

"It sounds as if you have things pretty well thought out," Lauren spoke up. "I admire you for wanting to push ahead."

"Don't. I was a wimp for so long, I'm still knock-kneed scared at going out completely on my own," Mitzi confessed. "Josh will back me up on that. I wouldn't have had the courage to go through with it if it hadn't been for his helping me in the beginning and helping me find a good divorce attorney. Brian has been so much calmer with the threat of his father running in and snatching him up. Now he's so confident I can do anything I put my mind to that I feel I can't let him down." She turned around. "Well, I'd better get back to our table before Brian gets worried." She looked from one to the other. "Actually, I think the brave ones are you two. After what's been going around the offices, I don't know if I'd want to be the target you are, Lauren. From everything I've heard, she sounds awfully dangerous."

"Mom! I'm finished!"

Mitzi turned red as her son yelled out her name again. "I have to go. Maybe if I take him out more often he'll do better. See you later."

"I can't imagine it's her," Josh said, when they left the restaurant and walked out to his car. "It doesn't fit. Besides, I can't imagine her leaving Brian alone at night. The two of them are too close. More so since the divorce."

"If you're desperate enough, there's ways. But I agree with you. Where she's concerned, there's something that doesn't seem right." Lauren wrapped her coat more securely around her shoulders.

"Admittedly, I like the idea of one less suspect to worry about."

Lauren slid across the seat to sit closer to Josh as

they waited for the car to warm up before he switched on the heater. "Only a few more days and hopefully it will be all over."

"And then we have a long talk about what the future could hold for us."

She had been sensing this coming for some time now. The attraction she'd fought and the one he'd pursued wasn't about to be ignored. Each time she thought about it, she probed her inner defenses and discovered it wasn't as intimidating as it used to be.

"Yes, and then we'll talk as much as you'd like."

"Do I get even a hint as to where we'll be going? Or did you decide making two sets of reservations at two different places could confuse her? That you'll end up going to one and I'd go to the other?" He felt a lot better to know she wasn't going to put him off anymore.

"It was definitely meant to confuse her, and at first, I thought of canceling the ones Sophie'd already made and then changed my mind. I thought Kevin might like to take his wife away for a couple days to a lovely resort that caters to couples. They could enjoy a nice, relaxing weekend. At the same time, Kevin would feel he's doing his job staking out the place. Especially if anyone familiar shows up."

Josh chuckled. "Lady, the more I'm with you, the more I like, and right now I know I like your style. Sharon's always bitching that Kevin never takes her anywhere, so it wouldn't look odd if they were there. Especially since we'd be out of town anyway. Hopefully, our little friend might think we changed our minds and turned the reservation over to Kevin and Sharon so it wouldn't go to waste. I've got to hand it to you, Lauren. Making two separate reservations was a pretty good idea. You're turning out to be one sneaky lady."

She teasingly ran her fingernail down his upper arm as she laughed along with him. "And don't you forget it!"

As Josh drove to Lauren's house, one eye was always glancing up into the rearview mirror. He still couldn't believe they weren't being followed tonight. He wasn't trying to feel paranoid, but after being at Lauren's house last night, even if Dana and Kevin were there, he'd expected to find a message from her on his answering machine. Nothing. And there'd been no indication she'd been inside his house. He wasn't sure whether to feel relieved or frustrated. All he knew was that he was relieved she hadn't tried anything with Lauren. He was positive the memory of her lying in that hospital bed with her face covered with tiny bloody cuts would haunt him for a long time.

"All right, we've established you're not going to divulge our destination. How about giving me a hint as to what to pack. Or what I can leave behind?"

"Dress warmly," was all she would say before suddenly answering an unspoken question. "She isn't back there."

He jerked himself back to the present. "I didn't think she was."

"Yes, you did. Just as I have at times. Which is why I want to finish this farce that she's begun. By our finishing it, we get to call the shots."

"I also admire your nerve," he complimented her.

"It comes from living with a cop's macho attitude. You learn about the times when you can't afford to back down. We've come to one of those times, Josh."

Thoughts of her ex-husband still didn't set well in his gut. "Yeah, I know."

It wasn't difficult to tell he didn't look happy about something. She wondered if he was worrying about what was going on. She playfully ran her finger down his cheek.

"You could look on the bright side of all this." She lowered her voice to a sultry level. "Just think about it, Josh, an entire weekend with me. Isn't that something you've been angling for? What you meant when you talked about us getting away later on? Think of it," she lowered her voice a bit more, "us, alone, no worries about cases for you, or autopsies and visiting crime scenes for me."

"Something tells me you'll get the better deal if you're not going to be worrying about dead bodies." Josh turned onto Lauren's street and pulled up her driveway.

He had just helped her out of the car when a patrol car drove by. It slowed to a crawl when it noticed them. When the spotlight briefly blinded them, Josh lifted his hand in a wave. The two officers nodded their acknowledgment and drove on.

"Shows they're on the ball." Josh walked with Lauren up to her door. He stood to the side while she disarmed the alarm and unlocked her door, but held her back when she would have entered. "Let me go in first."

Concern crossed her face. "You can't think she'd do something?"

"I hope not, and I don't intend to take any chances at this point." He eased the door open and walked in. He was startled when the light went on.

"It was Kevin's suggestion," Lauren explained. "While a couple of main lights go on at dusk, a few others are on motion sensors."

"A good idea." Josh made a quick but thorough pass through the house.

"I'm glad I didn't leave any clothes lying around." Lauren refused to stay in the entryway and remained on his heels as he checked out each room, ending with her bedroom.

"Then it's a good thing you haven't seen my place. I'm not exactly known for my neatness." He switched on the bathroom light and checked it out also. "Everything looks all right."

"How about some coffee?" She led him back to the family room. "I've got the coffee maker set up, so it won't take long."

"Sounds good."

She walked into the kitchen and pulled cups out of the cabinet. "All right, have a seat and I'll bring it in."

Josh sat on the couch, glancing at the magazines on the coffee table and picking one up out of curiosity. He fanned through the pages, pausing a few times when something interested him. He glanced at the books on the lamp table.

"Forensics, studies of bones, decomposed bodies," he muttered. "What do you read for enjoyment?"

Lauren carried in a tray holding a coffee server, two cups, and a bottle of Irish Cream. "Nancy A. Collins, Elaine Bergstrom, Clive Barker, Stephen King." She filled both cups with coffee, topped them off with a splash of Irish Cream, and handed him one.

"It sounds like a repeat of your work."

She couldn't wait until he started to drink his coffee before speaking. "We only drain the blood, Josh, we don't drink it."

It took him a great deal of effort not to spew out the coffee. He gulped and choked so badly he began coughing.

"Want me to thump your back?"

Josh rapidly shook his head, unaware his face was a bright shade of red.

"You did that on purpose, didn't you?" He wheezed once he caught his breath. "You went for the shock value just for the sheer hell of it."

"There's a lot of coroners out there with a very sick sense of humor that rivals, if not surpasses, any cop's," she said matter-of-factly, as she sat down beside him. She edged off her shoes and tucked her feet up under her. "You know, one of my favorite movies is *The Sting.*" She lifted her cup. "To a successful con."

Josh tapped her cup with his before taking hers out of her hand and setting both of them down on the tray. "Can't be anything but, although I have a better way of sealing the deal." He pulled her into his arms.

Lauren's smile grew as she allowed him to settle her in his lap. She looped her arms around his neck and brushed her lips against his until his mouth opened. Tongues tangled as they tasted each other with the hunger that had been building for some time.

Free to explore each other without worry of unwanted watchers, they loosened each other's clothing until Lauren's top was free of her shoulders and Josh's shirt was open.

"Now, this is more like it," he mumbled, nuzzling her ear.

"There's no beach."

He obligingly blew softly in her ear. "That's the ocean breeze. I'll work on the water part later, when we have more time."

"You know, Sophie's wrong," she sighed, running her fingers through the thick thatch of hair on his chest. She shivered when she felt him caressing the sensitive skin around her breast. "You're not such an old guy, after all."

"Believe me, I'm only too happy to prove it."

Chapter Seventeen

"Exactly what does a woman take with her when she goes away with a man for the weekend and she has seduction in mind?" Lauren studied the contents of her closet, wishing something would jump out at her. Wishing this wasn't the first time she'd done this. She doubted the long weekends she and Ron had taken during their marriage counted. Especially toward the end, when her idea of nightwear was a football jersey. She doubted it would be appropriate for what she had in mind.

She started to pull open the dresser drawer that held her sexier nightwear, but hesitated. She uttered a sound of disgust as she finally just jerked it open.

"Stop it, Lauren. She's not the type to leave something disgusting in here. Well, she is, but hopefully, not today."

She still carefully probed the contents as she pulled out a couple of nightgowns she felt would be more appreciated than a football jersey.

"It never hurts to be prepared," she murmured, as she folded them and placed them in her suitcase while keeping one eye on the clock. Josh would be there to pick her up in about fifteen minutes, and as usual, she'd left everything to the last minute and was now running around, getting everything together. She quickly packed up her cosmetics and threw them in her bag, along with a couple books. More, just in case. She looked at the clock again. "Damn!" She quickly pulled her hair back in a braid and dressed in tan stirrup pants and a burnt orange tunic sweater. She set her overnight case by the front door at the same time she noticed Josh drive up. She walked outside, noticing the early morning light had barely touched the sky. Her breath frosted in the cold air.

"Hi." He greeted her with a good morning kiss. "All ready?"

"I probably forgot something. I always do, so I won't worry about it." She closed the door and set the alarm. "I was tempted to leave a note. Just in case anyone decided to stop by while I was gone. Too bad I don't have a cat I could ask her to feed. Or maybe a python would be more fitting for her to cuddle up with."

"Well, hell, why not a black widow spider?"

"If we're talking about venom, I'd prefer something with a lot more kick." Once settled in the car, Lauren linked her arms around Josh's neck and pulled him toward her for a much warmer kiss than the one he'd given her.

When they finally broke free, Josh stared at her with glazed eyes. "Lady, I'd say that was hot enough to wake the dead."

Her smile was equally dazzling. "Now you know why I chose pathology."

Josh shook his head to clear it. "You are something. Now that we've gotten our hellos out of the way, you want to give me a hint? Are we going north or south?"

"North. It's a very nice bed-and-breakfast outside of Solvang, owned by some friends of mine."

"It sounds good to me." He nodded his approval. "I haven't been up there in years. Although I thought you'd choose something closer to the beach."

"I thought we'd save that for later." She couldn't resist glancing around as Josh headed for the freeway. "I can't believe she's stayed quiet and away from us for so long. I swear this is making me more paranoid than when every time I walked in the door I wondered if I'd find evidence of her having been in my house."

"I'm just glad there haven't been any more flowers," he told her. "Once I found out they had meanings, they bothered me almost as much as the other shit she pulled. But you know what I want to do?"

She slipped on her sunglasses against the sunlight now filling the car. "If it's anything kinky, you can forget about it, Brandon."

"Then you're safe, because I left the handcuffs and other little toys home. But I do want to state that no mention of our hellish friend will be made from the time we leave the city limits until we return. Deal?"

That was something Lauren was more than happy to agree to. "Deal. But if you want me to be an agreeable traveling companion, all I ask is you stop somewhere for coffee. I didn't get a chance to make any this morning."

Josh swung by the first fast-food restaurant open and ordered two large coffees. "Anything else?"

She shook her head. "Just the caffeine. I live on coffee so much when things get hectic at work, I don't feel normal if I don't have my morning fix to give me a much-needed kick start."

"I still can't imagine your work getting hectic. It's

not as if your patients can get up and walk out on you if you're running behind."

Lauren grinned. "I wouldn't be surprised if they did, since it does tend to get a bit chilly in the waiting room. They probably feel as if they're fur coats put away in cold storage."

Josh groaned. "That's really bad."

"You think *that's* bad, you should hear what some of us used to pull during medical school. One guy liked to pretend to be a corpse and lay on a gurney for the first session of gross anatomy class. The minute they pulled down the covering, he'd blink his eyes as if he'd just awakened from a nap and tell them the last thing he remembered was falling asleep upstairs in class."

"So the moral was not to fall asleep in class?"

"Exactly."

"You know, for a classy-looking lady, you have a very sick sense of humor and a strange idea of what's fun."

"Are you telling me you never pulled off any practical jokes in law school?" she challenged.

"There were days I felt I was lucky if I was awake enough to attend class, but we had one guy, Pat Hamilton, who was known to plant a mannequin holding a tape recorder in his seat during some of the classes."

"The tape recorder was to record the class?"

He shook his head. "Nope, he had a hidden recorder for that. This one was strictly playback, and it played back the sound of a man snoring. We were always surprised he wasn't thrown out."

"Don't tell me, he's a federal judge or something."

He shook his head again. "Even worse. He operates a storefront law office in East LA where he likes nothing better than going up against the big guys. Quite a few big-name law firms have tried to persuade him to go with them, but he's always turned them down. Says he prefers helping guys who can't afford the kinds of attorneys they need to sitting in a high-rise office where he couldn't dare put his feet up on the furniture."

"Sounds a bit like you, with your distaste for wearing ties to court."

"Yeah, there's some who're not too happy about that, so the day may come when I'll have to give in and wear one of those nooses. That new judge cornered me in the hall one day and said the day I show up in his court without a tie would be a day I'd spend in jail."

"Judge Burns?"

"That's the one. Talk about a stuffy old fart."

Lauren turned in the seat until she could comfortably rest her back against the door. "I had to testify in his court a couple days ago for the Winston case."

"The kid who OD'd on speed and the parents are suing his best friend's parents for knowing their kid sold drugs and not doing anything about it?"

She nodded.

"I was damn grateful I didn't get that case. It's tricky to prove the parents are at fault. If I remember correctly, Larry has that one."

"He does. But it was Judge Burns who informed me the next time to come to his court dressed in a ladylike manner. I'd forgotten the time and had to show up in my scrubs, something I never do and hated doing that time. During my testimony, he never called me 'Doctor,' but addressed me as Mrs. Hunter the couple times he asked me to clarify something, and he was so old-world stuffy that I was ready to hit him." She made a face. "Unfortunately, I made a smart remark under my breath that next time I'd show up in my crinolines, and he didn't appreciate it."

Josh chuckled. "I'm sure he didn't. The last few times I've seen Larry, he's been muttering to himself. He says his blood pressure has probably tripled since the case began. He figures the way his luck is going, he'd probably have a stroke right there in the courtroom. And get slapped with a contempt charge for staging courtroom dramatics. I told him if he's worrying so much, he should get some pointers from Ted. That guy is a genius when it comes to doing anything dramatic and outlandish."

"There was a judge in LA," Lauren began a story that soon had the two of them laughing. It wasn't long before they forgot the real reason behind this trip.

By agreement, they chose the coastal route instead of driving inland, where Solvang was. During the drive they continued to trade courtroom war stories. As a forensics pathologist, Lauren had spent more than her share of time in court, giving expert testimony, and could offer a different perspective from Josh's.

"I've spent enough time in courtrooms to know I'm much happier in pathology. Except for cops badgering my office for reports on posts not even performed yet or demanding them within the next hours. But since I have a habit of discussing my work in very basic terms, they tend to leave me pretty much on my own."

"Now I know where to hide out when I need peace and quiet."

"You'll be fine as long as you move around every so often so we don't think you're one of our residents," she assured him.

They chose to drive through Santa Barbara and take the mountain route to Solvang. As Josh drove the winding road, he couldn't help keeping an occasional eye on the rearview mirror. Especially since a dark-colored truck had been keeping pace with them since they'd left the highway. Traffic had been fairly heavy the closer they'd gotten to Santa Barbara, so he hadn't noticed it before.

"I thought we were going to leave our worries back home." Lauren's quiet voice startled him.

"I have."

"Liar."

"Are you calling me, an officer of the court, a liar?" He opted to keep it light.

She looked at him with a strange calm. "With the sideview mirror on this side, I can see that truck back there, too, Josh. The first time I noticed it, it was on the highway about fifty miles before we reached Santa Barbara. The windows are tinted so we have no idea who the driver is, and there's no plate on the front. Most of the time he stays too far back for us to get any kind of identification."

He put his foot down a bit more on the accelerator. The car shot forward. Right about now, he'd welcome a cop pulling him over for speeding. "Then you've observed more than me. There's no guarantee the truck has anything to do with us. He might be going to the same place and decided on the same route."

"That's right." Her eyes flicked toward the mirror again, then to the other side and downward, to where the cellular phone was nestled. "At least, we have a way to call for help."

Josh's expression was grim. "Maybe not. When there are mountains around, the reception can be between lousy and zip."

The silence around them grew tense as they each glanced in a mirror to see where the truck was. They didn't breathe a sigh of relief until it turned off onto a private road.

Josh exhaled a heavy breath of air. "Looks like our imaginations were working overtime."

Her own body slumped. "I thought I'd left it all behind. That the minute we reached the freeway I could forget about it. I can't believe I was so wrong."

He took his hand off the steering wheel and grabbed her hand, lacing her fingers through his. "You and me both."

But the tension didn't completely disappear until they were out of the mountains and Lauren gave him directions when they reached the outskirts of Solvang, California's piece of Denmark.

"Dave and his wife, Chloe, moved out here and started their bed-and-breakfast after Dave retired," she explained. "He was a federal prosecutor in Sacramento. They decided they wanted a quiet life after the fast pace of the big city. They used to spend a lot of time down this way and decided years ago this was where they'd retire to."

A name tapped the back of his mind. "David Sinclair?"

Lauren nodded.

He emitted a low whistle. "You know some pretty heavy-duty people."

"Actually, Dave and Chloe are friends of my parents," she explained. "Chloe and my mother met in college and became immediate close friends. They were each other's main attendants at their weddings, and the men soon became good friends, too. They're also Dana's parents. My parents come up here a few times a year and I have an open invitation."

"And they don't mind that you're bringing someone?"

She smiled. "Don't you mean, bringing a man I'm not married to?"

"Yeah. Is it going to bother them, or pardon me for being crass, have you done this before?"

"Don't worry about the pressure about being first." She suddenly pointed to her left. "Turn there, at the sign."

He slowed down to read the sign carved in the shape of a multipointed sun. "Sunshine Hollow?"

Lauren wrinkled her nose. "Unfortunately, that's been the name for the last sixty years, when the original owners opened it up and they requested the name stay the same. Dave and Chloe agreed."

"It's at the base of the hills. There are six bungalows set around the property so there's maximum privacy. They have a few horses for anyone who wants to try the trails nearby, a pool, and a large patio for those who don't want to do anything more than vegetate," she explained.

Josh slowed as he neared the end of the circular driveway. "Where are Kevin and Sharon this weekend?"

"They're in La Jolla, at a small and very nice beachside resort I heard about."

As Josh helped Lauren out of the car, a couple emerged from the front of the Spanish-style house and Josh got a good look at the man who was once known as the hottest federal prosecutor in the state.

"Lauren, how good to see you!" The woman threw her arms around her for a big hug. She stepped back and gave Josh an assessing look. "I'm glad to see you finally got some sense. He's a marked improvement over Ron."

Lauren shook her head in exasperation. "You've been talking to Dana."

"Of course we have. She's our daughter." Chloe Sinclair turned to Josh and held out her hand. "Hello, Josh, welcome to our home. I'm Chloe, the old man over there is Dave, and if Lauren has brought you up here, you must be all right."

He was immediately charmed by her slight southern accent and beauty he saw as lush in Dana and matured in Chloe. "I'm very pleased to meet you."

"Old man," Dave scoffed, coming forward with his hand outstretched. The man was tall, with iron-gray hair and sun-creased wrinkles etched in his face; Josh could see why he had been considered a formidable opponent in court. "I hear you're an ADA. We'll have to talk after dinner."

Chloe was incensed. She advanced on Dave, poking her forefinger in his chest. "You will not! These two are here to relax, not to talk shop. I'll tell you one thing, the last thing Lauren and I intend to do is sit at the kitchen table and trade autopsy stories."

Lauren held up her hands. "All right, you two, back to your corners." She looked at Josh. "Don't worry, they do this all the time."

"Hell, sometimes it's more fun than television." Dave winked at Josh. "Come on, I'll help you get your luggage inside. Bungalow four, Chloe?"

She nodded. "Now, don't worry, I'll make sure Dave doesn't intrude on your weekend," she assured Josh. "He used to hate to talk about the law. It was a forbidden subject at home. Then he retired, and like an old fire dog, the minute he meets a lawyer, he has to talk shop."

"She always makes me sound worse than I am."

"Considering your conviction record, I wouldn't apologize."

Chloe playfully clapped a hand over her husband's

mouth and pointed him toward the suitcases. "Do some work. Lauren and I are going on ahead."

The two women walked down the path with the men following.

Chloe lowered her voice. "Any more problems?" Lauren had explained the situation when she'd called to see if a bungalow would be available.

"No, thank God. But we both feel as if it's nothing more than a calm before the storm. She's never been this quiet before. That's why I wanted us to go away, to force her hand. And I knew there isn't any way she would know about this place."

"Well, you're in luck, because there's only one other couple here, and they'll be leaving in the morning," Chloe said. "We thought it was best not to have anyone else around."

"You didn't need to do that," she protested.

She waved away Lauren's concerns. "We prefer it this way. Besides, we also thought it would be safer."

Lauren shook her head. "Dave isn't going to sit up tonight with his twelve-gauge in his lap, is he?"

"Damn right I'll have that rifle out!" Dave shouted, obviously overhearing her. "An even better one than the twelve-gauge, too."

"Now he has an AR-18 locked away that he got from one of his cronies," Chloe explained. "I expect him to get a grenade launcher next."

"She makes me sound like a crazy survivalist when I only believe in protecting my property," Dave told Josh, as they entered a bungalow that was a smaller replica of the main house.

"We'll be serving drinks at the usual time on the patio if you're interested, and you already know you're more than welcome to have dinner with us,"

Chloe told Lauren, giving her another hug before taking her leave.

"I keep the real stuff somewhere else," Dave confided in Josh before following his wife.

Lauren dropped onto the couch. "Feeling a bit swamped?"

He slowly turned in a circle, noting the furniture chosen more for comfort than looks. A bathroom could be seen off to one side and a bedroom beyond that. A tiny kitchen was set in one corner with what he discovered had a refrigerator stocked with wine, beer, and soda.

Lauren tracked his movements. "The couch pulls out into a bed, if you're feeling a little nervous."

He shook his head. "No, I'm just trying to figure out how I got to be so lucky. Unless it's because it's all on your terms and it makes you feel more at ease with the situation."

Lauren looked down at her hands lying in her lap. "I suppose I do tend to control things at times." *Since the rape* remained unspoken between the two of them.

Josh wanted her to know he understood without voicing it out loud because the last thing he wanted was for her to feel uncomfortable.

He sat down beside her. "If I'd known you could come up with a great weekend getaway like this, I'd have wanted you for a travel agent long ago."

Relief flickered in her eyes as she realized he recognized and understood her reasoning.

"They gave us what I like to call the 'decadent bungalow.'" She hopped up and grabbed his hand.

"Hey, I was up early today and driving for the past few hours," he protested.

She walked backward as she pulled him into the bedroom. "Trust me, you won't mind."

"Well, sweetheart, I didn't think you'd be in such a hurry."

She shook her head. "Keep it tucked in your pants, Counselor." She allowed him only a glimpse of the king-sized bed with an old-fashioned quilt covering it before she pushed open a patio door and led him outside onto a small walled-in patio. *"Voilà!"* With a dramatic flourish, she gestured to a redwood hot tub. "It's a great way to relax."

Josh decided not to remind her he hadn't brought a bathing suit and could only hope she hadn't brought one, either. Instead, he wrapped his arms around her waist and pulled her against him.

"Yeah, I can definitely handle your vacation ideas."

They spent the balance of the afternoon relaxing and snacking on the refrigerator's contents before changing their clothes and walking toward the main house. Chloe and Dave were already there, seated at a large table and talking to a young couple. Several open bottles of wine were on a serving cart, along with snacks. Chloe made the introductions, merely saying Lauren and Josh were family friends, and indicated two empty chairs.

"The Parkers are from Oregon and on their honeymoon," Chloe confided to Lauren.

Lauren soon discovered the new Mrs. Parker was a kindergarten teacher, seemed to possess an incredible amount of energy, and talked nonstop. The foursome were relieved when the young couple left for dinner.

"An excellent reason why we run a bed-and-breakfast and don't have to worry about serving dinner," Chloe chuckled, refilling Lauren's wineglass.

"You have no idea who the woman is?" Dave's voice floated across the patio.

"David," his wife warned. "You promised."

"Hell, maybe I can come up with something no one else has been able to think of," he argued, gesturing with his beer bottle.

"Dana's the expert in that area, not you," Chloe reminded him.

He shook his head. "She's a wonderful doctor, but she reads charts and interviews sickos. I've dealt with them a hell of a lot longer and on more levels than she has."

"Josh and I made an agreement that we weren't going to discuss her this weekend," Lauren spoke up.

Dave walked over and put an arm around her shoulders. He dropped a kiss on the top of her head. "If you weren't like another daughter to me, I'd probably argue that point just for the fun of it. It's good you came up here to relax and get away from your problems, but deep down, you both know you haven't forgotten them. You've merely shelved them for a while. Which is a break you both need very badly. But I also want to help, if I can."

"You're right about the break. We thought someone was following us through the mountain pass, and even when we realized they weren't, it took us a few minutes to relax," she admitted.

Josh nodded in agreement. "I'm just grateful the stalker law is in full force, which gives us an edge if we can ever get this to court. We already have a lot of felony counts against the woman, but few clues."

Dave opened two more bottles of beer and handed one to Josh. "Fill me in."

"I give up," Chloe sighed, rising to her feet. "I'm going to put the finishing touches on dinner. Maybe food will get him to shut up for a while. Although I sincerely doubt it. Not when it's a subject he can go on for hours about. He's lucky I love him so much."

Lauren stood up to follow. "I'll help. Where would you like me to start?"

Chloe put Lauren to work fixing a salad.

"Is he the one?"

Lauren concentrated on tearing the lettuce. "I think so, but there's too much going on around us for me to be sure of our feelings for each other. It might be nothing more than heightened emotions because of what's happened. It's happened many times with others. Why not with us?"

"Probably because you two are a special case." Chloe placed her hands on Lauren's face and forced her around. She gently ran her fingertips across her cheeks and down her jaw line. "All the cuts were superficial?"

Lauren nodded. "They said I was lucky. If the glass pieces had been larger, I could have ended up with nasty scars."

"All I can say is, if the two of you manage to survive this, it can only mean you're meant to be together. He was even willing to go along with your plan, which I think we both know could prove disastrous if this woman falls completely apart if you all face each other. Even Dana said he seemed pretty near to perfect, and we both know she doesn't say that about any human being!" She chuckled.

"Just *please* don't use the word 'survive'!" Lauren hugged the woman. "Who knows? Maybe Dave is right; maybe he can come up with something we haven't thought of."

"If only we could be that lucky." Josh stood in the kitchen doorway just behind Dave. His eyes immediately sought out Lauren's and held them in a dark gaze.

"You've covered all the bases. I couldn't have done any better myself," the older man agreed. "All I can say is, if this plan doesn't smoke her out, nothing will until she's good and ready to show herself."

Lauren turned back to the salad. She tore the lettuce with vicious tugs that almost shredded the greens. "Somehow, that doesn't make me feel all that secure."

Chapter Eighteen

"How does one woman get so lucky? I tried for six months to get Josh's attention, and I couldn't get more than friendly conversation! Yet Lauren Hunter comes along and he falls for her like a ton of bricks. What does she have that I don't?"

"Besides Josh, you mean?"

"Someone once said he has some rule that he won't date anyone he has to work or deal with. Yet he deals with her, doesn't he?"

"All I know is I wish I was her this weekend!"

The words she'd heard the day before rang through her head like a taunt. She felt them burning through her skull like an acid destroying what little sanity she still possessed.

It wasn't fair! Hadn't she faithfully abided by her plan all this time? She had turned it into a game. Each hour, each day she stayed away from them was a triumph. She wanted them to worry about her, to wonder what she might do next. Whether she'd leave something even more dangerous at Lauren's house or enter Josh's house and stay there, awaiting his return. To let him see her. Realize she was the one he really loved.

She drove the streets blindly, unaware of her destination. Uncaring. She was too engrossed in the words searing her brain. Ever since Sophie had talked about Josh and Lauren going away for the weekend, speculation ran high. And people just loved to discuss it. Josh wasn't known for going away with any of his former women. Why her? Was there more going on than anyone assumed? Was Lauren going to be the one to tempt the forever single Josh Brandon to the altar?

"No! No, no, no!" She pounded the steering wheel with her fist, so furious she was unaware her car swerved over to the other lane until a car honked. She quickly regained control, whipped her head around, gave him the finger, and sped on. By the time she came to her senses, she realized she was just turning onto Josh's street. Her lips parted in a smile.

"It's fate," she whispered, looking from right to left as she drove slowly down the street until she reached his house. "Fate I intend to take full advantage of. The time has come for him to find out the truth. He needs to know that Celia will only destroy him if he stays with her. Unless I can destroy her first."

Chapter Nineteen

It wasn't until they'd returned to the bungalow much later that night that Josh felt a trace of awkwardness coupled with a little tension in Lauren's demeanor.

"Lauren, nothing has to happen between us just because we came up here," he said, once they entered the tiny living room. "After all, we've slept together before and nothing happened then. Damn."

She smiled at his attempt to lighten the mood without ruining it.

"I know that, Josh, and I thank you for that. I guess the full impact finally just hit me. And while I think we both might want more, the idea of just cuddling sounds very nice right about now." She looked over her shoulder. "I'm going to take a quick shower first, if you don't mind."

"Go for it."

Josh took his shower next, finding out that a steamy bathroom scented with Lauren's perfume was pretty taxing to the willpower. When he came out, he found Lauren in bed with a book propped against her drawn-up knees. He was surprised to find her wearing a pair of reading glasses.

"Medical textbook?"

She shook her head. "One of those murder mysteries that has a clever killer only one stubborn cop can find because, in certain ways, he's as crazy as the killer. It's pretty good. Want to read it after I'm finished?"

"No thanks, I think I'll stick to science fiction." The dimly lit atmosphere was definitely lending itself to the mood. "Want some more wine?"

"I shouldn't, but since I'm not driving, I'll go for it."

Josh poured the wine and brought the two glasses back into the bedroom. Lauren put the book away and accepted the glass.

"To better times." He tapped his glass against hers.

"I'll go for that." Lauren took a couple of sips and set the glass on the table. "Josh, we've gone through more in a short period of time than many people go through their entire lives."

He wasn't sure he liked the sound of that. "Meaning?"

"Meaning once this is over and we're back to living normal lives, we could very well feel differently about each other," she said softly.

"You said that once before, and I told you it was bullshit. I'm saying it again."

She leaned forward, bracing her elbows on her knees. "It's happened before, and it's perfectly natural. It's a situation that forces us into intimacy."

He sat on the end of the bed, resting his back against the bedpost. "I figured we'd be talking about this after things were settled."

She traced the quilt's pattern with her fingertip. "You've had relationships that are pretty open-ended. I'm not sure that's what I want. I may have had a lousy marriage, but that doesn't mean that I'm going to drift through one affair after another."

He leaned down to put his glass on the floor, then

crawled across the length of the bed until he reached her. He traced the line of her cheekbone with his thumb. "Good, because I don't intend for that to happen," he whispered, just before he kissed her. As before, the heat flared up between them.

"Josh," she whispered, linking her arms around his neck. "Why don't we just forget everything I said, and you come to bed and ravish me the way heroes do in novels."

"You know, Doc, you have some great ideas." He allowed his weight to propel them backward. Within seconds, Lauren's silk short gown flew through the air with Josh's briefs following it.

Lauren was still warm and sweet-smelling from her shower, her skin lightly scented with the lotion she'd used afterward. Josh's skin still damp from his own, his hair-rough chest abrasive against her softer skin.

They'd kept their hunger for each other locked up for so long they weren't able to hold back.

Josh silently urged Lauren to take the initiative. He pulled her over on top of him, settling her in the cradle of his thighs.

It was clear Lauren trusted Josh implicitly. She displayed no fear, no flashbacks to her rape, as she freely touched him.

"What do you like?" she whispered, running her tongue along his collarbone.

He wasn't sure he could breathe, much less talk. "Everything you're doing."

"This?" She brushed her fingertips against his erection. "Or this?"

Josh decided it was better to show rather than to tell. He reversed positions and soon had Lauren writhing under him.

"This might give you an idea." The moment he

thrust into her moist warmth he knew he was well and truly lost.

And the explosion that followed much too quickly for both of them was just as breathtaking as expected.

When Josh finally lay back with Lauren curled up in his arms, he felt completely drained.

"Either we had an earthquake up here, or we created one of our own."

"I think we created one of our own." She yawned as she lay in a boneless sprawl over him. "Why, are you complaining?"

"Are you kidding? I'm just wondering if it can happen again."

"Oh, I think so. Just as soon as you get your energy back." She nuzzled his ear.

"Then I guess we're about to find out, because my energy is coming back."

"And Sophie thinks you're too old!"

Lauren and Josh had no trouble forgetting the real world when they spent the next day exploring Solvang. Lauren pulled him through several fudge shops, fed him Aebleskivers, Danish puffed pancakes, and bought him a castle made of rainbow-colored crystal.

"Our refuge," she told him. "In this place, no harm will come to us."

His dark eyes studied her face. "A doctor who's whimsical. I like the idea, Doc."

But the weekend passed too quickly in their minds. They again had dinner with Chloe and Dave, but this time nothing was said of the real reason Lauren and Josh were there. Then they retired to their bungalow, where they wanted to recapture the magic of the night before. Afterward, they went outside to make use of the hot tub, sans bathing suits.

"This is just what I needed," he sighed, resting his head against the rim of the tub.

"*We* needed," she corrected from the other side, splashing a bit of water at him. She reached up and resecured a loose strand of hair that fell from the clips she used to pull it up in a loose topknot.

He opened one eye. "Don't do that."

"I want to talk."

He closed the eye, looking completely peaceful. "So talk."

She stood up and moved over to the other side until she could sit next to him, her hip bumping against his. She ran her fingers through his hair, brushing the overlong strands back from his face. "I want you to agree to something."

That got his attention. He opened his eyes and sat up straight. "Setting terms again, Lauren?"

"I don't want you to think of it that way. You've said things that indicated you're ready to settle down. And you seem to think I'm the one."

"I didn't realize it was a crime."

"It's not, but I still feel the situation is the catalyst. What I'd like is for us to give ourselves six months when this is over and see if what we feel for each other is real, or just part of the problem."

Josh stared at her squarely for so long she started to feel uncomfortable. "Part of the problem? That's an odd way of putting it. You see, I never thought of the two of us as a problem, Lauren. All I knew was that the first time I saw you at that retirement party, I felt knocked for a loop. And I never felt that way the first time I saw a woman. Sure, I've had my share of relationships, but that was because I never found what I was looking for. I thought I was doomed to be alone because that's what I felt a lot of times. I'd go back to my house and that's all it was; a house. Yet I go in yours and I feel life in there. The colors you used, the way it seems like a real home, even though your hours can be just as crazy as mine at times." He reached out, cupping the back of her head with his hand. "I was starting to run scared, Lauren. I thought I was doomed to have an unseen woman as a phantom lover who wouldn't allow the woman I'd love to enter my life. But you somehow got through, and if I sound corny or like something out of a bad movie, I'm sorry. If you put me in front of a jury, I'll knock your socks off with oration. Speaking from the soul is a hell of a lot harder, but I'm willing to give it a try if you're willing to put up with me. You feel you have to set terms, and I'll put up with them, to a point. As long as you'll go along with my terms, too."

"Such as?" she whispered.

"I want us to live together and be a real couple. It's the best way for you to find out if I'm the kind of guy you want to have around all the time."

She considered his proposition. "Six months."

Josh grinned and held out his hand. "Deal."

Lauren looked down at his hand and shook her head. "Counselor, you never learn, do you? You seal a business deal with a handshake. Our kind of deal requires a lot more than a handshake." She climbed onto his lap, fitting onto him perfectly. She rubbed her nose against his, then kissed him. "Now, isn't this much better?"

"Okay, but don't think this means you'll get your way all the time."

The next morning, they were both unusually quiet

as they ate breakfast with Chloe and Dave, then loaded the car with their suitcases.

"Next time, we'll leave the women behind and take a couple of horses up into the hills, where I don't have to listen to that old broad tell me what to do," Dave confided in Josh.

"If you want to sleep in that bed with me tonight, you'll be careful what you say," Chloe warned with little heat and lots of affection. She turned to give Lauren a goodbye hug and whispered in her ear, "You fight back, sweetheart. Don't let her win."

"I don't intend to."

Even the drive back was quiet. It seemed the closer they got to the Riverside County line, the more subdued they felt.

"Do you think we'll find anything when we get back?" Lauren finally had to break the charged silence. She knew she didn't have to elaborate.

His hands tightened on the steering wheel. "I'm hoping we won't. But then, I keep hoping she'll suddenly disappear from our lives, and she hasn't done that."

She lightly rubbed his shoulder for comfort and kept her hand there. "Then we'll hope she's gotten angry enough this weekend to come out in the open."

Except even Lauren couldn't keep up any pretense when Josh pulled into her driveway.

"It looks so quiet on the outside," she murmured, as she got out of the car. "And deceptive."

Lauren allowed Josh to enter first. He glanced through all the rooms and found nothing out of place.

"It looks good."

She still followed him as he headed for the front door. "Call me when you get home."

"I will." He kissed her several times as if putting off

leaving. "How about I check in for messages and if nothing looks urgent I come back over with a pizza?"

"No anchovies."

"Not a one," he vowed.

"Josh." She paused a beat. "If you want to move in next weekend, I'm willing to help carry boxes."

His grim features lightened considerably at her words. "Okay, we'll make plans this week."

Lauren didn't close the door until Josh's car left her sight. She walked through the house again, unwilling to believe someone hadn't been here. In her bedroom she found the perfume bottles undisturbed, her bathroom looking the same. She decided to unpack first and put her cosmetics away, then her clothing. It wasn't until she opened her closet that she realized her fears weren't imaginary. How she hadn't noticed the distinctive odor was beyond her. She covered her mouth.

"Oh, my God!" she choked, stumbling backward.

Every piece of clothing in the closet was covered with blood. When she spun around, she noticed the bedspread wasn't on properly. When she pulled it back she found a rose set in the middle of the pillow. A white rose, with two drops of blood marring one of the pristine petals, was the next obscene message.

"This time, you really have gone too far," she whispered, resisting the urge to grab up the rose and crush the petals. "Now it's time for you to realize you're not going to win if I have anything to do with it."

Lauren rummaged through her nightstand drawer, pulled out her gun, and promptly loaded it. Once it was loaded and comfortably in her hand, she called Kevin.

"It sounds like she didn't waste any time," he muttered.

"The blood might be able to give us a clue," she told him. "But I'd bet my reputation she used animal blood, unless she's either a vampire or works in a blood bank."

"At least we can finally cut down the list. Good ole Heather has been boffing her boss for the past two months. He had the hotel receipts and the desk clerk remembered her cleavage and the way the guy couldn't keep his hands off her. And the ex is out here on the sly, helping Daddy buy a new company or something. I'll call the crime scene guys and be right over."

It wasn't until she hung up and looked at the clock that she realized Josh should have called her by then. A bitter cold washed over her.

"No," she breathed, grabbing the phone and punching out the numbers. She drummed her fingers against the table until she heard the receiver on the other side of the line picked up. "Josh?"

"Lauren, look, we've said it all in the car, okay?" he spoke with the forced patience of a man who had little of it left to give. "This weekend proved we're not in synch. Let's just leave it that way."

The cold in her veins intensified. She spoke carefully as she felt her way through the verbal minefield. "I know we did, but I hoped you'd be willing to talk more. I don't think we said it all."

"There's nothing to talk about. There's no way we'll be able to not see each other, at least in court. But we're both adults, and I'm sure we can handle it. Your cop ex would know about these things, wouldn't he? Goodbye, Lauren. And please don't call again."

Josh pushed the phone away and slowly turned to the woman who had been unashamedly eavesdropping on the conversation. "Now do you believe me that we broke up?"

"It's for the best, darling, honest," she cooed in his ear, as she draped her arms around his neck. "You'll see, we'll be so happy together." She smiled as if she didn't have a care in the world.

No matter how badly he wanted to put his hands around her neck and tighten them, he didn't. Not when she held that gun so close to his chest.

The moment he walked in the front door and found her sitting on his couch, he knew this was the show-down.

"Hello, darling, you've been so curious about my identity that I decided to surprise you," she greeted him cheerfully. "Now that you have that slut out of your system, maybe you'll realize I'm the only woman you need."

Josh couldn't say one word to dispute her claim. The manic gleam in her eye and the way she held the handgun told him she was past listening. Even more than that, he felt sorrow over her being a woman he'd admired so much.

"We broke up," he told her, as he sat on the chair next to the couch. There was no way he wanted to be even close to her. "The weekend proved what a super-ficial woman Lauren is."

She laughed. "Oh, darling, I could have told you long ago how false Celia was, but you wouldn't have believed me. Just as long as you've come back to me. That's all that counts." She continued smiling. "We're going to be so happy together."

Lauren remained very still as she heard the click of the receiver disconnecting the call. It wasn't until a moment later she realized that she heard a softly distinct second click right after Josh had hung up. That was why he'd spoken so harshly. Someone had listened in on the call.

She started to grab for the phone again, then hesitated. What if this had pushed the woman over the edge? What if the sight of police at Josh's house had upset her so much she'd resorted to violence?

"Take deep breaths, Lauren," she ordered herself. "And think."

She quickly changed into jeans and a bulky pullover sweater that covered her gun when she stuck it in her waistband. Her hands shook so much as she pulled her hair back in a tight braid, it took several tries, but she kept focusing on what was ahead.

"I've run enough. I'm not running from this," she murmured, as she climbed in her car. While she backed out, Kevin's car and the crime scene van showed up.

"I have to run an errand," she told him.

"Wait a minute!" He grabbed hold of the door handle.

She shook her head. "I'll be back soon."

Kevin wasn't convinced. "What's up, Lauren? You're as white as a ghost."

"You would be, too, if you saw your entire wardrobe ruined. Even if the blood could come out completely, I wouldn't want any of it. I've got to go. You know the alarm code. Go on in." She stepped on the gas and he quickly stepped back.

"I still don't believe you!"

Lauren took a roundabout route to Josh's house and made sure to park her car down the street, out of sight. She crept up the yard near the garage, where there were no windows. She eased her way into the garage and made her way to the back door, praying it was unlocked. Holding her breath, she carefully twisted the knob and pushed the door open by increments until there was a space wide enough for her to squeeze through.

"You did what?" She heard Josh's raised voice coming from what she thought might be the living room. "Why did you do something so destructive to her clothing?"

"Darling, she had to be taught a lesson. The others hadn't taught her anything."

Lauren caught the sob traveling up her throat. She knew the voice. Then she quickly caught herself. She knew that in order to succeed, she would have to remain cool. Because if she failed, both she and Josh would remain victims of a woman whose identity would never be revealed. She took several deep breaths and hoped she didn't look as frightened as she felt. Before she could lose her nerve, she stepped into the room. The two inhabitants abruptly stopped talking and turned to face her. Josh looked ill, while the woman with him looked furious.

"Hello, Josh, I'm sorry to be barging in like this, but you refused to talk to me on the phone, and I felt we needed to have a talk face to face." She turned to face the other occupant, who stood stock still, staring at Lauren with malevolent hatred etched coarsely on her face. "Hello, Gail."

Chapter Twenty

Gail's face turned red with fury. "What are you doing here?"

Lauren tried to sound nonchalant. "I told you. I thought Josh and I should talk face to face." She took a few more steps into the room. For now, she kept her attention on Gail and the revolver lying in her lap, instead of on Josh. He stared at her with a look that told her how crazy she was to be doing this. "You should realize that blood isn't going to upset me the way it might other women. After all, I see it in my work all the time."

Gail's smile was too broad, too bright. "Yes, I was proud of that."

"Did you use animal blood? Something that wouldn't be easily traced?"

"You didn't think I'd use my own, did you?" Her laughter was high-pitched, with traces of hysteria. "I was amazed how some of the material just soaked it up. You're going to have to come up with a good story at the dry cleaner's." She glanced quickly at Josh as he sat forward. Her face softened and she gazed at him with the look of a woman in love. An insane woman.

"I think I'd rather buy a new wardrobe." Lauren

moved slowly, edging to the side until she could lean against the wall. A covert glance downward told her her gun couldn't be detected under her sweater.

"You've lost this time, Celia," Gail told her. "I want you to just go away so Josh and I can be alone. You'll find another man; you always do." Bitterness scored her words.

"What if I don't want to go away? Why should it be me? After all, Josh chose me, not you." She knew she had to tread carefully in her goading, but she sensed it was the only way she'd learn anything.

"Only because he didn't realize how much I really cared for him." Her breathing grew labored as she grappled with unseen demons. "You can't always win, Celia."

Josh tried to catch Lauren's eye, but she was afraid to look at him. She had to keep her attention on Gail.

"Sure, I can. I did before, didn't I?" She straightened up and slowly walked toward Gail. She wasn't sure if this was the time to push it more, but she felt she had to do something. "A lot of times, haven't I, Gail? Don't you think it's a bit odd that I always get the men? That perhaps the men wanted me more than they wanted you?" She swung her hips just a bit as she walked.

Gail's lips drew back. "You bitch, you evil-hearted bitch! You always said that, but we knew it was only because you'd put out for them. Whether it was in the back seat of their car or some sleazy motel, you'd just spread your legs and let them fuck you!" She jumped up. "I told Michael all about you, did you know that? I told him, but he didn't believe me, even when I could give him names and places. He still wanted to marry you, even when I told him how much I loved him. Wasn't it a shame the wedding had to be canceled?"

"You're sick, Gail. You need help." Josh spoke before he could realize the words could turn into a deadly trigger.

She spun around. "You're just listening to her again. You need to listen to me!" Her scream echoed in the room. "She's evil, a poison that will eat you alive! Why won't you listen to me? I want us to have a life together, Josh. Because I won't let her have you the way she's had all the others!" She blindly lifted her gun.

Lauren didn't think; she only reacted. Calling on the self-defense techniques Ron drummed into her, she launched herself at Gail, grabbing her gun arm and forcing it upward. The shot embedded itself in the ceiling as the two women fell to the carpet.

"Lauren!" Josh jumped up, but knew he was powerless to help her. He kept an eye on the gun in case he had the chance to at least kick it out of the way.

"No!" Gail felt the hard bulge at Lauren's waist and pulled out the gun. "You always cheat!" She aimed it at her head, then tossed it to one side.

Only by turning away did Lauren evade a direct blow, but she still was dazed by it. Ignoring the ringing in her ears and dazed vision, she fought back as hard as she could. She jabbed Gail in the nose, wincing when blood spurted.

"You can't win again! You can't!" Gail wailed, hitting and kicking violently. "I won't let you!"

Lauren had no idea it was coming until it was almost too late.

Gail suddenly scooted back with her gun in her hand aimed at Lauren. Except just as suddenly, she turned and shot at Josh instead.

"No!" Lauren grabbed for her own gun and shot without hesitation.

Gail's eyes widened with horror as she looked down and saw the blood spreading across her shoulder.

"It's not fair," she sobbed, rocking back and forth. "It's not fair."

Lauren crawled over to Josh, who lay back dazed.

"Shit," she hissed, pulling off her sweater and balling it up to use as a pressure bandage against the wound in his chest.

"Is that a good shit or a bad one?" he panted, wincing as she carefully laid him on his back. "Basically, I'm asking if you're saying I'm going to be sent down to your office?"

She gulped in air. "Not if I have anything to say about it. But you have to lie still, Josh." She looked blindly around the room for a phone, then spied it. "I've got to call for an ambulance."

"What about Gail?"

Lauren spared the woman a glance. She now lay in a fetal position, staring at her bloodstained hand.

"She won't be any trouble."

As she punched out 911, she heard sirens in the distance. "Maybe someone heard the shots and called the police. Or Kevin figured out what errand I was running." She quickly relayed the necessary information to the 911 dispatch and ran back to Josh. Tears ran freely down her cheeks. "You're not going to die, Josh. Not now."

"I thought I had six months." His voice was much weaker.

"I think that's just been shortened a great deal." She carefully lifted him in her arms and checked the bandage.

He coughed. "Hell, you mean all I had to do was get shot? There's one more thing."

"Anything."

"That's something else I'll remember." His chest rose and fell in erratic beats. "Would you please go in my closet and put on one of my shirts before they show up. While I like you wearing that next to nothing you wear you call a bra, there's no reason for you to share the wealth with the other guys." He managed a feeble smile. "You know, Kevin's going to be really pissed he missed out on this."

Lauren couldn't decide whether to laugh or cry. So she did both, cradling Josh in her arms, unaware he'd passed out.

Epilogue

"I am still pissed at you guys for pulling this without me." Kevin dropped a box of candy on Josh's bed tray. "I go to all that trouble to find out Heather and Stephanie weren't the ones and that Mitzi wasn't even close to being the right one, and you two have to go out and have all the fun."

"Believe me, it wasn't exactly planned." He winced as he groped for the bed controls and punched the button to raise the bed. "Have you talked to Lauren?"

He shook his head. "She wanted to meet with the doctors who examined Gail. She barely gave me enough time to take her statement. She's one good shot. I hope you remember that." His light-colored eyes darkened with concern. "You okay?"

"I was shot in the chest, my lung collapsed, and they said if Lauren hadn't put on a pressure bandage, I probably would have died. I've got stitches that are already itching, a catheter stuck up in me that's embarrassing as hell, a night nurse who belongs in a horror film, and I feel like shit. What does that tell you?"

"If you can complain that much, you're obviously getting better." Lauren breezed in and walked over to give Josh a kiss. "Patients always get cranky when they're feeling better. Although you still haven't gotten back all your color to my satisfaction." She gave him another kiss for good measure. "Mm, you're doing much better."

"Hearing that from you isn't all that comforting, Doc. You only deal with dead people." He gestured toward his friend. "Kevin's still pissed he was left out of the shootout."

"He'll get over it." She smiled at the detective, but the gesture was strained.

Josh didn't miss it. "How is she?"

Lauren carefully sat on the edge of Josh's bed. "She's lost in her own world. Her family arrived today, along with her sister, Celia. They were able to fill in the blanks for us about Gail's behavior. Celia's a couple of years older, very beautiful, hair almost the color of mine," she clarified the reason why Gail had fixated her hate on her. "And Gail always felt second best around her because she always made head cheerleader, homecoming queen, all of that. Celia said it was always put down to simple sibling jealousy until the girls got older. Gail started out by 'accidentally' spilling ink on Celia's prom formal and forgetting phone messages from her boyfriends, and then Celia fell in love and became engaged to a boy that Gail suddenly decided she loved and wanted. Gail spread ugly rumors about Celia, but her fiancé didn't believe them." Lauren sighed. "Two days before the wedding, he was in a bad car accident that left him paralyzed. He couldn't handle the idea of spending the rest of his life in a wheelchair, so he killed himself. Two weeks later, Gail left town, and although the family strongly felt she was behind his accident, they couldn't prove anything. They haven't spoken until now. They didn't even know she was working as a police officer."

"Maybe this was for the best," Kevin consoled. "Internal Affairs is checking her out further by looking into unsolved crimes in the cities she'd worked before. Who knows if she'd done this before, but got away with it that time." He looked from one to the other. "Besides, because of her, you two got together probably faster than you might have."

Lauren smiled at Josh. "Yes, we are together, but it's a shame it's at another's expense."

Josh reached out for her hand. "Kevin, can you get lost?"

He stood up. "I still need your statement, now that you're awake enough to give one."

"Tomorrow."

"This afternoon?"

"Tomorrow."

Lauren looked at Kevin. "Come back this afternoon. Josh has to learn he can't get his way all the time."

"So far, I haven't gotten it once."

"Sure you have. I gave up on the six-month limit, didn't I?"

"So it wasn't my imagination? You really did say that? It wasn't loss of blood that had me thinking the impossible. You actually changed your mind."

She edged herself closer. "I said that and a lot more, but you were unconscious by then, and I'm beginning to think it was a good idea you were. In fact, once you're out of the hospital, I'll prove to you just what I did say."

"You know, Doc, something tells me this is going to turn into quite a relationship."

She leaned closer until her lips touched his. "Oh, Counselor, you haven't seen the half of it yet."

YOU WON'T WANT TO READ
JUST ONE—KATHERINE STONE

WHO DUNNIT? JUST TRY AND FIGURE IT OUT!

THE MYSTERIES OF MARY ROBERTS RINEHART

Available wherever paperbacks are sold, or order direct from the Publisher. Send cover price plus 50¢ per copy for mailing and handling to Penguin USA, P.O. Box 999, c/o Dept. 17109, Bergenfield, NJ 07621.Residents of New York and Tennessee must include sales tax. DO NOT SEND CASH.

*"MIND-BOGGLING . . . THE SUSPENSE IS UNBEARABLE . . .
DORIS MILES DISNEY WILL KEEP YOU
ON THE EDGE OF YOUR SEAT . . ."*

THE MYSTERIES OF DORIS MILES DISNEY